LETHBRIDGE-STEWART

THE GRANDFATHER INFESTATION

Based on the BBC television serials by
Mervyn Haisman & Henry Lincoln

John Peel

Foreword by
Simon Clark

CANDY JAR BOOKS · CARDIFF
A Russell & Frankham-Allen Series
2016

Editor: Shaun Russell
Range Editor: Andy Frankham-Allen
Cover: Colin Howard
Logo: Simon Williams
Editorial: Hayley Cox & Lauren Thomas
Licensed by Hannah Haisman

Published by
Candy Jar Books
Mackintosh House
136 Newport Road, Cardiff, CF24 1DJ
www.candyjarbooks.co.uk

A catalogue record of this book is available
from the British Library

ISBN: 978-0-9935192-3-9

In memory of
Robert Banks Stewart
1931-2016

It Gets Under Your Skin

The writers of the Brigadier Lethbridge-Stewart era of *Doctor Who* would, as likely as not, have been familiar with the science fiction of the 1950s and '60s, represented by the likes of John Wyndham and John Christopher. They would also have probably read the classic 'scientific romances' of HG Wells and the vintage horror of Mary Shelley's *Frankenstein* and Bram Stoker's *Dracula*.

From this gene pool of story ideas it certainly appears to the watcher of *Doctor Who* that its script writers might have been influenced by what they read in their youth. Of course, it's impossible for writers not to absorb the work of their favourite authors and for their own work to carry a flavour here and there of adventures they read long ago. What's more, I'd stress that I'm not suggesting that ideas were copied, because like modern rock music owing a debt to the early blues guitarists, like Robert Johnson, certain plot ideas take on a life of their own; they get under the skin of successive generations of writers, and each new generation of writer reinvents stories for the age they're living in.

A favourite *Doctor Who* theme might be described as 'body horror', where people's minds or bodies are invaded in some way and transformed, so the person you believe to

3

be your friend or a family member is actually being transformed into a monster. This is perhaps the most subversive idea of all – that the person you trust changes into something that might become physically repulsive to us, and could also be a danger as well. I've certainly tackled this theme in the past. My second novel, *Blood Crazy*, deals with the notion that everyone over the age of nineteen becomes murderously insane almost overnight.

Perhaps some critics who like to, well, 'criticise' in a negative way might claim that writers have a tendency to poach the ideas of others. Generally, this is simply not the case. Story ideas are hardwired into all of us. We seem to have a genetic disposition to be interested in tales of love, chase, vengeance, survival and, yes, body horror, which is wrapped up in our fear of disease. There is a long tradition of body horror, of fiction that deals with some 'thing' that invades the human body, or psyche, and causes it to undergo a shocking and frightening transformation. And, as such, continues a long tradition that must stretch back to earliest days of the human race. It's easy to imagine our ancestors sitting around a campfire in an African jungle and someone beginning a yarn with, 'I remember once when my uncle went to sleep and an insect crawled into his ear and laid its eggs there', or, 'Did you hear about the boy who swallowed a seed and noticed, one day, that there was a leaf growing out from between his toes?' There would then be some particularly shuddersome descriptions to come, with plenty of 'Ee-yuk!' moments.

These body horror stories have developed over the centuries, becoming tangled up with fears of demonic possession. There are accounts in the Bible of devils

4

invading men and women's minds, seizing control and forcing the unfortunate individuals to act in bizarre ways. This very human obsession with the notion that our bodies can be invaded, transformed or taken over, literally took root in the minds of people down through the centuries in folklore, myth and religion. In the Middle Ages and Tudor times individuals were preoccupied by the fear of being infested by evil spirits as they slept (sleeping with your mouth open was considered a sure way of the supernatural blighters sneaking in!). Even as we entered more enlightened times in the nineteenth century, metaphors for disease and infestation were seen everywhere. Arguably, one of the most potent metaphors of this manifested itself in vampire stories. After all, the vampire infects those it bites to create more vampires – the victim then undergoes a physical and mental transformation.

Over a hundred years ago, Edith Nesbit (her most famous creation was *The Railway Children*) gave the vampire a very neat, and highly original, twist when she penned *The Pavilion,* where a vine growing in a pleasant country house creeps over people at night and drains them of their blood. This became one of the first stories to feature plants that turn out to be vicious man-hunters. On the face it, this seems absurd. We walk on grass, we eat fruit, boil cabbages. Plants always seem so harmless and inert. Do we ever look at an apple and think with a shudder, 'That looks a vicious little bugger. I'm keeping my distance from that'? And yet some of the most effective science fiction and horror stories present us with scenarios where plants become aggressive, dangerous, and, even shudderingly worse, have those plants either feeding on our flesh or invading us to either transform us into part-plant part-human creatures, or somehow taking control of our minds.

More stories of evil botany followed *The Pavilion*. William Hope Hodgson's deeply disturbing and thoroughly brilliant *Voice in the Night* appeared in 1907 – I really do recommend reading this if you haven't already. In this flesh-crawling tale, a young couple are shipwrecked on an island covered by fungus (I know, not a plant, but we're pretty much in the same ballpark). There's no food and eventually they try eating the fungus. Soon they notice blotches of fungus growing on their skin. It spreads, thickens until eventually they become walking, talking lumps of mould.

Plant monstrosities had truly taken hold in the consciousness of the reading public, almost becoming a sub-genre in their own right. Another fungus story, this time from John Wyndham, called *The Puff-Ball Menace* (though first published as *Spheres of Hell*) appeared in 1933. The fungus here is used as a terrorist weapon. After its victims died of apparent fungal poisoning more fungus sprouts from their graves, threatening to become a nation-destroying infestation.

Then, of course, John Wyndham wrote the plant monster daddy of them all, *The Day of the Triffids* (1951). There's nothing much for me to expand on here, because the Triffid has become embedded in our culture, and I'm sure you're familiar with the story – suffice to say, the Triffid has shuffled to the top of the food chain: this is the plant that walks, kills, communicates with its own kind, and appears to possess a reasoning mind.

Plants are on the march – at least in our imaginations,

they are. *Doctor Who* embraced the theme in *The Seeds of Death* and *The Seeds of Doom*, and, no doubt, you can identify many more. And now John Peel gives us *The Grandfather Infestation*, a fantastically entertaining, and horrifying novel, which suggests that everything that's green and grows from the earth might not be as harmless as we think.

Simon Clark
April, 2016

— PROLOGUE—

The attack came just after midnight.

The convoy was making its way through the Lake District, the roads washed in pale moonlight – three lorries and the two escort Land Rovers. Newly-minted Brigadier Alistair Lethbridge-Stewart was in the rear Land Rover, driven by 2nd Lieutenant William Bishop, fresh from his training at Mons College. In the back were half a dozen of his men. Lieutenant Colonel Walter Douglas was in the lead Land Rover, driven by Private Gwynfor Evans, with the rest of the squad in the back. The lorries contained every last scrap of Yeti, Dominator and Rutan technology that had been salvaged from both the Vault in Northumberland and the Vault's citadel under London. It was now being taken to the security of Dolerite Base in Scotland.

And, obviously, somebody knew this.

The transfer had been scheduled for overnight to avoid traffic, and prying eyes. There had been a few cars, of course, and some long-distance lorries, but for the most part these out-of-the-way roads had been clear. The strong headlight beams showed nothing more than tarmac and the odd house or stone walls.

From a side road that wound up into the hills, a big Bedford came crashing down just ahead of them, forcing

Evans to swerve and brake hard to narrowly avoid a collision. The lorry behind him swerved also, and the others hit their brakes. Bishop swung around the last lorry just as the Bedford exploded.

The Fifth Operational Corps reacted perfectly. The canvas over the rear of each of the Land Rovers was slung back, and the men within were ready when the attackers came out of the trees on either side of the road. Muzzled flames of automatic weapons added to the mix of moonlight, headlights and the blaze from the burning Bedford.

As always when there was action, Lethbridge-Stewart felt his pulse racing and his senses heightened. Though he always considered himself a peace-loving man, it was times like this that he felt fully alive. Using his door as a shield, he crouched, firing at any target he could see.

The attackers were professional, but they had badly underestimated the strength of their opposition, probably expected to have sown confusion with the lorry bomb stunt, Lethbridge-Stewart imagined. But his men were handpicked from the best he had at hand, and the attack might have surprised them all, but they knew how to react. The attackers were aiming their shots only at the men from the Land Rovers – clearly to avoid hitting the artefacts in the lorries. But the Fifth were under no such constraints.

Lethbridge-Stewart saw two of the attackers go down in the hail of bullets. The other attackers paused, and then a loud whistle pulled them all back into the woods. Several of his men started to follow, and Lethbridge-Stewart urgently called them back. It could be a ruse.

It was.

The attackers hadn't yet been dissuaded. As Lethbridge-Stewart watched, cautiously, the woods exploded once again with gunfire. This time their attackers were using the trees as camouflage and protection. The convoy was now a clear target, given the amount of light in play about it. The blazing Bedford blocked the way forward, and Lethbridge-Stewart suspected that the enemy had the back road blocked.

Which left him exactly one option.

'Douglas!' he yelled above the noise of the firefight. 'Clear us a road.'

Douglas caught on immediately, and started talking urgently to Evans. Ignoring him for the moment, Lethbridge-Stewart called to the other men near him. 'Grenades!'

Seconds later, there was a series of explosions amongst the trees. At least one of the attackers screamed, and the blasts were followed by the crack and groan of a tree falling. By this point, Douglas' Land Rover had surged forward and onto the side road, keeping up a withering fire into the trees as it did so.

Their enemy had to be aware that they were now in danger of being flanked. A couple of Lethbridge-Stewart's men were down, but there was no telling how many of the attackers were similarly fallen. There were two in the road, and undoubtedly more in the woods. How much punishment would these men take before they gave up?

Would they give up?

Several bullets thumped into the Land Rover, and one of the soldiers cried in pain. Lethbridge-Stewart fired back at the muzzle flashes, then had to pause to reload. There was so much noise all around, though, that it was impossible to tell what was happening. But there were no more whining bullets close to him, and he called out, 'Cease firing!'

Silence descended. The woods appeared deserted. Cautiously, he waited. This could be another ruse.

Then he saw one of his own men emerging from the trees, waving the all clear. Douglas stepped into the circle of light a moment later.

'They're all gone,' he reported. 'Taken their wounded, left four dead.'

Lethbridge-Stewart signalled his own men to stand down and joined Douglas. 'Our own casualties appear to be relatively light,' he said. There were at least four wounded, but none dead that he could see.

'They were after the technology,' Douglas said quietly.

'Obviously.' Lethbridge-Stewart scowled. 'They knew what we were carrying, and the time and the route. Only conclusion is that there's a leak of intel from our side.' He crossed to one of the fallen attackers. He was dressed in black, with a woolly hat and his face smudged up. 'Professionals. Hired mercenaries, no doubt.' The man's face was blank, dead.

'We have a traitor,' Douglas stated, simply. 'I wonder who these men worked for?'

Lethbridge-Stewart shrugged. 'There are a number of people interested in alien technology. Some of them even work with us.' He sighed. 'Get the men ready,' he ordered. 'We'd better get on our way.' He glanced around the battle scene.

They had come through this because they were trained and prepared. And, in the end, a little lucky.

But next time...?

11

— CHAPTER ONE —

Venus in Blue Jeans

'And, for the benefit of those of you who've spent the last decade on some other planet, that was, of course, the King.' Mary Wilde flicked the switch to silence Elvis. 'Well, py-rates and py-mates, we've come to the end of another show. Stay tuned to Radio Crossbones, though. Long Larry Legend is up next with the week's new releases. This is your py-rate wench Mary Wilde signing off for now; but never forever.' She started up the fade-out music – Johnny Kidd and the Pirates (what else?) hammering out *Shakin' All Over* – and pulled off her headphones.

There was barely room in the closet of a studio to yawn and stretch, but she managed it without skinning her knuckles this time. Grabbing her play list and a couple of new sevens she'd been handed earlier, she slipped out of the room as Long Larry entered, deftly dodging the inevitable slap he aimed at her backside. He laughed, not at all bothered by her annoyed scowl.

She needed a smoke, badly. Nodding to Pres, the engineer, she headed down the corridor and then up onto deck. She shivered; somehow she always forgot how bloody cold it got out here at 10pm and three miles or so off the Scottish coast. She considered going down to her cabin for a coat, but decided she could put up with the shivers for the time it took her to smoke a Players.

She hoped.

The first drag, as always, made her feel better. Being on the air was a real high, but the second the show was over, she started to plummet from the high, ready to crash for the night. She needed this smoke before turning in, to allow her time to come back to Earth. She leaned on the railing, looking across the dark waves to the vaguely lit horizon where Scotland lay.

'Hey, Mary.'

She glanced around and then relaxed when she saw it was Alan Scott approaching. Alan was the head technician for the ship and an okay guy. He was middle-aged and his thin blond hair was turning grey in places. He was one of the few men on the ship who hadn't made a pass at her, for whatever reason, and he seemed content to just be friends. She appreciated that, and she liked him. She fished out her packet and offered it to him. 'Smoke?'

'Ta.' He took one and lit it before leaning on the rail beside her. 'You should be wearing at least a cardigan,' he suggested.

'It's too hot in the studio if I do,' she replied, blowing smoke. She grinned. 'You should whip up some air conditioning in your copious free time.'

He laughed. 'Right. I'll make a note of that.' He pretended to scribble in the air. 'It's number two hundred and seventeen on my to-do list.'

'That high? You must really like me.'

'Everybody likes you, Mary,' he said. 'Especially the listeners. Your show is always good; I enjoyed tonight's.'

'You had time to listen?' She grinned again. 'Don't let

the bosses know, they'll think you're not working hard enough.' Then she shook her head. 'I don't know, Al, it's just silly stuff, really. Music for the masses.'

'Don't say that!' he snapped, sharply. She looked at him, surprised by the anger in his voice. 'Don't put yourself down like that.'

'Al, love, thanks for the vote of confidence, but what I do isn't important. I play music, I engage in silly banter and I show off my cleavage for the visiting journalists. I'm just pirate radio's dolly bird, that's all. Nothing special.'

Alan threw his cigarette out to sea with a surprising violence. 'If you really believe that, Mary, then I'm very disappointed in you. I thought you were smarter than that.'

'I'm smart enough not to have any illusions left,' she informed him. 'It's a man's world, and I'm only here because they tolerate me. I'm not a threat to them; just a glamour girl playing in their sandbox.'

Alan stared out to sea for a moment. 'Did you know I'm married?' he asked her suddenly.

'Married? No. Is that why you don't have wandering hand trouble?' She laughed, bitterly. 'Plenty of other men aboard are married, and it doesn't seem to stop them.'

'I take being a husband and father very seriously,' Alan informed her. He gestured out to the lights on the distant horizon. 'You're right, Mary; that's a man's world, at least for now. But it's changing, and you're helping it change. Maybe just a bit, but you *are*. There are girls out there right now who see you competing in a man's world and winning. It will help inspire them. One day it won't be a man's world any longer; it'll just be a human world. And it won't matter what sex you're born, you'll still have a chance to achieve

14

your dreams.' He looked at her very seriously. 'I have two daughters – eight and six – and I very much want them to grow up into that kind of a world. And you're helping that world arrive. Don't *ever* think you're nobody special.'

Mary looked at him in amazement. 'You've got a very high opinion of my abilities,' she said, laughing nervously. 'I'm not sure you should be putting me on such a pedestal.'

'You put yourself there,' he said. 'Use it to your advantage. Live your dreams.'

'Like you?'

'Me?' He shook his head. 'I never dreamed I'd be working radio; I always wanted to be an astronomer. I applied to Jodrell Bank, you know.'

'Wow.' Then she realised what he meant. 'You didn't get in? But you're a genius with our equipment.'

'Only so many jobs, Mary, and I didn't make the cut. They're more interested in tracking the latest Soviet lunar module than hiring me.' He gave her a wry grin. 'But it *is* why we have such a powerful transmitter on this ship. Built most of it myself.'

'Jodrell Bank should be jealous,' Mary said, only half-joking. 'I was always good at the sciences in school, but music was a much bigger pull. So I'm glad you're here; at least one of us gets to use their brain.' She placed her hand over his. 'You're one of the good guys.'

'And you're bloody freezing!' he exclaimed, gripping her hand tightly. 'Get down below immediately.'

'Yes, Daddy,' she said, in pretend meekness. Then something caught her eye in the sky. 'Hey, a shooting star! Make a wish, love, for that brand spanking new world of yours.'

Alan followed her gaze and then frowned slightly. The light, burning brightly, was dropping steadily down the dark sky. 'That's no meteorite,' he said, puzzled. 'Wrong colour.'

Mary shrugged. 'It doesn't look like plane lights.'

'It's not,' he agreed. 'Still the wrong colour.'

'One of those lunar modules, maybe?' She laughed. 'Or maybe the moon people are returning the junk we left there back to us?'

Alan shook his head. 'Not a lunar module,' he decided. 'It's definitely in the atmosphere, but it's not going fast enough for re-entry.' He frowned again. 'I honestly don't know what it could be.'

Mary stood beside him and they watched the pure white light descend from near the zenith where Mary had first spotted it. It was growing slightly larger as it fell, so Alan was right; it was certainly in the atmosphere, not something bright orbiting the Earth. It was hard to keep track of all the stuff that was above the Earth these days, but this wasn't a part of any orbital junk. At least, not any longer. It was still growing in size.

'It's not going to hit us, is it?' Mary asked, only slightly worried.

'I shouldn't think so for a minute,' Al said. 'It's a big ocean, and we're a very small target. But it does seem to be getting closer.'

Mary found herself fascinated. She was by no means a space person. Oh, she'd been as excited as anybody a few months back when the Americans made it to the Moon, and she read the occasional article about the British Rocket Group and their Mars programme with a certain amount of national pride, but she always thought of herself as down-to-earth. But somehow, seeing this glow in the sky, it seemed to feel more real to her. It was one thing when people went up to meet Space, but quite another when Space came down to meet you.

It was difficult to tell how far off the light was, but there was a reflection in the water, shimmering with the waves, that suggested it was getting lower and closer. It was heading toward the dark and distant coast of Scotland.

'Damn,' Alan muttered.

'What?'

'It's coming down in the sea,' he said, clearly disappointed. 'There will be no way to reach it. I was hoping for an impact on land so it could be recovered.'

'Hoping to give Patrick Moore a tip, were you?' she joked.

'I was thinking more of Lovell. Or maybe Bernard Quatermass, or perhaps even...' His voice trailed off. 'Blast, there it goes.'

He was quite correct; whatever it was that had fallen from the sky slammed into the water a couple of miles closer to the shore. For a moment there was a diffuse glow in the water, and then it faded away.

'Well...' Alan sighed. 'That's another lost opportunity, eh?' He glanced back at her. 'The water's far too deep there to even think about a recovery attempt.' Then he saw her shiver. 'Right, we were getting you inside before you froze to death, weren't we? Come on, young lady.'

He put a protective arm about her – and it *was* protective, not a pass – and steered her toward the doorway. Did they call it a doorway on a ship? She couldn't remember if there was a technical term and didn't much care if there was. He closed the door behind them and latched it, cutting off the cold draft.

Now they were inside, they could hear the show going on currently, piped through speakers. The bosses liked everyone to listen in to their product. Long Larry was playing some of his experimental stuff. Sooner him than her. She liked rock and roll, not this newer stuff. She was one of the few people who thought The Beatles were better before *Rubber Soul*. And as for Jimi Hendrix... he'd never last!

'You ever see Johnny Kidd live?' Alan asked her as they walked toward her room – *cabin*!

'No,' she admitted. 'I wish I had.'

'I did, once,' he informed her. 'In Leicester.' He grinned. 'He dressed up like a pirate and swung a cutlass around as he performed. I always thought he'd slice his mike cord clean through. It was all show, of course. The fans loved it. He could really relate to them.' He glanced at her again. 'You can, too. And if it wasn't beneath him to pretend a bit, surely it's not beneath you?'

Mary threw up her hands. 'Okay, I surrender. I promise not to knock the pirate wench stuff anymore, okay? I'll be a good, docile role model for your daughters.'

'See that you are,' Alan warned her, a twinkle in his eyes. Then he was serious again. 'I was really upset when I heard about the car crash.' Seeing her blank look, he explained: 'Johnny Kidd. Such a shame.'

'You know what they say,' she told him. 'Only the good die young.'

'Then you watch out for yourself,' he warned her. 'Dress

18

warmer!'

'I –'

There was a loud hammering sound and the corridor shook. Mary yelped, and tried to brace herself against the wall, but slammed into it instead. Alan, unbalanced, fell to the floor and cried out in pain.

Another noise echoed about them, as the ship rang like a bell. This time she, too, fell. Her left shoulder slammed into the metal plate of the floor and she squealed in pain. 'What's happening?' she cried.

The song had abruptly ended on the air, and she could hear Long Larry yell, 'What the hell?', before the ship shuddered again.

'It feels like we hit something,' Alan said, confused.

'What?' Mary tried getting to her feet, but the corridor shuddered again, and she decided she was safer staying on the floor. 'But we're miles out at sea, there's nothing to hit!'

There was a loud groaning sound, as if the ship were somehow being squeezed, and the corridor started to tilt slightly. 'Are we sinking?' she cried, feeling scared.

'I don't see how we can be,' Al answered. He had grabbed a handhold on a closed door and was levering himself to his feet. 'Maybe another ship…?' He held a hand out to her, and she grabbed it eagerly, glad for the human contact.

'Wouldn't somebody have seen another ship?' Mary yelped as the vessel shuddered again. Larry's voice had gone quiet, and there was the hiss of static over the loudspeakers. The bosses wouldn't be happy that he wasn't transmitting.

'Who knows?' Alan nodded back the way they had come. 'Maybe we'd better get up on deck. If anything's happened to the ship, we may need to abandon it.'

Abandon ship? The thought hadn't occurred to her. For a second she had a memory of seeing *A Night to Remember* as a teenager; the sinking of the *Titanic* suddenly seemed too horribly real, and she shook her head to try and put the picture of people dying in freezing water out of her mind.

'Shouldn't we get our life jackets?' she asked. 'And warmer clothing?'

Al glanced at her bare arms and hesitated. 'Maybe we should,' he agreed. Then the ship shivered again, and another loud clang almost deafened them. 'On second thoughts, maybe we shouldn't wait. There's probably stuff in the lifeboats.'

She nodded, still clutching him. Thank God she was with calm, sensible Al and not some moron like Larry. Together they started back up the corridor.

The lights died abruptly, and she could see absolutely nothing. The speakers went completely dead, not even static. All she could hear for a moment were gasping breaths from herself and Alan, and then distant yells and screams.

The floor under her feet shifted, and she felt herself falling into darkness. There was a second of blind panic as Alan was ripped from her grip and she hit metal, hard, and then there was nothing.

— CHAPTER TWO —

I Like It

'Today, sir?' Lethbridge-Stewart couldn't keep the annoyance out of his voice. He glared at the telephone wishing he could pull his service revolver and just shoot the damned thing.

'I know it's an inconvenience, Brigadier,' Major General Hamilton growled. 'And I wish there was something I could do about it, but I can't. You answer to me, I answer to Whitehall and Whitehall answers to Downing Street. If they say they want a last-minute inspection… well, then, we just have to polish our shoes, shine up our buttons and put a happy smile on our faces. Well, *your* faces, actually. Try and look like you're happy to co-operate.'

'But they're *civilians*,' Lethbridge-Stewart protested. 'They don't understand military reasons for doing things, and they ask such damnably foolish questions. Plus, we only opened the place two days ago and you know the snafu factor.'

'Believe me, man, I ran the same arguments past Whitehall barely ten minutes ago,' Hamilton informed him. 'And what they told me, I now tell you; this is a surprise inspection of the new Dolerite Base. They were ordered not to tell me, and I was ordered not to tell you, so do try and act surprised.'

'Believe me, General, I am.'

'That's the spirit. I'll talk to you again after they've left.'

Lethbridge-Stewart cleared his throat. 'And when do they *arrive*, sir?' he asked.

There was rather an urgent rap on the door.

'Ah, I believe I already have the answer to that,' he said, and hung up. 'Enter!'

Private Evans opened the door. 'Apparently we have visitors, sir,' he announced. 'I didn't know any were to be expected.' He glanced at Lethbridge-Stewart accusingly, as if the arrival had somehow messed up his plans for the day. Typical Evans, probably hoping to find some quiet corner to nod off in.

'They weren't,' Lethbridge-Stewart said drily. 'But they are now. Send Colonel Douglas to me immediately, and find Miss Travers. I don't care what she's doing or what excuse she pulls; I want her here. And I suppose we'll need Sergeant Maddox as well.'

Evans looked at him expectantly. When he saw Lethbridge-Stewart hadn't caught on, he added, 'Shouldn't you be sending someone to meet the visitors then?'

'Oh, right. Better have Bishop do that. Tell him that I'd appreciate it if he could point out a couple of the sights on the way down.' That should buy a bit of briefing time, at least.

'Right you are, sir.' Evans saluted and left the office.

Lethbridge-Stewart looked down at the latest letter from his nephew, Owain; it would have to keep. He followed Evans and found Douglas already in the outer office. 'Ah, Douglas, glad you're here. You've heard the news, I suppose?'

'Visitors, sir? Yes.' He grimaced. 'They didn't give you much time to get things in order, did they?'

'Politicians,' Lethbridge-Stewart explained. 'Probably hoping to catch us with our pants down so they can gleefully complain about the military's share of the budget again.'

'Well, nothing's gone wrong today, has it?' Douglas asked. 'I mean, apart from the fact that they're here, of course.'

'No, not yet.' Lethbridge-Stewart took a deep breath. 'But they're bound to want to question Miss Travers, and you know how she takes to her work being interrupted.'

'I don't suppose there's a chance we could just stuff her in a cupboard somewhere?'

'They'll be looking for skeletons in cupboards. I'd sooner not supply them with one. Straighten your tie, Colonel,' Lethbridge-Stewart ordered. 'We'd better go and meet them. Bishop's bringing them down.'

'Yes, sir!' Douglas made a show of straightening his already straight tie.

'How did you find the course at Old Sarum?' Lethbridge-Stewart asked, as he led the way up the corridor.

'Useful, not had much cause to work directly with naval officers before,' Douglas said. All officers of the Corps were, as per General Hamilton's orders, required to attend a ten-day training course at the Joint Warfare Establishment to help facilitate the smooth operation of the Fifth, which was made up of the three main British Army services. 'The next section is on the way there now, which leaves only a couple more sections. All officers should be up to speed by the end of the month.'

'Good to hear.'

'Mr Quebec is an... *interesting* instructor, sir,' Douglas said, struggling to keep a straight face.

Lethbridge-Stewart tapped his swagger stick in his gloved palm as he glanced at the indicator panel on the lift. It showed that neither lift was moving, so Bishop seemed to be buying him some time. The visitors were still on the surface.

'Brigadier!' He winced slightly at the anger in the voice, and turned slowly to see Anne Travers striding down the corridor that led from her laboratory. She was a small, attractive woman with a pixie-like face and – generally – an amiable smile, but when she was annoyed she could get quite tart. She was clearly annoyed. 'That flunkey of yours interrupted me at an important moment and *ordered* me to come here.' Evans had never been one of her favourite people; it was difficult for her to forget his cowardly behaviour during the Yeti incursion in London.

'Private Evans was obeying my orders, Miss Travers,' he explained. 'We have visitors.'

'What do you expect me to do?' she snapped. 'Serve tea and cucumber sandwiches?'

There was the whine of the lift starting up. The visitors would be here in moments, and he didn't need a tantrum.

'No, just be your usual charming self,' he suggested. 'Remember, they are the ones paying the bills for your important experiments.' Wisely, Miss Travers elected not to reply. Instead, she turned silently to face the lift doors. Sergeant Jean Maddox hurried up to join them; she briefly saluted Lethbridge-Stewart before taking her place at the rear of the small group.

A moment later, the doors opened and Bishop ushered

24

two men out into the reception area. One was tall, imperious and impeccably dressed. His receding hair was brushed back and he had dark, penetrating eyes. The other was shorter and stockier, with brownish-blond hair. He was the first out, and he glanced around impatiently.

'All this way,' he complained. 'Why did they have to build a secret base all this way from London?'

'It's easier to keep it hidden from the Fleet Street Johnnies the further we are from Fleet Street,' Lethbridge-Stewart answered. He recognised both men from earlier meetings. 'Mr Grant, Mr Bryden, may I introduce my senior staff? Lieutenant Colonel Douglas, my 2-in-C. Sergeant Maddox, in charge of communications. Lieutenant Bishop you've already met. And this is Miss Anne Travers, Head of Scientific Research.' He turned to her. 'Miss Travers, this is Mr Peter Grant, a representative of the Ministry of Defence, and Mr Peyton Bryden.'

Miss Travers inclined her head slightly. 'I've already met Mr Bryden,' she said. She didn't sound very pleased to see him a second time. 'Though I didn't know he was overseeing us.'

'I'm not,' Bryden said. 'I'm simply the man who pays the bills.' He smiled, but there was something feral in his expression. 'It's nice to see some pretty faces around here.'

'Always liked a girl in uniform,' Grant commented, cheerily. 'Nurses, police women... soldiers.' He smiled at the impassive Maddox. 'Not at all fond of all-male clubs.' He glanced at Bryden. 'I'll wager you belong to a few of those.' Without waiting for a reply, he turned back to Lethbridge-Stewart. 'And I suppose you've an equally good reason for building this place directly under Edinburgh

Castle?'

Bryden didn't give Lethbridge-Stewart a chance to reply. 'It's easier to hide troop movements in an area that's already swarming with them anyway,' he said. 'And, of course, refitting the old Longbow facility was more cost-effective than building from scratch, especially considering the secret nature of all this stuff. All of this was in the briefings and in the documents we've been sent. Don't you read any of that material?'

'A man would have to be crazy to read all the stuff the Ministry puts out,' Grant replied.

'*I* read it all.'

Grant rolled his eyes and then nudged Bishop gently with his elbow. 'Don't you think he'd make a great straight man to a comedian like Eric Morecambe?' he asked. 'Who can resist a comeback to a line like that?'

Douglas managed to somehow keep a straight face. 'Did you two gentleman travel up here together?'

'Yes,' Bryden replied through clenched teeth. 'God help my sanity.'

'He's not doing a very good job of it so far,' Grant muttered.

Lethbridge-Stewart had quite enough bickering. Clearly these two men didn't like one another, and that would make for a very tense visit. 'Perhaps you'd care for a tour, gentlemen?' he suggested. 'There are still a few rough edges to file down, so to speak, but the majority of Dolerite Base is up and running.'

'That's what we're here for, Brigadier,' Bryden said. 'I'd like to see how you military chaps have spent our money.'

Grant deliberately stared at the big sign on the wall

behind the reception desk that read *Home-Army Fifth Operational Corps – Dolerite Base*. 'Good to see you're keeping this place hush-hush,' he said.

Lethbridge-Stewart had to restrain himself. 'As you no doubt recall,' he said, drily, 'you passed through a security check as you entered the Castle. There was a second as you entered the New Barracks and a third before you were allowed in that lift. I'm certain that Lieutenant Bishop asked to see your passes once more when he met you. By the time anyone reaches this level, gentlemen, I think we can be fairly sure they already know where they are.'

'Then I suppose the sign is a bit redundant, eh?' Grant suggested. He started to move off, but the two soldiers that were stationed in reception moved to intercept him.

'Pass, please, sir,' the corporal asked.

Grant glanced at the brigadier. 'Isn't this a bit redundant as well?' he asked.

Lethbridge-Stewart resisted a smile. 'You were the one who mentioned the need for security,' he pointed out.

'Is this going to happen every time I take a step?'

'This will be the final time,' Lethbridge-Stewart assured him. 'Unless you wish to enter the restricted area. And even I have to produce my pass for that.'

Bryden pushed past Grant and offered his pass. Grant followed suit. The corporal examined both and then handed them back and saluted. 'Thank you, gentlemen.'

'Now,' Bryden growled. 'Let's get on with it.'

Lethbridge-Stewart nodded at Douglas, and he took the hint to play tour guide.

'Of course,' he told the two visitors, 'this is just for HQ staff. We're not up to full strength yet, but even so we couldn't house even one battalion here. HQ is made of about fifty people. Senior staff, of course, and the rest are mostly security and communications. Three watches, so there are hand-overs every eight hours. This area…' Douglas gestured down the corridor they had entered '…are offices for the quartermaster on the left, senior staff on the right. My office is right there, and the brigadier's is at the end.'

'Let's take a peek,' Grant suggested. 'See how the money's being spent, eh, Bryden?' Bryden managed to avoid a nudge from Grant's elbow.

'Why not?' he agreed.

Lethbridge-Stewart moved into the lead and opened the door. The two men looked around at the simple desk, the filing cabinets and the large wall map of the British Isles.

Grant shook his head. 'It's a bit… bleak,' he observed.

'It's not meant to be a luxury hotel,' Lethbridge-Stewart replied. 'Besides, I've only just moved in. I'm sure it will accumulate a little clutter in time.'

Bryden's eyes narrowed. 'I'm not so sure about that,' he said. 'You don't seem to be the collecting type. Let's move on, shall we?'

Douglas took the lead again. 'At the end is the communications centre,' he explained. He nodded to Sergeant Maddox, who opened the door. This was her realm, and it fell to her to introduce it.

This room, at least, was impressive. It was some sixty feet long and twenty wide. There was a bank of communications gear in the centre of the room, with the stations manned, though none of the equipment was yet in use. At the far end of the room, taking up a large table, was another map of the United Kingdom, this time laid out. It was some ten feet by about eight. On the board were three sets of markers and a small model aircraft.

'Corps deployment,' Maddox explained. 'Dolerite Base,' she said, pointing out their position. '1 Battalion is stationed at Stirling Castle, and 2 Battalion is currently at… Salisbury Plain. There's no permanent base for them, and they can be mobilised quickly and moved to wherever they are needed.'

'We're selecting carefully for our forces, so, as I said, we're nowhere near full strength yet,' Lethbridge-Stewart added. 'Thankfully, things have been a bit quiet the past couple of weeks and we've not needed to mobilize. Plenty of training going on, of course.'

'And the toy aircraft?' Bryden asked, sarcastically.

'Mobile HQ,' Maddox explained. 'It's a modified Hercules; can fly to wherever we're needed with everything we need to set up a forward base.'

Grant grinned and rubbed his hands together. 'Terrific spy stuff, eh?' he commented. 'Got a niece who's mad keen on that sort of thing. Got a crush on Sean Connery, don't you know?' He winked at Maddox. 'Then again, all the lasses do, I expect. Isn't he a local?

'I do believe he's from Edinburgh, yes,' Lethbridge-Stewart said, just about exhausting his knowledge on the subject. 'Perhaps we'd better move on?' he suggested.

'Yes, I think we've quite exhausted the conversational options in here,' Bryden agreed.

Out in the corridor again, Douglas approached the final door. This was a reinforced blast door, currently closed. Douglas unlatched and opened it, to reveal a long, bleak corridor ahead of them.

Grant's face fell. 'It's a bit of a walk.'

'Then the exercise will do you good,' Bryden said. 'What's down here?'

'I call it SAR; Science and Research,' Miss Travers said, since this was her area. 'We have to keep it as separate as possible from the rest of Dolerite.'

'Why?' asked Grant. 'Is this where you store the alien bodies?'

Miss Travers managed not to roll her eyes, and Lethbridge-Stewart was grateful. 'No, I think the Americans have the monopoly on dead aliens at the moment,' she said. 'But we do store special technology down here.'

Bryden came to life sharply. 'Dominator technology?' he asked.

'Yes, that's been moved here,' Anne said. 'That's in the restricted area, though.' They had reached the door at the far end, and this was also closed and sealed. Douglas set to work opening it.

'Why the thick doors?' Grant asked.

'Blast doors,' Miss Travers explained. 'They're afraid that some of my experiments might blow the place up, so we've got extra-thick walls in this area, as well as the protective doors.'

Grant patted her shoulder. 'Oh, I'm sure they're just overreacting, my dear,' he said.

Miss Travers frowned at him. 'Actually, I think they're *under*-reacting, Mr Grant. We're handling alien technology, and there's no way of knowing what might happen. Personally, I'd feel a lot safer if this section could be placed on the dark side of the Moon.'

Somehow, Grant didn't seem to take offense. 'But if you were there, we'd never get to see you. Besides, if anything went wrong, you might blow the Moon clear out of orbit.'

'Out of orbit?' Miss Travers looked sadly at him. 'That's a bit far-fetched.'

'Well, I suppose you should know,' Grant said. 'Being the boffin, and all that.' He looked slightly puzzled. 'Why don't they call you *Doctor* Travers?'

Lethbridge-Stewart winced; this was another subject Miss Travers could go on about almost forever. Her disdain for the university system and her education in the more esoteric branches of research. He had a suspicion that neither Bryden nor Grant would be impressed. Thankfully, before she could begin, Douglas swung the door open.

'Right,' Lethbridge-Stewart said, trying to hide his relief. 'Now for the labs, eh, Miss Travers?'

Thankfully, she caught on. 'Of course, Brigadier,' she agreed. 'Gentlemen, if you'll follow me...?'

They were in yet another corridor beyond the door. There were doors lining either side, starting about forty feet down. Miss Travers gestured to the doors on the right. 'Mechanical Rooms,' she explained. 'We're tied into the national grid for our power generally, but there are back-up generators. That also houses the air circulation and so forth. My labs are on the right.'

Grant frowned slightly. 'So if you were to... ah... blow the place up, Dolerite Base would lose power and air? That seems a trifle... unwise. Without power to the lifts and with the air circulation out...' Lethbridge-Stewart realised that Grant wasn't as genial and dim-witted as he had been acting. He wondered how much of it was a façade.

Miss Travers, too, looked at the ministry man with a trifle more respect. 'There are backups on all floors,' she explained. 'If we were to go into lockdown for any reason, they automatically come on line. If this level explodes, it shouldn't affect the other levels aversely. At the very least, we'd be able to evacuate Dolerite.'

'That's good to know.'

Miss Travers opened the first door on the right. 'This way, if you please.' The corridor led into the main laboratory space.

Lethbridge-Stewart had very little idea what all the equipment inside was actually for, but he had to admit it looked nice and shiny and impressive. The lab was a large one, sixty feet by twenty. Electronic equipment lined the walls, and there was some sort of a test rig on a table close to the door. Several other tables held equally esoteric materials. There were three low bookcases laden with texts and magazines.

Bryden looked impressed. Lethbridge-Stewart imagined that the businessman had some idea what he was looking at; he was, after all, in electronics himself, making much of his money from consumer electronics. His firms were second only to International Electromatics in the world markets. 'And is all of this... human technology?' he asked.

'It is,' Miss Travers replied. 'All the exo-tech stuff is kept under lock and key.'

'But you *are* examining it?' he asked.

'Define *examining*,' Travers said. 'I'm *studying* it, but we're far from doing anything else to it.'

The industrialist looked angry. 'Do you have any idea what incredible strides forward we could take if we learned the secrets of Yeti technology?' he asked. 'Why, it's light-years ahead of us in robotics alone!'

'I don't think you quite comprehend the dangers involved here, Mr Bryden,' Miss Travers snapped. 'The Great Intelligence is somehow connected to that *technology*. If we were to examine it, to power it up without stringent precautions, it could give the Intelligence an anchor point and allow it to reach out again.'

Bryden glared at Lethbridge-Stewart. 'I thought you said the Great Intelligence was dead? It's in all the reports.'

'Which I didn't write,' Lethbridge-Stewart pointed out. 'They originated from General Hamilton's office, not mine. I am not so certain the Intelligence is dead, though it *has* withdrawn, as far as we can tell. But when you are dealing with non-human forces, Mr Bryden, it is quite difficult at times to be entirely sure that *dead* is an appropriate description.'

Bryden glared from Lethbridge-Stewart to Miss Travers. 'So you do *nothing* with this potential Aladdin's cave of wonders?' he asked, incredulously. 'It's just sitting there, untouched?'

'For the moment,' Miss Travers agreed smoothly. 'That is my recommendation.'

Bryden turned to Lethbridge-Stewart. 'And you allow women to set your policy?'

'When they are right, I listen to their recommendations,' Lethbridge-Stewart answered. 'And, on this matter, I am quite convinced that Miss Travers is perfectly correct.'

Bryden shook his head. 'When I get back to Whitehall, I shall have a few things to say about this,' he warned. 'We need to protect this country, and we should use every tool at our disposal. *Every* tool,' he stressed.

'Of course, you are entitled to say whatever you wish,'

Lethbridge-Stewart agreed. 'And if I am ordered to, we shall begin to cautiously commence more direct studies, subject to Miss Travers' advice and precautions. She is, after all, our Head of Scientific Research, and we would be foolish to ignore her advice.'

'As you say,' Bryden murmured. 'She *is* your scientific advisor. At least for now.'

Miss Travers couldn't fail to get the implied threat, but, thankfully, didn't raise to the bait. 'Shall we continue, gentlemen?'

The next laboratory was the chemical one, filled with the sort of equipment Lethbridge-Stewart hadn't really seen since his school days – test tubes, retorts, pipettes, Bunsen burners and so forth – as well as a large stock of chemicals and testing agents. Everything so far was absolutely spick and span as there had been no call on its services. Miss Travers was about to lead the way to the next room when a soldier hurried up, saluted and then handed a message to Sergeant Maddox. Maddox glanced at it and then looked up.

'It's the message you've been waiting for, sir,' she reported. 'HMS *Kraken* is entering the search area.'

'Excellent,' Lethbridge-Stewart replied, and meant it.

'What's this about?' Bryden asked, sourly.

'I'm afraid we'll have to curtail the tour, gentlemen,' Lethbridge-Stewart said, hopefully managing to hide his relief. 'Dolerite Base may be getting its baptism.'

— CHAPTER THREE —

Poor Me

'Set 'em up, Joe,' Harold Chorley snapped, pushing a couple of well-used pound notes onto the pub's very stained counter.

'Do you think you should, Mr Chorley?' the landlord asked. 'You've been acting a bit... odd lately. And my name's not Joe, it's Thomas.'

Chorley glared at the thick-set man – who obviously enjoyed his own beer – and frowned. 'Odd in what way, *Joe*?'

The landlord sighed, but then evidently decided not to argue. 'Scotch or bourbon?'

'What did I have last time I was here?'

'Scotch.'

'Then let's be fair, and make this one bourbon,' Chorley decided. Joe took a bottle from behind the bar and poured a stingy measure. Chorley leaned across and tipped the bottom of the bottle to double it. The landlord glared, corked the bottle and took the money.

As he had the previous three times he'd been in here, Chorley sat the drink down in front of himself and simply looked at it. When his troubles had started all those months ago, he'd begun drinking, hoping this would help him somehow. It hadn't, and he'd now hit upon a new plan, one which clearly bothered the landlord.

'Are you drinking to forget?' he asked, a minimal amount of sympathy in his voice. 'Or forgetting to drink?'

Chorley barked a rough laugh. 'No, my friend, I was drinking *because* I've forgotten.'

'Beg your pardon?'

'Granted.' Chorley stared at the bourbon. 'There are chunks of my memory missing, Joe.'

'The booze'll do that to you.'

'It went missing *before* I started drinking. Well, the second time I started drinking, anyway,' Chorley informed him.

Joe blinked. 'How did that happen, Mr Chorley?'

'I have no idea.' Chorley waved his glass at the man. 'And *that* is why I drank. And now I am *not* drinking instead. Kindly leave me to do so in peace.' The man glared at him, but did as he was told, moving to serve another less puzzling customer.

Chorley liked this pub. He thought it was *The Three Cripples* – the name seemed appropriate for the state he was in – but he wasn't entirely sure. The lights were dim, the customers few, the smoke thick and the jukebox thankfully silent, and that was all he cared about.

Chorley had *needed* the drink. Of course he had known he was overdoing it, but that was rather the point, wasn't it? It was utterly impossible to explain to any other person how he felt, but he *knew* there was a section of his memories gone, wrenched from him. But how and why? He didn't even know who had done it, although it most certainly was due to being sent on a mission to Dominex by Colonel Lethbridge-Stewart. Dominex was gone now, and so was a part of his life, most likely never to return. He felt violated and terrified. If it had happened once, who was to say it couldn't happen again? And again? And what if –

'Blimey, Mr C, you 'ere again?'

Chorley winced. This was the last thing he needed, the mood he was in. 'Go away, Markham. You're the last person I want to talk to right now. I have contemplation to... contemplate.'

Markham ignored the order. He hooked a stool with his foot and dragged it over so he could sit beside Chorley. 'Mind you, a chance to stare into glasses would be a fine thing, Mr C.'

'I'm sure it would,' Chorley grunted. 'But I don't feel like contributing to the Markham Thirst Quenching Fund tonight. So shove off, like a good little nark.'

'Mr C!' Somehow Markham's little ratty face managed to look affronted. 'I ain't no nark. I'm the purveyor of information what's of interest to other folk.'

'I'm impressed. You must have been reading. I didn't know you knew any three syllable words. But I'm not interested in buying any of your tips tonight. Tonight I am thinking.'

'Seems to me you're not getting anywhere fast. What you need instead of thinkin' is a nice, juicy story.'

Despite his protestations, Markham *was* a nark. He had a habit of listening in on things without being seen, and had a large network of 'friends' who supplied him with items from time to time. His general course of action was to sell what he learned to the police first, and then to find Chorley or another reporter to resell the information. For such a low-life, Markham was actually rather reliable, and normally Chorley would have been happy to hand over a fiver.

'Allow me to proceed in peace, then,' Chorley requested. 'I am interested in nothing else tonight.'

'You sure?' Markham peered intently at his face. 'Well, 'ow about the ship what sunk?'

'What ship sunk?'

'The pirate ship.'

'That was hundreds of years ago,' Chorley said, irritated. 'Hundreds and hundreds. There are no pirates anymore.'

'Not *that* kind of pirate, Mr C. You know, the ones that play music.'

'Oh, *those*.' Chorley shook his head, keeping his eyes on the drink that he really didn't need. 'Noisy brutes. They should all sink.'

'Well, this one did, yer see. Accompanied by shooting stars.'

'I can think of a few stars I'd like to shoot,' Chorley muttered. 'Starting with Ken Dodd. If I hear that song *Tears* one more time…'

'Not *them* stars,' Markham said. 'Ones what fall out of the sky. Right next to this 'ere ship. The one what sinks.'

Despite himself, Chorley discovered he was starting to get interested. This sounded like it might be right up his alley. And, more to the point, right up Lethbridge-Stewart's alley. He needed a decent reason to contact that man again – the one man who *did* have answers. He looked at his glass, and pushed it towards Markham. 'No sense in wasting this,' he said, amiably. 'Tell me more.'

Markham grabbed the glass fast, in case it might be withdrawn, and downed it in a single gulp. Then he began to talk.

'What is this all about, Brigadier?' Bryden asked, as Lethbridge-Stewart led the group back to the situations room.

'One of those so-called pirate radio stations went off the air last night in the middle of a show. The last transmissions suggested they were sinking. The RAF did a flyover at first light; there's no sign of the ship.'

'It's probably just some sort of publicity stunt,' Bryden muttered. 'They're always doing silly stuff to get their name in the papers and attract more listeners.'

'That might be the case if they came back on the air,' Miss Travers said. 'But where's the advantage to getting publicity if you're not transmitting? And where is the ship? Even if we assume this *is* some sort of publicity stunt, the ship was out past the three-mile limit last night; it was seen by a passing freighter.'

'Put in to shore somewhere?' Grant suggested.

'Not at any port on the east coast of Scotland,' Lethbridge-Stewart said.

'It could be halfway across the North Sea by now,' Grant mused.

'That's a possibility. But not a very likely one. We've got an alert out; if any other ship spots it, we'll get a call. So far, nothing.'

'Very well,' Bryden said, as if he were the decision-maker. 'Let's assume that these nuisances were telling the truth, and their ship *did* sink. What's that to us? Surely it's something the maritime authorities should deal with?'

'Normally, yes,' Miss Travers agreed. 'But this *isn't* normal. The freighter that spotted *Crossbones* also saw a shooting star in the same area, at the exact time the ship reported it was sinking.'

'So?' Bryden scowled. 'Shooting stars are hardly uncommon.'

Grant's face lit up. 'Ah! You don't think it *was* a shooting star, do you?'

'It was travelling awfully slowly for a meteor,' Miss Travers said.

The ministry man rubbed his hands together in glee. 'You think it might have been a flying saucer?' he asked, clearly excited by the prospect.

'Well, I think we should try and rule it out, at least,' Miss Travers replied. She appeared to be enjoying his response, all of her earlier irritation now vanished.

'It's most likely a wild-goose chase,' Bryden point out.

'That's what we're hoping *Kraken* can tell us,' Lethbridge-Stewart said.

They reached the situations room, and Sergeant Maddox hurried across to confer with her girls. The large table map was illuminated now, and a model ship had been placed off the Scottish coast. There was an air of quiet tension in the room.

Maddox straightened up from the board. 'We have contact with *Kraken* now, sir,' she reported crisply.

'Splendid,' Lethbridge-Stewart said. 'Put it on the speakers; let's hear what they have to report.'

'Let's have a look-see, eh, Mr Mellors, shall we?' Captain McKenzie held out a hand and his first officer placed the binoculars in them. They were on *Kraken*'s bridge as the frigate made its way into the target area. As ever, the seas were a little choppy – the North Sea was never over-calm – and McKenzie barely noticed the sway in the deck. After thirty years at sea, it would take more than a little swell to disturb his calm.

'Nothing showing on radar, sir,' Mellors reported.

'No.' McKenzie scanned the horizon, and visual inspection confirmed the radar report; there was nothing visible at all beyond grey skies and greyer waters. 'Well, we've barely arrived, so there's no telling what we'll find. Put a couple of hands for'ard to check for debris.'

'You think the radio ship might have sunk, sir?'

McKenzie shrugged. 'Don't know what to think yet,' he admitted. 'This is probably nothing more than a wild-goose chase. Those radio chappies are probably ashore having a pint somewhere and don't have a clue the amount of fuss they're causing.'

'You're probably right, sir.' Mellors grinned. 'Could do with a pint myself, now you've mentioned it.'

'Pint?' McKenzie gave him a mock-glare. 'Whisky is the only true drink for a man.' He glanced across the bridge toward the radio shack. 'Are we still in touch with that Fifth Operational crew?'

'Yes, sir, we're keeping an open line, as ordered.'

McKenzie nodded. He had no idea why he was reporting their findings to an army unit – nobody bothered to explain anything, of course – but Admiral Hennessy had been quite explicit about this. Even if they *did* find a problem – which McKenzie didn't expect – what could those land-bound fellows do anyway? Probably just more official nonsense, but… 'Better send them a report telling them we've arrived in the search area and we're proceeding. Then see if you can rustle up some tea, eh? We may not be able to have a tipple, but I need something to help out. This could be a long search.'

'Sir.' Mellors shot off to do as he'd been told. He was a good chappie, handy to have around.

McKenzie brought up the binoculars again and took another sweep of the horizon. Not that he expected to see it changed from the last one.

Chorley was feeling more like his old self again with the arrival of the dawn. Maybe it was symbolic, or maybe he was simply clutching at straws, but at least there was now something for him to look forward to again; a story. He hadn't managed anything substantial since his frustrating interview with Big Billy Lovac.

He'd checked the early editions, and there was just a short note in *The Mirror* about Radio Crossbones going off the air in mid-broadcast. The writer had (in typical *Mirror* tradition) jokingly suggested they may have been captured by real pirates. It wasn't news, of course, just a quick joke. None of the other papers even gave it that much space. They probably figured it was just some silly publicity stunt and dismissed it.

Chorley wasn't so sure. That shooting star aspect intrigued him. Maybe it was only because of his run-ins with Lethbridge-Stewart and his let's-keep-it-all-an-official-secret brigade; maybe he was seeing conspiracies where they didn't exist. But he'd always been proud of his instincts, and right now they were telling him that there was definitely something to this story. He just didn't know what – yet.

He'd put in a call to General Hamilton's office and been

stone-walled. To his mind, that meant they were up to something. There was no point in avoiding the press if you didn't have something to hide. It didn't mean it was this Crossbones affair, of course, but there didn't seem to be much else going on: the usual troubles in Northern Ireland, of course, and the aftermath of the IRA bombing of the London Hilton five days ago. But right now, though, he'd lucked out; he'd interviewed Doctor Cullen at Jodrell Bank about a year back, and when he'd called the radio telescope, it turned out that this was one of Cullen's days at the Bank, so he'd been able to claim friendship. That was stretching things a bit, but it had ensured they hadn't hung up on him.

'Chorley?' The voice was loud in his ear, and he moved the phone an inch or so further away. Cullen was a large man, and he didn't talk, he boomed. 'What the devil do you want?'

'Just a quick bit of information,' Chorley said. 'I was wondering what you might know of a meteor that fell last night off the east coast of Scotland, a couple of miles from Peterhead.'

'I've heard nothing about that.' Cullen's voice lowered a bit. 'I'll ask around and get back to you. But why in the blazes are you interested in meteors, man? Don't tell me you've decided to report some real news at last?' Chorley told him about Radio Crossbones going off the air at the time of the meteorite. 'What? You think the blasted meteorite sank the ship? Do you have any idea how improbable that is?'

'Well, you know the old line from Sherlock Holmes,' Chorley said. 'When you've eliminated the impossible, whatever left, however improbable, must be the truth. Or

43

something like that.'

'You're a dunderhead, Chorley,' Cullen growled. 'But if there *was* a meteor fall last night, I'm certainly interested. I'll call you back.'

Chorley hung up, thoughtfully. 'Meteorite Sinks Pirates' would certainly make a great headline. If matters were quite that simple.

Captain McKenzie sipped the steaming tea as the search continued. They were inside the probable zone now, and so far had seen no indications that a ship had even been there. If *Crossbones* had sunk, there ought at least to be debris, but nothing out of the ordinary had yet been spotted. How long, McKenzie wondered, did the Admiralty and this Fifth Operational Corps want him to continue the search?

One of the men he'd posted forward suddenly waved an arm, and gestured with the other. 'Objects ahead!' he called out. 'Slightly to starboard.'

McKenzie put down his tea, and snatched up his binoculars. He couldn't make much out, but there did seem to be some sort of a silvery sheen to the water. 'Three points to starboard,' he called out to Mellors, who repeated the order on.

Slowly, *Kraken* turned and surged forward, toward the silvery spot. As the frigate ploughed through the waves, McKenzie saw that the sheen was turning into individual shapes. Something floating on the surface of the water.

A few moments later, the lookout called up, 'It's fish, sir, dead fish.'

What the blazes? 'All stop,' McKenzie ordered. To the observer, he said, 'Get the nets and bring some aboard. I want to know what killed them.'

It took a few minutes and a few extra men, but eventually one of the nets was hauled aboard, with a few dozen fish in it. The lookout pulled one out and examined it.

'Well, man?' McKenzie called.

The man looked confused. 'I hope the cook's made plenty of chips for dinner tonight, sir,' he finally said.

'What do you mean?'

The sailor shrugged. 'These fish, sir, they've all been cooked.'

CHAPTER FOUR

We've Gotta Get Out of This Place

Mary's head felt like it was being hacked open from the inside. She groaned, and then she felt wet. Something pushed at her.

'Don't move.' It was Alan's voice. 'You cracked your head pretty badly. The bleeding's stopped, and I don't think you've broken any bones. But you should stay still for a bit.'

'Not bloody likely,' Mary said, struggling to sit up and open her eyes. 'What happened?'

'I don't know. I recovered about ten minutes ago.'

Mary managed to get her eyes open. Water was dripping down from her forehead, and she put a hand up. It encountered some sort of bandage.

'Wet compress,' Alan informed her. 'To stop the bleeding.'

Mary grunted, and looked around. They were still in the corridor on *Crossbones*, but main power seemed to be out. The emergency lighting was on, but flickering, and she felt like she was in a metal cave; a cold, damp, dark metal cave. The speakers were dead. Then she realised that the deck underneath her was tilted at about a thirty-degree angle.

'Are we listing?' she asked, worried. 'Maybe the ship hit something?'

'I don't think so,' Alan replied. 'There's no movement.

Feel.'

He was right; the deck was tilted, but absolutely steady. If they were floating crippled, there would be rise and fall from the swell.

'Maybe we ran aground?' Mary suggested.

'We were outside the three-mile limit. Power went out; it's still out. I doubt we've been unconscious long enough for the ship to have floated that far.' Alan glanced at his watch. 'It's six twelve,' he informed her. 'Can't tell if that's am or pm, though I suspect the former, as I've not wound my watch and it's still going. That implies we've been out for maybe seven hours.'

'Maybe we ran ashore on an island?' She tried to remember her geography. 'Are there any out here?'

He shrugged. 'There's Strommach,' he said. 'Smallish place a mile or two off the coast. I suppose we *might* have drifted that far. As I recall, there's just one village, a fishing village, but if we *are* there, then somebody most likely would have a phone.' He looked at her in concern. 'I'll just have a look up top and then come right back, I promise. You just rest and gather your strength, okay?'

Mary wanted to protest, but she really didn't have the energy. And he was right; one look from the deck would tell them a lot. 'Okay.'

'Be right back,' Alan repeated, and patted her arm. Then he set off up the sloping corridor to the door that led onto the deck.

She smiled at his back. He really was one of the good guys. She couldn't imagine what would be happening now if she'd been stuck with Larry instead.

Which made her wonder; how come they were the only

47

two around? The ship had a crew of about a dozen, and the radio station at least as many again. *Crossbones* wasn't a large ship, so surely there ought to be more people stumbling about by now? It couldn't be that only she and Al were ambulatory, surely?

She heard the clanking of the door to the deck being opened. That was Al, poking his nose out. Maybe he'd have news for her in a minute. If *Crossbones* had run aground on Strommach – or some other place – then there were bound to be locals investigating, weren't there? If a strange ship had run aground in *her* backyard, she'd certainly have taken a look!

Then something occurred to her; the door was only at the end of the corridor, and it opened directly onto the main deck. If Alan's watch was correct, it was six o'clock. Morning or evening, it should be light outside. And if it were light outside, there should be sunshine streaming down the corridor toward her.

But it was still dark and gloomy.

Then Alan was back with her. Even in the dim lighting, she could see the worried look on his face. 'Where are we?' she asked him.

'I don't know,' he said, his voice shaking a bit. 'It's pitch black outside; much darker than it should be. I can't see a thing. Literally no stars, not a flicker of light out there.'

Mary shivered, and it didn't have much to do with the fact that she was cold. 'That doesn't make sense.'

'No,' he agreed. 'But, honestly, has *anything* made sense so far?'

Good point. 'What are we going to do?'

'We need light,' Alan said. 'Maybe with a strong torch

we can see something to give us a clue. And the only place I can think of that might have a torch is the bridge. I know the way there, so I'll just –'

'No!' Mary realised she sounded on the verge of hysteria, but she didn't care. 'Not *I* – make it *we*. I'm not staying here all by myself.'

'Mary you need…' he began, but she cut him off.

'I need to be with you, Alan,' she said, as firmly as she could. 'I can't stay here on my own. Please, Al, don't make me beg.'

He looked as if he was going to argue again, but he shook his head and sighed. 'Okay,' he agreed. 'If I were in your position, I'm sure I'd feel the same way.' He gave a weak grin. 'Actually, probably a lot more hysterical.'

'I find that hard to believe.'

'What, that I can get hysterical?'

'No, that you can out-hysterical me.' She accepted his help and stood up, gingerly. Her head felt light, but then it calmed down, leaving her with just a dull throb. 'It's okay,' she decided. 'I think I can walk unaided. To the bridge!' A thought managed to seep through into her aching head. 'Hang on. If there's no light outside, how will we be able to find our way?'

'You can get to the bridge staying inside the ship,' Alan pointed out. 'And the emergency lights are working in here, thank God.'

'Great.' Mary brightened up a bit. 'And we might run across some other people, too.'

'I'm kind of surprised we haven't already,' Alan admitted. 'Well, we have to go past the studio first, and there ought to be somebody around there.'

'Hey!' Mary said, as another thought hit her. 'We might be able to send a signal from there. Get help.'

'Not until we can tell people where we are. But that's not a bad idea. We should check the transmitter as we go past, that's for certain. Somebody must know we're off the air by now. I know our audience figures could be better, but I'd think one or two people might have missed us by now. There might even be people looking for us already.'

Mary was managing to walk reasonably steadily. The deck felt funny, partly because of the angle it was inclined at, and partly because it wasn't swaying. She was used to that by now, and it felt odd when the motion was missing. Alan supported her from time to time if it looked like she might fall, but otherwise left her to manage by herself, and she appreciated that.

They made it to the studio without seeing anyone else. The door was closed. Alan opened it. 'Uh, better stay back,' he advised her.

'Why?' She ignored the hand he threw up and pushed into the doorway.

The room was a shambles. Records had been jarred free and hurtled across the room, shattering like black snow over everything. The stacked record players had fallen, as had several portions of the transmitter. Larry was still mostly in his chair, crushed there when an electronic panel had collapsed onto him. His skull was partially caved in. Mary felt sick.

The producer, Tom Wentworth, had died also. He still had his earphones on, and the long, jagged shard of a 7-inch record was buried deep in his left eye. There was less blood around him, but still far too much.

'There's nothing we can do here,' Al said, grimly. He pushed her back and closed the door again. 'You okay?'

'No,' Mary admitted. She was light-headed, but she felt terrible that the uppermost thought on her mind was *thank God that wasn't me!* She hadn't been fond of Larry, but he was at least less obnoxious than Tom; it was still horrible that he was dead, though, but he had died quickly. A small relief. 'Well, the transmitter looked pretty much beyond repair,' she managed to say. 'Not to mention Larry and Tom.'

'Yes,' Alan agreed. 'But the radio on the bridge might still be operational.'

'We'd best carry on, then.'

Alan nodded, and she suspected he was just as glad to get away from this scene as she was. She remembered Alan telling her a couple of times that he'd served in the last war, so he'd probably seen dead people before. But that didn't mean he was inured to the sight. She'd never seen anyone dead, not even her grandmother, who'd died twelve years earlier. Mary was certain her dreams from here on would be... disturbing.

'Can we be the only survivors?' she wondered aloud.

'It would be unlikely,' Al said. 'Larry and Tom might be the only... casualties.'

'Then where is everybody?'

Alan shrugged. 'Anyone alive and awake would probably head where we're heading. If there is anyone else, that's the likeliest place to find them.'

That made sense. Mary hoped that there were more survivors. Not just for their sake, but so that she and Al wouldn't be the only living people on a shipload of corpses.

*

Alan led the way to a set of stairs – did they call them stairs on a ship? Sailors seemed to have odd names for everything – and then up a deck. A second set of stairs later, and they emerged into a short corridor. At the end of it she could see stronger lights, and this time they appeared to be moving.

More people!

'Hello!' she called out. 'Hello!'

A face appeared in the doorway and then a bright light shone right in her eyes. She yelped, and threw up her hand.

'Sorry, lassie.' The light was lowered. Through the yellow blotches flashing in her eyes she could make out a sailor, dressed for heavy weather. 'I dinnae think. Are the two of you well?'

'As well as can be expected,' Alan said. He was blinking heavily, obviously having been caught in the torch's beam as well. 'How many of you are there?'

'Six,' the sailor replied. 'I dinnae ken if we're all that's alive, though.'

A second sailor poked his head around the door. 'We were about to go and have a wee look,' he said.

'Do you know where we are?' Mary asked, anxiously. The bridge was clearly quite small, so she couldn't get inside. She desperately wanted to look out.

'No idea, lassie,' the first sailor said. 'We're no longer at sea, mind.'

'Can't you see anything out there?' asked Al.

'Oh, aye,' the second man said. 'But it doesnae make much sense.' He shifted a bit, creating a slight gap. 'Ye're welcome to take a look,' he offered.

Neither of them wanted to miss out, and they crowded

into the cramped space on the tiny bridge. Mary saw the other four men – two were working on the radio, a third held a torch so they could see – and gave a quick nod before looking out of the window. The second sailor shone his heavy-duty torch through the glass.

As Alan had informed her, it was pitch black outside. The beam played across a portion of the deck, and then over the side of the ship. She could make out vague shapes of rocks, but literally nothing else. Alan pushed the man's hand slightly to get him to shine the light further out. But all that was visible was more rocks.

'Did we run aground?' Mary asked, confused.

'No, lassie,' the first man replied. 'If we had, there would be a sight of water on one side of us. But there's only the rocks as far as we can see.'

'Aye, and if ye look, ye'll see they're all dry,' the second sailor pointed out. 'Wherever we are, they should be wet.'

The more she discovered, the less sense any of this made. 'And where's the sky?' she asked.

'A good question, lassie. I wish I had as good an answer.'

'Some of us should take a look outside,' Alan said. 'We might get a few answers that way.' He glanced at the men working on the radio. 'Any idea how long it'll be before you get that working?'

'No telling, lad,' the spokes-sailor replied. 'It doesnae appear to be broken, but neither does it appear to be working.' He shrugged. 'Mind, I agree wi' ye about taking a wee look around down there. Perhaps the two of us?'

'Three,' Mary said, very firmly. 'I want to know what's going on.'

'Isnae that just like a woman?' the sailor muttered. 'Well, aye, why not? Ye'll just be in the way here if ye stay.'

It wasn't the most gracious acceptance Mary had ever had, but right now she'd take whatever she could get. And pray that they would find some answers to all of this.

Now that Chorley had a plan of action, he felt more like his old self again. Maybe there was nothing to this story of the missing ship, but every journalistic instinct he had was informing him that this was indeed a trail to be followed. He'd been keeping an eye on Lethbridge-Stewart since he'd stitched Chorley up with that Big Billy Lovac interview, and Chorley doubted it purely a coincidence that Lethbridge-Stewart had been sighted in Scotland. Stirling, in particular, but that was besides the point. Scotland was still Scotland. Chorley hated the word 'coincidence', though it sometimes happened.

The phone rang, and he answered it. It turned out to be Cullen calling back.

'There does seem to be something to what you heard,' he confirmed. 'Several people reported seeing a meteorite last night in that area. Unfortunately, it seems to have gone down in the sea. I'd have loved to have had a chance to collect a fresh sample. And the timing is right with that radio ship going off the air. But it doesn't mean the meteorite hit the ship and sank it; that would be too much of a long shot.'

'I'm willing to bet on long shots sometimes,' Chorley admitted. 'And I'm going to check on this. I'll call you back.'

'If you need more help,' Cullen finished. 'I know, I know. You'll be disappointed up there, though, trust me. This story isn't what you think it is.'

'I really don't know what it is yet,' Chorley admitted. 'But I'm going to find out.' He hung up and finished packing his suitcase. He had just enough time to get to the station for the *Flying Scotsman*. He'd be in Edinburgh in less than nine hours. He could rent a car there for the rest of the journey.

It felt really good to be on the hunt again. And if this turned out to be nothing but a will o' the wisp in the end, at least he'd be able to drown his sorrows with some very fine Scottish whisky. He might need it.

'Well, what do you make of this, Miss Travers?'

Anne gave Lethbridge-Stewart a cheeky grin. 'I've heard that the Scots do strange and disgusting things with their cooking, Brigadier, but I don't think even they would cook fish while it's still in the ocean.'

'Then what might?'

'Well, there's the obvious explanation. That meteorite.' She shuffled through the stack of reports on the desk. Maddox quietly slipped her the right one. 'Thanks. Yes, here it is; glowing object in the sky, hits the water... Meteors can build up terrific speed and heat when they pass through the atmosphere. When it hit the water, the ocean conducted a great deal of that heat away, and the fish were cooked.'

'In other words,' Bryden said tersely, 'there's a perfectly simple and rational explanation for this, and we needn't get involved?'

Anne shrugged. 'There's *a* simple explanation,' she agreed. 'I can't confirm it's the right one, of course, though it does look fairly obvious, doesn't it?' She glanced apologetically at Lethbridge-Stewart. 'Sorry, Brigadier.'

'No apologies needed,' he assured her. He made a quick decision. 'Well, it looks like the Navy has matters well in hand here. Let's leave them to their search for the missing ship. It doesn't look like anything we need concern ourselves with.' He turned to Maddox. 'Nevertheless, keep an eye on the situation, Sergeant, and let me know if anything changes.'

'Yes, sir.'

Lethbridge-Stewart dismissed the problem from his mind. 'Right then, anybody fancy a brew?'

The sailor who finally introduced himself as *Jock* led Mary and Alan to the main deck. The thirty-degree tilt meant that the port side was lower than the starboard, so that was the way he led them. He clutched the rail in one hand to steady himself and shone his torch over the side. There was dry land down there, and several large boulders scattered about. It looked to be about a twenty-foot drop; too far for them to jump, and then they'd have no way back.

'You have a rope?' she asked Jock.

'Better, lassie,' he said. 'There's a ladder we use for when we've a tender out. That should about reach the ground there.' He moved to a stowage locker, hauled out the end of the rope ladder he'd mentioned, and threw it over the side. 'I think even ye can scamper down that, eh?'

'No problem,' she assured him. She put out a hand to grasp it, but Alan knocked it aside.

'I'll go first,' he said, gently. 'Just in case.'

Mary couldn't be angry with his chauvinism; she knew he meant well, and was trying to be protective. 'After you,' she agreed.

He handed her his torch and scuttled down the ladder

with surprising agility. When he was on dry ground, he held up his hands, and she dropped the torch into them. She followed it up with her own torch, and then descended the swaying ladder herself. Jock came after her; thankfully, he was wearing heavy-duty pants and not a kilt as she had no desire to discover what Scots wore under them.

They stood in a small group together for a moment. Mary turned her torch onto the side of the ship. The ground they were on was loose, and she could see that the weight of the ship had made it sink five or six inches into the loamy soil. She played her light down the side of the ship. The ground was dry dirt as far as she could see.

'Al,' she said, softly. 'Look at the ship; it's sunk a few inches into the soil.'

'So?'

She played her light again along the bottom of the hull. 'If we'd run aground here – wherever *here* is – shouldn't the ship have dug a groove in the soil?' It was untouched.

'That's… strange,' he admitted. 'Then *how* did we get here? It looks as if the ship was somehow just plonked down on this spot.'

'That seems to be as likely as anything else that's happened to us so far,' Mary muttered. They all shone their torches around, but all that could be seen was the flattish ground and the scattering of rocks. Mary glanced upward, but there was only blackness; neither sun, moon nor stars to be seen. And there was no breeze, the air was still and slightly smelling of the ocean. When she listened, she heard nothing.

None of which made any sense. It looked as though the ship had come aground somehow – though the *how* wasn't at all apparent – so there should be *some* signs around of where they were. But there was nothing, absolutely nothing. And *nothing* didn't make any sense. Mary had been something of a tomboy growing up, but she'd done some reading, mostly science fiction, which she enjoyed. Clarke, Hoyle, Wells… This was like something you'd read in one of their stories. Was it possible that they had somehow been taken – ship and all – to another world? Even if she could accept that, there still ought to be at least a sky above them and not nothing. Frustrated, she shone her torch upward, expecting to see more nothing.

It was hard to estimate distance, but perhaps a hundred feet into the air was a wall of rock. No, more accurately, a *roof* of rock.

'Dear God,' she gasped, as the bizarre truth hit her.

Alan and Jock followed her beam upward with their gaze. Both stiffened.

'It's a cave,' Mary said softly. 'Somehow, the ship is inside a cave.'

'Technically, I think it's a cavern,' Alan said. He seemed to be as stunned by this as she was, and wasn't really thinking about what he was saying. 'Could we somehow have *fallen* into it?'

'It doesn't seem likely,' Mary pointed out. 'I mean, how could the ocean just open up and drop us into a cavern and then for the cavern to close up again?'

'It couldnae,' Jock said, firmly. 'The ocean's hundreds o' feet deep where we were. It couldnae just vanish and let us drop, now, could it?'

'You have a valid point,' Mary agreed, still dazed. 'But since we *are* here, there must be some sort of entrance. And that means that there must therefore be an exit. We just have to find it. If we can get out of here, maybe some of this will start making sense.'

'Sense?' Al smiled. 'That would be nice. So, which way do we go?'

'Does it matter?' Mary asked. 'Whichever way we go, we're going to hit rock sooner or later. Then we just follow it until we find the exit.'

'Sounds as good an idea as any,' Alan agreed. 'Well, as the only lady present, why don't you pick a direction?'

Mary shrugged, and shone her torch beam at the ground in front of her. 'This way, then, I guess.'

Mary tried to rack her brains and remember any facts she could about caves and caverns. How big could this place be? That rock ceiling about their heads couldn't be too extensive, or it would collapse under its own weight. She vaguely recalled that you needed some sort of supports on arches or they'd collapse, but she had no idea how far apart the supports would have to be. Still, at least a couple of things were explained by their being in a cavern; the lack of light and the lack of vegetation. Without sunlight plants couldn't grow in here, although she thought there were some fungi and mosses that didn't need sunlight. Her science rarely went above A-level, and so wasn't sure if she was remembering correctly. Oh well, it wasn't important.

She smiled to herself. Her mind was rambling a bit. Shock, obviously.

The beam from her torch illuminated a pillar. It was tall and thin and carved from rock.

Carved? Well, maybe eroded?

'Fellas,' she said. 'Look at this.'

Alan and Jock shone their lights onto the pillar also. It was made from some sort of darkish rock, and was oddly lumpy. As her beam travelled up it, she saw that it wasn't supporting the ceiling at all. It ended some fourteen feet in the air, which didn't make any sense.

'There are more of them,' Alan said, shining his light about. 'Maybe some ancient building once stood down here?'

The pillar moved. Mary gasped. The bumps and hollows in the rocky surface weren't carved or eroded. They were limbs and features.

The rock-thing looked straight at her.

'Humans,' a thin, wavering voice said, quite distinctly.

— CHAPTER FIVE —

Yellow Submarine

'Well, thank goodness they're gone.' It had been quite a strain on Anne, dealing with their visitors. They hadn't asked as many inane questions as she'd been dreading, but she was glad she'd be able to get back to the important things now, like finishing setting up her labs. Then she saw the look that Lethbridge-Stewart was giving her. 'What?' she asked.

'They *are* paying the bills for your little toys, Miss Travers,' he said.

'And they were keeping me from playing with my *little toys*, Brigadier,' she informed him. 'If it's all the same to you, I'd like to get back to doing some real work around here.'

'So would we all,' Lethbridge-Stewart assured her. 'But if you don't mind, I've a couple of questions I'd like cleared up.' Douglas and Jean Maddox made a move to leave the office, but he waved a hand. 'No, this may concern the two of you as well.' He glanced at Bill, who was standing quietly in the background. *No need to tell him to stay*, Anne thought with a smile. The brigadier turned back to Anne. 'You were a trifle… abrupt with Mr Bryden.'

Anne was annoyed that she had to explain herself to him, especially since she was having trouble putting her feelings into words, which was unlike her. 'I've met the man before,' she said. 'I didn't like him then, and I've seen no reason to alter that opinion. He's arrogant and sexist, and a trifle shady.'

'In what way?'

'I simply don't trust him,' Anne said. 'He was awfully keen on seeing the alien technology, and didn't seem happy when we refused.'

'He's a businessman, Miss Travers,' Lethbridge-Stewart replied. 'He's always on the lookout for fresh products and opportunities. That's all.'

Douglas grinned. 'I heard he's been taking a bit of a pounding from International Electromatics these days. He probably just wants something he can market and out-sell their transistor radios.'

What they were saying made a lot of sense, and Anne wondered if she was allowing her personal distaste for the man to weigh down her judgment of him. 'Perhaps that's all it is,' she conceded. 'I'll try and conceal my revulsion in the future.'

'Thank you,' Lethbridge-Stewart said.

'What about that fellow, Grant?' Douglas asked, clearly trying to stifle a grin. 'Bit of a buffoon, wouldn't you say?'

Anne wasn't certain the remark was meant for her, but she answered it anyway. 'He's not as silly as he makes out, Walter,' she said. 'He paid attention when it mattered.'

'Yes,' Lethbridge-Stewart agreed. 'He's deeper than he appears to be.' He rapped his swagger stick into his gloved palm. 'Well, I think that's all for now. Back to work, everyone.'

'Ah, sir?' Jean said quietly.

'Yes, Sergeant?'

'There *is* one thing I think you should know. The Navy's been lying to us.'

That gave him pause. 'What?'

Jean hurried on. 'Well, *technically* not lying as such, sir, merely that they didn't tell us all that they know.'

'Explain yourself.'

'It's true that *Kraken* is doing a surface check on the missing ship, sir.' Jean paused and looked around the room; Anne nodded for her to continue. 'But they neglected to mention that they have a sub in the area also.'

'Indeed?' Lethbridge-Stewart raised an eyebrow.

'Yes, sir. *Venom*.'

HMS *Venom* slipped through the murky offshore Scottish waters, its occupants completely unaware that they were being tracked. Captain Browne prowled about the controls like a caged tiger, waiting for reports. Officially – and, in fact, mostly actually – their mission was sonar imaging of the seabed. They had been diverted from this routine and, to be honest, boring work by Admiral Hennessy, who had ordered them to look into the disappearance of a pirate radio ship. HMS *Kraken* on the surface had found no signs of the ship, and it was presumed to have sunk. *Venom*'s up-to-date sonar equipment was top of the line (at least according to the manufacturer, Bryden Industries) and it should be a doddle to pick up a freshly sunken ship, especially since they'd mapped this area just a couple of weeks back.

'Steady as she goes,' Lieutenant Devon murmured to the helmsmen. 'Keep us nice and even.'

'Sonar,' Browne called. 'Anything yet?'

'No, sir,' the rating replied. 'Everything's as before.'

Devon moved to join Browne. 'Any idea why we're doing this, sir?' he asked. 'A bit out of our line, isn't it, looking for sunken ships?'

'Orders, Number One,' Browne replied. 'What else? The brass don't see fit to explain themselves. I'm sure there's a good reason for this.'

'Are you, sir?'

Well, to be honest, no, but that wasn't the sort of thing you let your subordinates know you were thinking. 'Got something better to do, Mr Devon?'

'No, sir.'

Browne nodded, and Devon moved on to hover over the helmsmen. Devon was a good man, but he had to learn to restrain his curiosity. The Admiralty rarely bothered to explain their reasons to the rank and file, or even to mere captains. *Ours not to reason why...*

The search went on.

Anne studiously ignored Lethbridge-Stewart's look of annoyance. 'And if they didn't think to mention this to us, then how exactly do you know about it?' he asked.

'Um, that would be my doing,' Anne admitted, with a slight grin. Lethbridge-Stewart did not return it. 'I may have forgotten to mention the new decoding device I added to the mix in communications.'

'Yes, you may indeed have forgotten to mention it.' Lethbridge-Stewart gave her a very frosty glare. 'Perhaps you'd care to mention it now?'

'Yes, well, Jean happened to mention to me that the other branches of the Services have been a trifle less than co-operative from time to time, notably the Navy.' Anne didn't know quite why he was making her feel guilty. 'So I built a decoder for her that helps her track their vessels. You know, in case they forgot to tell us about them. Which they appear to have done in this case, so it's really probably a good thing, right?'

Lethbridge-Stewart cast his eyes upward as if appealing to Heaven for help. 'Miss Travers,' he said. 'If you're going to break the Official Secrets Act in future, I'd like to know about it. Preferably in advance.'

'You're saying I *shouldn't* have built the decoder?' Anne was a little annoyed. 'How was I to know it would break the Official Secrets Act? It was a *secret!*'

'Submarines are *supposed* to be hidden,' Lethbridge-Stewart said. 'If the Navy knew we could track them, they'd be furious.'

'Well, then, let's not tell them,' Anne said brightly. 'It can be *our* Official Secret!'

Douglas was clearly having a hard time keeping a straight face. 'She does have a point, sir,' he said wryly. 'They don't tell us; we don't tell them. Sounds fair to me.'

'We're supposed to be co-operating,' Lethbridge-Stewart pointed out.

'They're the ones who didn't co-operate first,' Anne objected.

'Which is all getting very much off the point.' Lethbridge-Stewart turned back to Jean. 'Maddox, are you sure that this submarine is investigating the missing ship?'

'Yes, sir. It's just entering the search zone. Can't be a coincidence.'

'No, it can't,' he agreed. 'Well, you'd better monitor it

and keep me informed. Ah... you *can* listen in on their communications, too, I suppose?'

Jean cast Anne a quick *sorry* look before saying, 'Yes, sir. That's one of the functions of the decoder.'

'Carry on, Sergeant.' Lethbridge-Stewart glared at Anne. 'Perhaps you'd better return to setting up your equipment, Miss Travers,' he suggested.

As Anne nodded and turned to leave, Douglas muttered to her: 'Good thing our visitors weren't here when that news came out.'

Jean wasn't stupid; she'd deliberately refrained from mentioning it until they were gone. Anne was grateful. 'Yes,' she agreed. 'Bryden would probably want to market it.'

Browne paced, waiting for some sign that his sub had found something. He knew that some people found working in submarines to be confining and even claustrophobic, but he found the experience exhilarating. The slow, steady heartbeat of the engines, the pulsing of the air circulators, the soft pinging of the sonar. It was a world of its own, a world he was familiar with and more than comfortable in. Even the half-light of the control room, so the operators could see their screens better, was normal to him. Down here, everything was calm and organised, smooth and predictable. *Venom* was unaffected by storms or swells, dwelling forever in a world of gentleness and placidity.

The sound of the sonar abruptly changed. 'I'm getting...' the operator started, and then: 'Obstruction dead ahead!'

'Hard a'port!' Browne snapped. 'Sonar, report.'

The engines howled, and the helmsmen responded

instantly, starting to turn the sub. Browne grabbed the nearest solid object – the faring about the periscope – and held on.

'Unknown, sir,' sonar called.

'The missing ship?' Browne asked.

'Too large, sir, much too large. It's on the seabed, but not on our maps.'

'Helm?'

'Turning two-eight degrees, sir,' the chief helmsman called.

'Closing,' sonar announced. 'Two hundred feet... One eighty...'

Browne made a decision. 'Prepare for impact,' he ordered. 'Sound the alert, Mr Devon.'

'Aye, sir.' Devon leaped to obey, hitting the klaxon alarm. The blaring sound began immediately. Between bursts, Browne heard sonar counting down.

'Eighty feet... Sixty-five feet...'

'Helm?'

'Thirty-four degrees, sir.'

They should have cleared the obstruction by now, but sonar was still counting down. 'Thirty feet... Twenty-two feet...'

'Brace for impact!' Browne called, making certain he had a firm grip himself. His ordered world was coming apart at the seams.

Venom slammed hard into the obstruction. Despite his grip, Browne was wrenched free and went flying. Everything that hadn't been fastened down flew across the control room, slamming into the machinery. Men cried out, the lights flickered, died and then came back. For a second or two, the heartbeat of the engines sped up, sounding like a heart attack in progress, and then reverted to their former steady beat.

Browne banged his head on a low pipe, leaving him a trifle disoriented. But he knew his routine, and even with a ringing in his ears, he could almost think straight. 'Mr Devon, report!'

His first officer picked himself up off the deck and glanced at the panel. 'No breech, sir,' he reported.

'Left plane is damaged, sir,' the chief helmsman called out from his seat. 'Not responding to controls.'

'Power seems fine, sir,' Devon added. 'Air... operational.' He glanced up, a look of relief on his face. 'Whatever it was we hit, it didn't cause too much damage, sir. We're about ninety-five percent operational.'

One damaged plane? Well, that wasn't too bad. Maybe they'd be limping back to Holy Loch, but at least they *would* be heading back.

'Sonar,' Browne called. 'Any idea what it was that we hit?'

'No, sir,' sonar answered. He looked shaken, as well he might. 'Luckily, it seems to have been resilient; it gave a little as we struck.'

That explained the low level of damage. 'Are you still reading it?'

'Yes, sir. It's still in place...' Sonar's voice trailed off.

'Well, what is it, man?'

'It appears to be *moving*, sir.'

'What are you talking about?' An idea crossed Browne's mind. 'Could it be a whale?'

'No, sir, the readings are all wrong for that. The shape's

indeterminate, not entirely solid.'

For a second Browne wondered if there was some truth to the stories about a Loch Ness monster. Had they collided with a prehistoric creature of some kind? Then reality returned to his mind, and he dismissed the absurd notion.

Venom shook and rang with a deep booming sound. Browne grabbed out again, clutching the edge of a panel to avoid being thrown from his feet a second time. The lights dimmed briefly. The hull groaned.

'Something from the object,' sonar confirmed. 'Ropes or chains or something.'

This whole situation was making less and less sense. 'Speed?' Browne asked.

'Dead in the water, sir,' Devon reported. 'Engines engaged, but we're making no headway. Whatever has got us has got us good.'

Venom was trapped somehow, caught by whatever it had hit. Maybe some sort of Soviet undersea base? Something they'd built for spying, or smuggling agents ashore. But Browne had heard nothing of the Soviets having the technology to build anything like this.

'Can we free ourselves?' he asked his first officer.

'We could try over-running the engines,' Devon suggested. 'That might be enough to pull us free.'

'Give it a shot, Mr Devon.' There was no telling what had them, but it might be possible to break it. *Venom* had a top-rate power plant.

'More movement!' sonar reported. 'More of those… whatever's heading our way.'

'Get us out of here, Mr Devon,' Browne said, firmly.

'Working, sir.' Devon nodded to the helm. 'Full ahead

now.'

The engines howled with the strain, and the sub shook again. But Browne could tell that it was not because they were freeing themselves. Loud bangs on the hull indicated that more restraints had attached themselves to the sub.

'Cut engines!' he ordered. He didn't need them overheating, they had enough problems as it was. The whine died down to the normal background pulse. 'How about torpedoes?' he asked, fearing he knew the answer.

'We're oriented badly,' Devon replied. 'The whatever-it-is is behind us. We couldn't aim.'

Browne was running out of ideas. 'Can we get divers out with cutting tools?'

'I'll check to see if the hatches are free.' Devon hurried off.

If only they knew what had caught them, Browne might have some idea of how to deal with it. It was the not knowing that caused the most problems. Whoever had said that ignorance was bliss didn't have the slightest grasp on reality. He crossed and stood behind the sonar station. 'Any idea what that thing is yet?'

'No, sir,' the operator admitted. 'It's not like anything I've seen before.' He pointed to the image on the screen, which presumably meant more to him that it did to Browne. 'The reflection's not hard, like metal or rock. It's more yielding. And whatever has us in its grip is mobile.'

Browne shook his head. 'Are you saying it's some sort of giant squid or something?'

'I doubt it, sir. Squid's are real deep-sea creatures, and we're only in a few hundred feet of water. One wouldn't be able to live this close to the surface. But something living, yes, sir. Just don't ask me what.'

Browne grumbled. That was *precisely* the question he wanted to ask, of course. But if it was something living, then it was something that could possibly be killed. And *that* would free them.

Devon was back at his elbow. 'Forward hatch is clear, sir,' he reported. 'I've got a team suiting up now. They should be ready to go out in less than five minutes.'

'Well done, Number One,' Browne said. *Now* they could do something. 'Sonar says that thing out there is probably some sort of living creature. Make sure the team has some high explosives with them. Last resort, we take it out.'

'Understood, sir.' Devon saluted and hurried off again.

Browne looked down at the image on the sonar screen with some satisfaction. Whatever had hold of them, some HE rammed in its face would make it change its mind.

The groaning on the hull sounded louder. There was the sound of metallic failure.

'We're being pulled backwards, sir,' the helmsman reported. 'Very slowly, but we're being reeled in.'

'Come on, Devon,' Browne muttered to himself. This was getting more and more urgent. He turned to the second officer. 'Better get on the blower with Holy Loch and let them know what's happening,' he decided. 'I'll prepare a short report; let me know when you have them.'

'Aye, sir.'

What was he going to say about this? Browne winced, whatever it was, this was not going to look good on his record.

Lethbridge-Stewart hurried to the communications room,

71

following an urgent summons by Maddox. He strode through the doors, and the sergeant looked up in relief.

'*Venom*'s in trouble, sir,' she reported.

'Trouble? She's a sub, Maddox, what kind of trouble could she possibly be in?'

'Hard to say, sir. The captain doesn't seem to know. He just reported in that they've been caught by... something.'

'That's a bit vague.' *Not to say worrying*, Lethbridge-Stewart considered.

'Sorry, sir,' Maddox said, as if it were her failure. 'But they say they've been stalled in the water by some sort of creature. It's pulling them in.'

Creature. There was a word that never boded well as far as Lethbridge-Stewart was concerned. He thought back to the Rutan on Fang Rock and, more recently, the Factotum beneath Wembley. Neither would have been capable of stalling a submarine, but still, there were other creatures, *aliens*, out there that he was so far unaware of. The very reason the Fifth was set up.

'They're sending out divers to try and cut themselves free,' Maddox added.

'Right.' It was looking like a job for the Fifth after all. 'Put it on the speakers. I think we'd better listen in. Get hold of Colonel Douglas and Miss Travers and have them join us.'

Seaman First Class Tom Jackson was an expert scuba diver, and he thought he'd seen pretty much everything the sea had to offer. He'd dived the Caribbean on his holidays, where the water was crystal clear and the fish were fearless. He'd dived the Mediterranean, whose rich, dark waters were

72

almost intoxicating. And he'd dived the North Sea too many times to bother counting. The waters here were cold and peaty, but held no surprises.

Until today. He and his two companions were floating in the dusky waters outside *Venom*, and he had finally been startled by something aquatic.

He triggered his radio. '*Venom*, Jackson. Sir, the sub's been caught by some sort of immense plant. It's wrapped fifty-foot tendrils about the craft.'

The receiver crackled in his ear. 'Say again, Jackson,' came Lieutenant Devon's voice.

'It's a plant, sir. The biggest damned thing I've ever seen. It must be something like three hundred feet across. I can't quite tell in these waters. But it's got tendrils wrapped around *Venom*, that's what's dragging her in.'

'Then cut through them, man!'

'Understood, sir.'

He gestured his companions on, and they swam to the nearest of the bonds. The tendril was about six feet across, the size of a man. Jackson fired up the cutting tool he carried, the heat causing ferocious bubbling that blinded him for a second. He started to cut into the plant growth.

Instantly the tendril jerked, tightening its grip. Jackson ignored this, concentrating on cutting the thing. For some reason, it was very slow going. Normally any plant growth would shrivel and die almost instantly, but this was hardly marked, even when he concentrated the beam.

His whole world suddenly churned. He felt a sharp slap across his back that sent him spinning through the bleak waters. He lost his grip on the cutter, and it automatically cut off. He spun helplessly in the water, and scrambled to try and correct this. He was starting to get himself under control when another tendril slashed through the water and wrapped itself tightly about him. He had no idea how this could be happening; plants could never react with this kind of speed! Even carnivorous plants didn't have this kind of response time.

He couldn't breathe. The tendril had spun itself about him so tightly that he couldn't even take a breath. He struggled, futilely, and tried to grab the cutter which was floating tantalizingly just out of reach. Hypoxia was setting in, and he found himself unable to take a single breath. He struggled, but could do nothing. Lights exploded in his head as he started to slip from consciousness.

Lethbridge-Stewart stood ramrod-straight, listening intently to the signals coming over the communications system. Douglas had joined him, wordlessly standing beside him. Miss Travers was here, standing beside Maddox, both of them pale. Petty Officer Wren Maisie Hawke manned the radio.

'We've lost contact with the divers,' the voice said.

'Pressure on the hull increasing,' a second rating reported. 'Captain, we're starting to lose hull integrity.'

'Alert *Kraken*,' another voice – obviously Captain Browne's – ordered. 'Maybe they can drop depth charges.'

'We're too close to the target, sir,' the second voice said. 'It's likely to damage us.'

'More than we're being damaged now?' Browne snapped. 'Get moving, man.'

'Doesn't sound good, sir,' Douglas murmured to Lethbridge-Stewart.

'No.' There was nothing any of them could do, of course, but it felt galling to hear good men being attacked and to have to simply stand by, helplessly.

'Pressure now—' The radio abruptly cut off.

Hawke looked up from her panel. 'We've lost the signal, sir.'

'Can you get it back?' Lethbridge-Stewart demanded.

'No, sir, it's cut off at the source.'

Maddox looked over Hawke's shoulders. 'We've completely lost *Venom*, sir. It's off the screens.'

Lethbridge-Stewart focused on the matter at hand; he didn't like to consider the possibility that they'd just overheard the death of many sailors. 'Switch over to *Kraken*,' he ordered. 'They must be going to investigate.'

'Sir.' Maddox looked down at Hawke. 'If you could, Maisie,' she said.

Hawke nodded and did as commanded; the radio crackled to life again.

'...to *Venom*,' said a voice. 'Come in, *Venom*.' They had clearly lost the signal, too.

Lethbridge-Stewart looked at his people. 'What the devil is happening in the North Sea?'

Captain McKenzie scanned the surface of the choppy water, knowing that disaster was underway below the waves. 'Sonar?' he called across the bridge.

'Nothing, sir. No sign of *Venom*.'

'What about the plant?'

'Nothing, sir. Just seabed.'

McKenzie couldn't understand it. A submarine didn't simply vanish, especially not *Venom*. It was one of the most state of the art attack subs in the world. It couldn't be taken out so simply by some kind of underwater flora. That was impossible!

'Object off the starboard bow, sir,' one of the lookouts called.

'All stop,' McKenzie ordered, immediately. 'Let's take a look.' It had to be something from the sub, some sort of evidence of what had happened to it. And it might even explain what had happened to that pirate radio ship. It would be stretching coincidence a lot if two different fates had befallen two separate vessels in the same small area of the ocean.

He couldn't help thinking that anything that could take out a sub like that could also take out a surface vessel with just as much ease. Maybe even the *Kraken*...

'It's a body, sir,' the lookout called up a few minutes later as *Kraken* came alongside. Netting had been thrown over the side of the ship, and two hands scuttled down. In a few moments, they were back up, hoisting the body onto the deck.

McKenzie had hurried down to the deck, and arrived at the same moment as the body. It looked... wrong. The man was in scuba gear, but his face-plate had been smashed in, his tank crushed. The body was totally limp, the limbs splayed on the deck in a very unnatural fashion.

One of the hands who had recovered it looked up at him. 'He's been crushed, sir,' he reported, his voice sounding sick. 'His bones have been pulverized.'

— CHAPTER SIX —

Island of Dreams

'Hawke, keep monitoring in case there are more developments,' Lethbridge-Stewart said, and turned from the radio operator. 'If there are, Sergeant Maddox, let me know immediately.' She nodded and Lethbridge-Stewart looked to Miss Travers and Douglas. 'Right, conference room in one hour,' he ordered. 'Miss Travers, I want ideas from you as to what might be happening.'

'You think this is a case for us?' Douglas asked, eagerly. Lethbridge-Stewart couldn't blame him for that; as a lieutenant colonel, Douglas was a field soldier, but he hadn't been in the field since Hamilton called him back from Northern Ireland in June. As important as setting up Dolerite Base was, and administrating the training of the new recruits, Dougie was itching to get back in the field. Lethbridge-Stewart knew how he felt.

'It certainly looks like it,' Lethbridge-Stewart said. 'Is Samson back yet?'

'No, sir, he's still down Salisbury conducting training with Mr Quebec.'

'Very well, get him to report back here ASAP. Get on to Captain Bartlett at Stirling Castle and prepare B Company. I want them ready for action by the time Samson gets back.'

'Yes, sir!' Douglas saluted and hurried off.

Aware that Miss Travers was eyeing him, Lethbridge-Stewart turned back to her. 'Don't you have work to do?' he asked her.

'Always,' she agreed. 'But I was just wondering... Where *is* the conference room I'm supposed to report to in an hour?'

Oh... 'Good point,' he conceded. 'Well, until we have an officially designated one, I suppose we'd better make it my outer office. Is that acceptable?'

'Perfectly. I'll see you there and then.' She turned and walked away.

Lethbridge-Stewart rounded on Maddox again. 'Get me General Hamilton,' he ordered. 'Patch it through to my office.' He spun on his heels and marched back. He had to figure out just how he was going to word this call, especially since it was extremely doubtful that the general knew of the loss of *Venom* yet.

Like Dougie, though, he felt a tingle of excitement. Action at last!

'Ah, Kirstie, there's nothing to do here. There's no future for either of us.' Rabbie Duncan sat on a large flat rock and sent one of its smaller brothers skipping over the waters of the North Sea. The sun was setting, sending a blood-red glow across the western skies. The wind was rustling the sparse grass and plucking at his hair. It was stirring Kirstie McKellan's lovely golden locks across her pretty face, so she had to keep brushing them back.

She sighed. 'I cannae tell ye no' to go,' she said, softly. 'But I cannae lie and say it makes me happy.'

'It's just a mickle unhappiness now, love, and a muckle o'joy afterwards,' Rabbie assured her. 'Six months is no' so bad.'

'When it's six months without ye, it can be,' Kirstie murmured. 'But I can be brave.'

'That's ma lassie.' Rabbie leaned forward to kiss her gently. 'And then—'

He broke off as he heard a low, loud crashing sound. A moment later a soft hum pervaded the air.

'What the devil can that be?' he wondered aloud. It had come from the direction of the village below them.

'I've nae idea,' Kirstie said. She was shivering slightly. 'But it cannae be anything good.'

Rabbie grabbed her hand and half-dragged her to the edge of the rise looking back at the village. When they were almost at the island's highest point, a couple of hundred feet above sea level, the pair turned, gasping for breath. Below them spread the small cluster of homes, the stone jetty where the fishing boats were tied up stretching out into the sea. They were still there as it was too early for them to be heading out. Within minutes, the cause of the crash became obvious as boat wreckage floated towards fishing boats on the troubled surface of the waters.

Moving slowly up the beach from the sea was a metallic… slug-looking thing. It reflected the redness of the dying sun from its wet body. It had to be forty or fifty feet long, and about twenty high. There was no visible means of locomotion, but it was dragging itself up towards the first houses of the village.

A second and then a third popped above the surface of the waves, obviously crawling ashore along the sea bed.

Rabbie had never seen anything like these things. They appeared to be completely smooth, and were the cause of the low humming sound that filled the night air, like the buzzing of a million angry bees. A small dingy that had been left on the beach lay in the way of the second object. It simply crawled over the boat, crushing it beneath its weight and leaving the wreckage behind.

Kirstie clutched Rabbie hard. Normally, he'd have loved it, but he could feel her shaking, heart pounding. 'What are they? They scare me.'

They scared him, too, if he was honest, but he had to pretend otherwise. He had to be strong for her. 'I dinnae ken,' he admitted. 'But we're safe up here.' He hoped that was true.

'But our kin,' Kirstie whispered, and she was right; everyone they knew and loved were down there, facing… what?

The villagers had heard the humming and crashing sounds by now. There was nothing as modern as television on the island, and precious few radios. The sound carried well, and people were leaving their homes to see what was causing it. A woman screamed when she saw the advancing things. One old man reached inside his door to grab a shotgun. At this distance, Rabbie couldn't be sure who they were. The man levelled the shotgun and fired at the closest of the objects. If the shot had any effect, it wasn't apparent. He tried again, with just as little result.

Several more of the slug shapes emerged from the water, crawling after the first three. All were tinged blood red by the sunset as they hummed their way ashore.

The first object reached the closest house. It neither

changed direction nor slowed in its advance. The nose of the machine bore away at the stone of the house, and the wall gave way. It collapsed onto the thing, which shrugged off the stones as if they were feathers. It crashed onward, ploughing straight through the house, and leaving only crushed stones and sticks that had been furniture.

Other men grabbed their hunting rifles and opened fire at the machines. As with the first shots, the advancing objects simply ignored everything and moved onward. Anybody who hadn't left their homes to see what was happening because of the humming now emerged as they heard the house collapsing. The people milled about in confusion, uncertain what was happening or how to respond.

'Dear Lord, Rabbie,' Kirstie said in a hushed voice. 'What are those monstrosities doin'? That's our homes they're destroyin'!'

'I dinnae ken,' Rabbie admitted, shocked and appalled at what was happening. 'But I should be doon there, helping.'

'And what could you do?' Kirstie asked him. 'Bullets don't harm them.'

'No, but I've got to do somethin'.'

The slugs were ignoring everything; intent only on wrecking the village, house by house. There were eight of them now, all crawling and crushing as they went. They appeared to be ignoring the milling people, focused only on destroying everything standing in the village. All too swiftly, their grim purpose appeared to be accomplished; not a house or wall was still in one piece. Every home had been flattened, every person driven on to the streets.

'Stay here, Kirstie,' Rabbie ordered. 'I have tae help, somehow.'

She grabbed his arm and wouldn't let go. 'Dinnae go,' she begged.

'Lassie, that's our folks down there,' he said.

'But it's too late.'

'I dinnae care!'

'Then I'm comin' wi' ye,' Kirstie vowed.

Lethbridge-Stewart reached his office to find the phone ringing. 'Lethbridge-Stewart?'

'Hello, Alistair.' It wasn't the general, it was Lance Corporal Sally Wright. 'General Hamilton will be with you in a moment, he's just finishing up a call to Whitehall. How are things?'

There were times when he found it difficult to speak to Sally, even though she was his fiancée. And he *should* be missing her, and be grateful to hear her cheery voice, but the truth of the matter was that he was attempting to focus on what could be a dangerous situation, and light-hearted romantic chit-chat was never his strong suite.

'Bit of a flap on, I'm afraid,' he replied. 'Need to speak to the general really.'

'This might be a good time to bring up the matter of my transfer again,' Sally suggested.

'Transfer?'

'Honestly, Alistair, there are times when I don't think you really want me with you.' Sally's tone was light, but Lethbridge-Stewart knew her well enough to know when she was annoyed. He shook his head, and let her carry on. 'I've applied to join the Fifth, as you well know, and a bit of prompting on your part wouldn't hurt my chances, you know.' There was a slight pause. 'You *do* want me with you, don't you?'

Trust the woman to put him on the spot! It was a good question, though, *did* he want her with him? Hamilton had told him about the way Sally had overstepped her bounds when he'd been placed in the safe house back in June. Luckily Hamilton still had faith in her, and even more in Lethbridge-Stewart, but... He was attempting to formulate some kind of an answer when she broke in.

'Ah, Brigadier, the general is ready now. I'll just put you through.'

Saved; for the moment.

For the first time the slugs slowed, and then halted in grim unison. There was a pause, and then they began to turn again, this time to face the unsettled and defeated crowd. It looked to Rabbie as if everybody on the island – himself and Kirstie excepted – were gathered there in clumps, as if being in a small crowd would help somehow. Or maybe just for human contact. There were a couple of hundred people, no more. Their voices had gone quiet as the invading objects spun with unknown intent.

One group on the fringe broke and started to run toward the ridge where Rabbie had momentarily paused, watching helplessly. As they began to move, so did all of the other people. None wanted to stay in proximity to the machines.

Instantly the whine from the devices increased in pitch. The smooth surface of the slugs broke apart, and a gaping maw somehow appeared on each of the things. There was a soft explosion, and then netting flew from the prows of all of the machines, spreading and soaring over the fugitives. It fell on them like leaden rain, enveloping groups of them in their grasp. Then, with a fresh whine, the nets began to retract.

'They're *fishing*,' Kirstie breathed.

She was right – men, women and children, screaming and howling, were being dragged in by the nets, pulled inside the slugs. The maws closed, cutting off all sound from their victims. Rabbie was terrified. He had no idea what was happening, but it couldn't be anything good for his kin and the folk he had known all of his life.

There were dogs barking, terrified and yet wishing to protect their owners. The machines simply ignored them.

Rabbie stared aghast after the shining things as they glided onwards. There was nothing that he could do. Kirstie's hand found his, but Rabbie wasn't sure if it was for her sake or his.

— CHAPTER SEVEN —

There's a Kind of Hush

There was no one left, and no sound but the lapping waves and the low hum from the eight machines. They seemed to hesitate. And then further hatches opened in the smooth surfaces.

What next? Rabbie wondered numbly.

Loud puffs of air followed by small, ball-like objects ejected from the slugs. Hundreds – perhaps thousands – of the things flew everywhere. Into the ruins, onto the beaches, up the hills… More and more were fired from the machines, flying up into the air, and then descending and bouncing, rolling, before they came to a halt.

Several fell near Rabbie and Kirstie. Instinctively, they flinched back from them. Rabbie clutched Kirstie.

They were all half-way in size between a cricket ball and a football. The surface was pocked rather than smooth, and there were ridges around the objects like the lips of a clam shell. For several minutes, nothing happened. The slugs stopped firing the spheres, and the fallen balls simply lay where they had dropped or rolled. The dogs still barked, the only sound in the descending night, save the low hum from the machines.

Rabbie screwed up his courage and started moving again, his hand still firmly clutching Kirstie's, but he barely took two steps when, with a puffing sound, one of the balls exploded into life. Then a second, and then more of them, their shells cracking open with puffs of air.

A vague cloud of vapour emerged from the balls, and Rabbie and Kirstie took an uncertain step back. The vapour dissipated in seconds. The balls appeared to be turning inside out. They cracked along the ridged lines of their surfaces, and the outer shell peeled back to reveal their tightly woven innards.

'What is it, Rabbie?' Kirstie whispered.

'I dinnae ken,' he admitted. 'But it does no' look dangerous.'

Kirstie clung to his arm tightly. 'Don't go near one!' she begged.

'I wasn't,' he lied. Instead, he picked up a fallen stick, aiming to poke one and see what would happen.

'Don't!' Kirstie begged. 'Dinnae provoke it!'

Rabbie considered for a moment, and realised she might well be right. These things, whatever they were, weren't likely to be harmless, given what had happened so far. Maybe even poking one with a stick could start some kind of retaliation? After a moment's hesitation, he dropped the stick again, and Kirstie gave a sigh of relief.

Then the ball sprung to life. In a whirl of motion, it seemed to somehow grow in size. Rabbie realised what was actually happening; something in the centre of the ball was unfurling. He peered through the gathering gloom, and could make out what looked like leaves and tendrils, opening up and moving. They started to creep out of the broken shell and crawl until they found dirt.

'What's happening?' Kirstie asked, urgently.

'They're some kind o' plants,' Rabbie replied. 'They're putting out roots.'

'Plants don't grow that fast.'

'Aye, normal ones don't,' he agreed, shivering. 'But these are uncanny plants, love.'

All around, wherever they had fallen, the pods had broken open and the plants were growing, seeking earth in which to bury their roots. In macabre silence, they scuffed away until they could begin to bury themselves.

The slugs sprang to life again. Whirring away, they all turned at once until they were facing the ocean. Then they trundled back, out of the ruined town, and slid slowly into the coal-dark waters until all of them had vanished from sight. Several dogs dashed to the water's edge, barking furiously and ineffectively.

Gone. Their families, everybody he had known all of his life... gone.

'We'll get them back,' he promised. Kirstie shook, tears running down her face. 'I promise ye tha' we'll get them back.' Rabbie had absolutely no idea how to even start achieving his goal, but he *had* to have one, otherwise all that would be left to them was deep, empty despair. Their homes, everything... gone.

And everywhere in sight were those plant-things, growing and rooting themselves.

Except...

Rabbie pointed. One of the balls hadn't broken open like the rest. It still lay where it had fallen, inert. He started to move forward, but Kirstie dragged him back again.

'Let it be, Rabbie,' she begged him. 'It's *evil*.'

'It's just a wee vegetable, love,' he assured her. 'It cannae hurt us.'

Samson Ware was still getting used to being a warrant officer first class, a step up from his old rank of sergeant, and he was certainly enjoying it. A month ago he'd been simply a stunt man at a TV studio, but his old CO Alistair Lethbridge-Stewart had recruited him for the fledgling Fifth Operational Corps, and even given him a boost from his old rank as thanks for his services. He'd then been assigned to help train the growing ranks of the Corps, and had only recently returned from the training course at the Joint Warfare Establishment. Training was all very well, and something he'd always excelled at, but Samson much preferred the life of action, which was why he'd become a stuntman in the first place. It was also why he'd bought his canary yellow sports car, a 1967 Lotus Seven. When he'd received his orders from Colonel Douglas to report in at Edinburgh HQ, he'd immediately hopped into the car and driven through the night.

It was dawn when he pulled up into the parking area outside the New Barracks. There were two guards on duty, both dressed in ceremonial kilts – well, there would be lots of tourists around later. Both seemed quite impressed with the Lotus.

'Keep an eye on her, lads,' he said, cheerfully saluting them.

'Not a hardship, sir,' one replied. 'She's a beauty.'

'That she is,' Samson agreed. 'Keep up the diligence, and one day you might be able to afford one, too.'

'By the time I'll be able to afford one,' the sentry grumbled, 'it'll be an antique, and I won't be able to afford one.'

Samson grinned. 'We all need dreams.' He hurried on into the Barracks and took the lift down to the Fifth's HQ. After he'd passed through the guard stations, he hurried down to Lethbridge-Stewart's office and knocked on the door. A voice called for him to enter.

Despite the early hour, it was Lieutenant Bishop on duty. 'Morning, Sergeant Major,' he said.

Another thing Samson had to get used to. When he'd last seen Bill, the young man was only a lance corporal, but he'd since completed his training at Mons and was now an officer, and thus Samson's senior. 'Morning, sir,' he said with a smile.

Bishop reached out and shook Samson's hand. 'Congratulations on the promotion, Sam,' he said.

'You, too, Bill,' Samson said, glad that Bishop was not letting his rank go to his head. 'His nibs in?'

'The brigadier's in communications right now, but he'll be back shortly.' Bishop raised an eyebrow. 'You made good time.'

'Good? I'd call it excellent.' Samson grinned; Bishop was rather envious of the Lotus, as so many were. 'One of these days, I may let you drive her.'

'That might be the last you'd see of her, and me,' Bishop informed him with a grin.

'Warning duly noted, *sir.*'

The door opened and Lethbridge-Stewart strode in. If he'd been up all night, it wasn't apparent. 'Ah, Samson! Good man. You made good time.'

'Thank you, sir.' Samson grinned. 'Does it mean action at last?'

'It certainly looks like it. We've lost a commercial ship and a Navy sub in the North Sea under mysterious circumstances.'

'Certainly sounds like our remit.'

'Briefing at oh-nine-hundred. Get some rest and a bite of breakfast in the meantime.'

'Aye, sir.' Samson saluted and left. Now that Lethbridge-Stewart had mentioned it, he was a bit peckish. He hadn't stopped off on the way for anything to eat, and he could just murder a cup of strong, hot tea. He had to think a minute to recall where the mess hall was in the base – he'd only been here once before being sent south to supervise training – and then set off cheerfully. He wondered if Anne would be around at this time in the morning, or if she was getting her beauty sleep.

Wherever she was, it wasn't the mess hall. Aside from the staff, there were only two people there. One was a corporal he didn't recognise, sitting alone at the far end of the room. The other was Private Evans, staring gloomily at a plate of porridge. That wasn't too surprising, Evans wasn't at all popular with his fellow soldiers after his actions during the Yeti invasion. It had been months ago, but it wouldn't be forgotten for a long time yet. Samson grabbed his own porridge, salting it in the Scottish way, and a steaming mug of tea and reluctantly joined Evans. He had to set an example to the enlisted men, whether he wanted to or not. After all, he was still technically an enlisted man himself, despite his new rank. And – let's face it – he knew what it was like to be ostracized, even if it was for a completely different reason.

'You don't look too happy, Private,' he said.

'Well, what do you expect?' Evans complained. It was typical of the man that he not bother with 'sir'. 'We're off to war again.' He sighed. 'It's all very well for the likes of you, but who'll bear the brunt of it? The likes of me, see?'

'I can't say I've ever heard that you're overworked, Evans,' Samson replied, working on the porridge.

'Of course you'd say that,' Evans grumbled. 'Privileged, that's what officers are. Not the downtrodden masses, like us poor saps.'

'Oh, yes, I'm just wallowing in privilege,' Samson said, tucking into his breakfast. The porridge wasn't bad, but the tea was lovely. It was just what he needed.

The mess door opened, and a couple of men started to enter. One caught sight of Samson and stopped. He muttered to his companion, they cast one baleful glance at Samson, and then left. Samson sighed, but Evans looked annoyed.

'Aren't you going to do something about that?' he asked.

'About what?'

'Those two men, they disrespected you just because you're coloured, and you being RSM and all.'

Samson sighed. 'No, I'm not going to do anything about it,' he said gently. 'They won't eat with me because I'm a negro? Fine. Who are they hurting? I'm the one eating breakfast, and they're not.'

'It's disrespect, that's what it is,' Evans insisted. 'Look you, I know something about prejudice, see? They all call me *Taffy*, and treat me like I'm an idiot, just because I'm Welsh.'

'No, they treat you like an idiot because you're a lazy, dodging little shirker,' Samson pointed out.

'That's just what they *say*,' Evans argued. 'If I were an officer, I'd give them what for.'

'If you were an officer, I'd transfer to another regiment,' Samson said. 'Look, the brig gave me a job; train the new recruits. I don't mind coming down hard on men who screw up as soldiers, but I'll be damned if I'll try and educate them out of their prejudices too. If they won't respect me because I'm black, I want them to respect me as a soldier.'

'You're an optimist,' Evans replied. 'I'm a realist, that's what gets me into trouble.'

'Oh, that's it, is it?' Samson was starting to feel tired. 'Look, Evans, I'm going to get some quick shut-eye, wake me up by oh-eight-thirty.' He glared at the Welshman. 'And don't forget.' He took one last swig of the tea and left. As he did so, he heard Evans' mutterings.

'And that's me a blooming room service now. Talk about privilege.'

It was a nightmare.

Mary stared at the – well, whatever it was, in shock. She could see nothing that looked like eyes, but somehow she knew that it was staring back at her. Now she had got over her shock, she could see that it was vaguely humanoid in shape – two arms, two legs, and what had to be a head – but it looked as though it were made of rocks jumbled together, all grey and brown and black. There were no features, just crags and fissures at various places over its body.

And it was over twelve feet tall!

'What the hell is that?' Alan gasped. All Mary could do was to shake her head.

'Yon thing is a living gargoyle,' Jock muttered, crossing himself. 'Spawned from Hell i'self.' Mary found that difficult to argue with.

'Humans,' the thing repeated, its voice like gravel grating together, though the words were distinct enough, and in English, too. 'You will listen to me and do as you are instructed. Disobedience will not be tolerated.' The head turned slightly, as though it were looking at each of them in turn.

'Why... Why should we listen to you?' Mary demanded, trying to sound far, far braver than she felt.

'You have no choice,' the creature replied. 'We bear you no malice, but we will kill you if you do not follow our instructions.'

'It's not even armed,' Alan muttered. 'And I'm not taking orders from... from a living rock.'

Mary gripped his arm. 'I don't think you should provoke it,' she whispered back. 'Look at it. It could kill you by just sitting on you.'

'That's absurd. Mary, I think we should stand up to it.'

'I have a feeling that would be a very bad idea,' she informed him. 'It sounds so certain of itself.'

'That is enough talking,' the rock-thing said. 'You will accompany me.'

'Where?' Mary demanded.

'Back to the vessel you were on,' it answered. 'There are further humans there, and the Grandfathers require all of them.'

'Some are injured,' Mary informed it. 'And some are dead.'

'All are required,' the creature replied. 'Those that

cannot work will be given to the Grandfathers.'

'And the dead?' Alan asked.

'They will, of course, be the first taken to the Grandfathers.'

This wasn't making a great deal of sense. 'What will the Grandfathers do with the dead?' Mary asked, puzzled.

Somehow the creature managed to sound amazed. 'Obviously they will be devoured.'

'What?' Mary asked, her voice barely a whisper of shock.

'Do your own Grandfathers not devour the dead?' the creature asked, still sounding surprised.

'Of course not!' Mary exclaimed. 'I don't even *have* a grandfather; they're both dead.'

That seemed to stun the rock being. It finally looked at her again. 'A living being without a Grandfather,' it mused. 'This must be examined. It is… inconceivable.' Then it straightened up again. 'But enough talking. You will now accompany me.'

Jock backed away slightly. 'I'm no' goin' wi' you anywhere.'

'You were warned,' the creature said.

It thrust out its right arm, and the rocky fist enveloped the sailor, and then closed. Jock screamed and struggled for a second or two. There was a terrible stench of burning flesh, and then silence. The rock-thing opened its hand, and a blackened, charred, smoking body fell to the ground.

'We will return for that later,' the creature stated. 'Now you will accompany me.'

Mary felt herself shaking, and she wanted desperately to throw up. Jock had just been casually murdered and tossed aside like so much rubbish.

'Easy, love, easy,' Alan said, gently, putting an arm about her. 'Be strong, Mary. Don't let it see it's scared you.'

'I doubt it can understand human emotions, Al,' she managed to say, fighting the urge to puke, or the utterly irrational one to lash out against the thing. She was certain it wouldn't even feel any blows from her fists, and for her troubles she'd simply scar and burn her hands.

'Will you accompany me,' the thing asked, 'or shall I be forced to kill you both also and find others to contact?'

'We'll go with you,' Alan promised. 'We just need a minute. That was our friend you just murdered.'

'Murdered?' The creature seemed puzzled. 'You are not of my kind. How then can it be murder? Do you not kill inferior species yourselves? Is that murder?'

'He was an intelligent, living being!' Alan growled.

'Intelligent? Hardly.'

Mary felt a form of righteous anger bubbling inside her. To be so dismissive of people! 'Yet you speak to us,' she pointed out. 'You know our language.'

'You speak to dogs and cats,' the thing said. 'They heed you, but they are not intelligent by your standards. You are not intelligent by ours. And your language is ridiculously simple to learn, as are all human languages. Now, we must go or you must die. Make your choice.'

'We're coming,' Mary said, shaking free of Alan's protective arm, reverting to type. Deep down she knew it was shock, that she appreciated the kind thought, but she didn't need any man's help. She set off back the way they had come, not even looking back to check that Alan was accompanying her.

Lethbridge-Stewart called the briefing to order as he strode into his outer office. Dougie was there, along with Samson and Bishop. Miss Travers was seated at the table, rounding out the group.

'Time for action,' Lethbridge-Stewart informed them, and saw the gleam of anticipation in all of their eyes. 'I've spoken with General Hamilton and he's clearing things with the other Services. The Navy isn't happy, but they've agreed to co-operate. The loss of their sub seems to have shaken them up, and they don't seem to understand how we already knew about it.' He glanced at Miss Travers. 'I didn't bother explaining it, but they're bound to ask again.'

'Are they planning a search for it?' she asked.

'At the moment, I believe they're – ah – evaluating the situation.'

'Sitting on their behinds and wondering how to cover them,' Miss Travers suggested. Lethbridge-Stewart said nothing; she was undoubtedly correct. The Navy would want someone to take the blame for the loss of their vessel.

'Are they sending in more ships?' Dougie asked.

'No,' Lethbridge-Stewart answered. '*Kraken* is still in the area and looking for – well, pretty much anything at the moment. They've found the divers – dead, unfortunately – but no wreckage. There's no evidence yet of what happened. The Navy is reluctant to commit more vessels until they've some idea of what they're up against.'

'And they'll never *get* any idea unless they investigate,' Miss Travers pointed out.

'That is now officially our job,' Lethbridge-Stewart said. 'The Air Force have agreed to do an early morning flyover out of RAF Buchan. Sergeant Maddox will monitor it and let us know the results. Other than that, we have pretty much a free hand.'

'What do you have in mind, sir?' Dougie asked.

'Lieutenant Bishop, you are to take charge of the detachment that Colonel Douglas has selected. Sergeant Major Ware will go with you. You're to head immediately for Peterhead and hold yourselves in readiness. By the time you arrive, decisions should have been made, and I'll give you further orders then.'

Bishop grinned and saluted, pleased to receive his first command. 'Yes, *sir!*'

Dougie – understandably – looked a bit peeved. Even though he was acting as a staff officer, due to his position as Lethbridge-Stewart's 2-in-C, he still held a field rank and was used to being out there getting things done. 'And me, sir?'

'Start work on assembling another team. Anyone with any kind of sea training especially. I'll want you to be ready to head in as soon as we have further information and know what might be needed. Miss Travers?'

'Brigadier?'

'Do you have any thoughts to offer?'

'Apart from the one that you're going off half-cocked?' She smiled to take some of the sting out of the comment. 'Look, the problem would appear to lie under the surface and, good as your men are, they can't hold their breaths long enough or dive deep enough to find out what's happening. I've an acquaintance I know who might be able to help out here. His name is Professor Brinstead, and he's built an experimental bathysphere. I know he's been planning on testing it; he's a bit of a Francophobe, and he's had some arguments with Captain Cousteau. Thinks the French have rather taken over the field in oceanic exploration, and wants to one-up them. If he's not started his tests yet, I might be able to get him to agree to take a look with us in the target zone.'

'Experimental?' Lethbridge-Stewart raised his eyebrow. 'It *will* work, won't it?'

'How do I know?' Miss Travers snapped. 'That's the point of experimenting, isn't it?'

'I see. And what sort of weaponry does it possess?'

'Weaponry?' She glared at him. 'Good Heavens, Brigadier, is war all you can think about? This vessel is a scientific one; why on earth would it have any weapons?'

'Miss Travers, people have already been killed in that area, I don't think it's out of line to be thinking of armaments.'

'Well, then, you just think about them. I'll contact Brinstead and find out if the bathysphere is even available, shall I?'

Lethbridge-Stewart sighed. 'Yes, that's a good idea. And if it *is* available, find out how long it would take to get it into the target area, too.'

'Relax, Brigadier,' Miss Travers advised him. 'I know the thought of sending an unarmed craft into the search area bothers you, but *Venom* was well-armed, and it didn't do her much good, did it?'

'That's hardly reassuring, Miss Travers.' But she did have a point, much as it pained him to admit it. 'Right, gentlemen – and lady – let's get to work, shall we?'

Mary and Alan followed the creature through the dark. It

seemed to be willing to communicate. 'What are you?' Mary asked it.

'I am what I am,' it replied. 'We call ourselves the Ones.'

Hardly helpful. She looked up at the huge creature; how could beings like these remain hidden for so long? They were hard to overlook. But maybe they *had* been seen, and the accounts dismissed as fantasy. Wasn't there a line in the Bible about there being giants on the Earth once upon a time? And a bit closer to home, there were giants in many myths and stories, from Jack the Giant Killer to the Norse ice giants. They were pretty close to this spot, weren't they? Maybe the Vikings had spotted these creatures sometime, and stories of them passed into myth.

'There's a legend among my people,' she said. 'Well, not *my* people, but...' She was babbling. Mary cleared her throat and started again. 'Stories of a race of ice giants called the Ymir. Would that have been inspired by you?'

'No,' the creature answered. 'We have only just arrived on your planet. It could not have been us.'

The meteor... Then these creatures hadn't been here forever, hiding from humans. They were only... 'Then you're...' Her words were reluctant to come out. 'Monsters from outer space?'

'We are not *monsters*,' the creature replied. 'Though we are from outer space, yes.'

'And you're here to invade our planet?' she asked, amazed at how well she was standing up to this. Meeting a monster from outer space and chatting with it as if it had invited her over for tea.

'Not in any way you imagine,' the monster replied. 'We have studied your fables about creatures from other worlds.

99

They all have the same flaw; they assume that human ingenuity will enable humans to defeat these... monsters. But the fables are written by humans, for humans. They do not understand alien minds. In your tales, you humans either outwit the aliens or else simply dispose of them using atomic weapons. Neither will work with us.'

'Oh? And why not?'

'In the first instance, because we are your intellectual superiors, the chances of your outwitting us are about the same as the chances that your ants might rise up and defeat the human race. In the second instance, yes, a properly placed atomic weapon would probably destroy our ship and perhaps kill us all. But your authorities do not know where we are. We are monitoring all human-used frequencies and we are aware of what they know and plan. And if they do discover our location, then any weapon used against us would need to be so powerful that it would destroy a greater portion of the island we are in proximity to and kill millions of your own race. I doubt that would be sanctioned by your authorities.'

Mary didn't like the creature's confidence. 'You seem very sure of yourself.'

'We are your superiors,' it replied. 'I have considered your idea, and I approve of it.'

Mary was puzzled. 'What idea?'

'Calling us the Ymir. The irony is amusing to me.'

Oh. 'And what irony would that be?'

It regarded her with what must have been pity. 'You have seen, yet you do not comprehend. The irony is that while we are indeed giants by your standards, we are not *ice* giants; quite the contrary. Your internal body temperature is several hundred degrees below ours. We are actually heat giants.'

Something was starting to make sense. 'And that's how you killed Jock. But why aren't you freezing, then? Walking around like this?'

'Our skin is not thin and feeble like that of humans,' the Ymir – she might as well start calling it that – replied. 'It protects us from a great range of temperatures and pressures. Your bodies are quite delicate compared to ours. That is another advantage we possess over humans.'

'Then why are you invading our planet?' she asked it.

'That is enough conversation,' the Ymir announced. 'We have reached your vessel. You will go aboard and inform the rest of your companions that they are to exit the ship. The dead and injured are to be carried out. Then the ship will be destroyed.'

'And if they don't believe me?'

'They have ten of your minutes. If they do not emerge by then, I shall destroy the ship with them in it. Tell them that if they wish to live longer, they must emerge and obey my instructions.'

'I can't guarantee that they will agree,' Mary informed the Ymir.

'Then offer them your goodbyes and return to me if you wish to prolong your own existence,' it suggested. 'I do not wish to kill you – I find you quite entertaining – but I shall do so if you do not obey implicitly.'

'You'd make a lousy dog trainer,' Mary muttered. She glanced around and saw Alan standing there. He seemed shocked and withdrawn. 'Come on, Alan, we'd better do what the Ymir says.'

'He will remain with me,' the Ymir said firmly.

Mary raised an eyebrow. 'A further incentive for my return?' she asked.

'No. More humans are arriving. If I am forced to kill you, then he will be my next messenger.'

'Charming,' she deadpanned, her heart racing suddenly. She eyed the climb ahead of her to get back onto the ship. 'Okay,' she said, determined. She grabbed hold of the end of the rope ladder.

'There is no need to climb.' The Ymir's great hand reached for her.

Mary had a swift second of utter panic as the killing hand closed about her. She tensed, expecting to burn to death like Jock. But that didn't happen. Instead, the hand closed quite gently about her and lifted her to the level of the deck and released her. Shaking, she fell to the deck.

'Why are you disturbed?' the Ymir asked her.

'Because I thought you were going to burn me to death!' she screamed at it.

'Why would I do that? I informed you that I need you to carry my message. It would have been foolish to then incinerate you.' It then seemed to realise what she had said. 'Ah! You have forgotten that I informed you that I can regulate my outflow of heat. My touch does not always burn.'

'It would have been nice if you'd reminded me of that *before* you picked me up!'

'Yes,' it agreed. 'I had almost forgotten how feeble your mind is. It is my fault for not recalling.'

Some apology! But Mary was starting to feel slightly better, and she was able to control her shakes enough to regain her feet. 'Right,' she growled. 'Ten minutes, starting now.' She spun on her heels and headed for the bridge.

CHAPTER EIGHT

Trains and Boats and Planes

Chorley caught a taxi from the train station to the docks. If anyone here in Peterhead knew what had happened to the missing pirate radio boat, it would be the fishermen and the other dock workers. He knew he'd get nowhere talking to the authorities, he'd simply be handed from one department to another until he gave up in disgust. No, the docks were where the real info would be.

He'd managed to doze a bit on the train. He was slightly tired, but he could cope with that. Plenty of time to sleep once he'd figured out what the angle of the story would be. He was getting back into the swing again; there was nothing as invigorating as being hot on the track of a real story. And every journalistic instinct he'd honed over the years was telling him that there was something in this one, it was just a matter of *what*.

Peterhead docks had seen better days, and probably would again, now that oil had been found out in the North Sea. As soon as the rigs came on line, there'd be plenty of action here again. For the moment, though, there were mostly just the fishermen, returning with the dawn to ready their catch. There was a stench, of course, that most of the men probably didn't notice, but Harold Chorley certainly did.

There was no point in trying to talk to the fishermen, they wouldn't appreciate any interruptions. Chorley looked around, knowing there'd be some retired mariner or three hanging about the docks, the pull of the sea far too strong for them to stay home with their wives. They'd be the ones to know and pass along any news. As he suspected, he spotted one white-bearded old fellow, leaning on a bollard, watching all of the action, smoking the inevitable pipe.

Chorley ambled over to join him. 'Morning.'

The old man looked at Chorley – realising immediately that Chorley was neither seaman nor local – and knocked out his pipe. He began to clean it and refill it before answering the greeting. 'Morning.'

'Busy place,' Chorley commented.

The man lit his pipe and took a long pull. 'Aye,' he finally allowed.

'I heard that they lost a ship. One of those pirate radio thingies.'

'They do say.'

'Know anything about it?'

Another pause. 'Nope.'

'I've a fiver for anyone who can tell me about it,' Chorley said.

'Pity,' the sailor replied.

'Why's that?'

'Could have used it.' He managed a grin. 'Could make something up, if you'd like.'

'I'm a journalist,' Chorley informed him. 'I'm after the truth.'

'Thought as much.' The fisherman was gazing out to sea. 'Now that's odd.'

'What is?' Chorley followed the old mariner's gaze, but he could only see yet another boat coming in.

'Not a local,' the old man said. 'Not a fisherman, either. Boy and girl, by the looks of things.' He moved finally, ambling down toward where the nearest fishing boat was unloading. He whistled, and the captain looked up from his work. The retired sailor nodded out to sea, in the direction of the approaching boat. Chorley followed and saw the fisherman stiffen, and then call to his crew. They abandoned their work for the moment, and moved into action.

The approaching boat came closer, and Chorley could see that the old man had been correct, it was too small to be a fishing boat, barely large enough to hold the exhausted youths. Probably just a courting couple who'd gone further than they'd expected, and spent the night at sea. On the other hand...

One of the fishermen jumped across to the little boat, holding the end of a line. The young man gave a start as the boat rocked, but the young woman didn't even stir as the other men hauled in the boat.

'Careful,' the youth said, his voice cracking. 'It's a terrible shock she's had.'

'Wha' happened, lad?' the captain called. 'Yon boat got away wi' ye?'

'Nay,' the boy said. 'We were attacked, mon.'

'Attacked, you say?' Chorley called out, pushing his way down to where the young man and girl were being brought up. 'Where was that?' Every journalistic instinct he had was yelling out in triumph now.

'Strommach,' the youth replied. 'They're all gone.'

'Who's all gone?'

106

'Everybody.' The boy shook his head wearily. 'They came out o' the sea and took them all away. Kirstie and I, we got barely away.'

'Who came?' Chorley demanded urgently.

The boy reached into the haversack slung over his shoulder. Gently, carefully, he pulled out what looked like a battered ball. 'These,' he said.

Chorley stared at the thing. It was some kind of a pod, but like nothing he'd ever seen before. Not that he was much of a gardener, but he was certain most plant pods were a lot smaller than this one. The young man carefully placed it back into the battered haversack, and then he just collapsed.

'They're in need of a doctor,' the captain decided. He motioned Chorley away, but the journalist didn't care. He'd seen and heard what he needed. He turned back to his informant, who was leaning against a post and smoking his pipe again.

'Would you happen to have a boat?' Chorley asked him.

'Happens I do,' the old man said.

'Then it's your lucky day,' Chorley told him. 'I'll pay you to take me to this Strommach place.'

Mary climbed up the stairway to the bridge. The surviving sailors were still there working at trying to get the radio operational. One of them looked up as she entered.

'Ah, ye're back, lassie,' he said. 'Did ye find out where we are?'

'Yes,' she said. 'We're in a trap. You have to abandon the ship, right now.'

'But we've almost got the radio operational,' a second sailor said. 'There's just some sort of interference. I think I

107

can overcome it, though.'

'I doubt it,' Mary informed him. It didn't sound like the sort of thing the Ymir wouldn't have taken into account; it had told her that it was monitoring all human frequencies, so it was undoubtedly blocking the radio from working. 'We have to get off this ship immediately, it's about to be destroyed.'

'What are ye sayin'?' the first sailor asked. 'We're perfectly safe here. There's no water, but no danger, either.'

How could she say this without sounding crazy? 'We're in a trap,' she said. 'We were brought here. There are... things outside, and they will destroy it. You have to get off *now*, or you'll die with it.'

'Did ye bang your head, lassie?' the sailor asked, sympathetically.

'You idiot!' Mary snapped. 'They've killed Jock already, and you'll be next!'

'Jock's dead?' the second sailor asked, jumping to his feet. 'How?'

'Stick around and you'll find out,' she told him. 'Let's go now.' Then she paused. 'And we have to take the injured and the dead also.'

'Slow down, lassie,' the first sailor said. 'Ye sound like ye've had a wee shock. Maybe ye'd better take somethin'.'

'Yes,' she agreed. 'You. Off this ship. Now.' She grabbed his arm. 'Come on, time's running out.'

He shook himself free. 'There's no need to be so hasty.'

'There's *every* need to be hasty!' Mary had an idea. The sailors couldn't see the Ymir in the darkness, but the alien probably hadn't moved. She lit her torch. 'Here, look!' She shone the beam at the spot where the Ymir had been standing.

The light illuminated the craggy creature, standing beside the ship, towering over Alan's smaller form. Alan shielded his eyes from the glare, but the Ymir barely moved.

'Jesus, Joseph and Mary!' the first sailor swore. 'What is yon thing?'

'*Yon thing* is your death, unless you start moving,' Mary assured him. 'Let's go. Now.'

'It's a monster,' the second sailor gasped.

'You're starting to get the idea,' Mary said, approvingly. 'So let's get out of here.'

'I'm no' going near that thing,' the man replied. He turned back to the radio. 'I'll have this working in a minute. We can call for help.'

'No, you can't. That creature out there will stop you. We have no chance against it. We have to go!'

'Dinnae fret, lassie,' the first sailor said. 'We'll protect ye.'

'I'm trying to protect *you*, you moron!' Mary looked at the handful of sailors on the bridge. 'I'm going now, any of you who wants to live, come with me.' She looked around, but the sailors made no move to join her. 'Don't you understand? That thing will kill you if you stay!'

'We can defend ourselves,' another sailor said.

'Not against that thing, you can't.' Mary wasn't getting through to them! 'Please, *please*, come with me and live.'

'We're going nowhere,' the sailor said. 'Not without a fight.'

'The time is ended,' the booming voice of the Ymir announced. 'Leave now or perish.'

Mary looked helplessly at the sailors. None of them were

moving. With a helpless gasp, she turned and fled the bridge.

She reached the deck and the huge hand plucked her up again. She had another second of horrible terror, and then she was down beside Alan, who clutched her to comfort her.

The Ymir looked down at her. 'They will not come?'

'No,' she gasped. 'They didn't believe me.'

'A pity,' the alien said. 'It is a shame to destroy workers.' It reached out toward the ship. Tall as it was, she knew it couldn't reach the bridge. Somehow, one of the sailors had found a pistol, and opened fire. The bullets chipped bits of the stony skin from the Ymir, but caused it no pain. It gripped the ship's railing in both hands and pulled.

Groaning, creaking, the ship started to sway and then move. Mary and Alan staggered backward, afraid it might suddenly swing over and crush them, but the Ymir stood firm. As the vessel toppled toward it, the alien started to radiate heat. The bulkhead melted around it. Mary could feel the incredible heat, and she shuffled backward until it was endurable.

She could hear the sailors yelling even over the grinding of metal. One of them fired the pistol directly into the Ymir's face. The alien didn't even flinch. It continued to melt the ship, and a moment later was able to reach the window of the bridge. It thrust out a hand and the glass melted away before it.

The screams of the sailors increased for a moment and then cut off abruptly. Once more, there was the appalling stench of burning human flesh that made her want to throw up.

Then there was blessed silence.

At least the sailors were suffering no more. But Mary found little comfort in that.

The Ymir let go of the ship. The heat started to abate, at least from the creature. There were pools of incandescent metal still throwing off high temperatures. A large section of the bow of the ship was gone, melted to slag.

'That was foolish and wasteful,' the Ymir stated. 'More humans are coming. I trust they will be less obtuse. Workers are needed.' It returned to stand with Mary and Alan. 'We shall leave the dead for now,' it decided. 'When the other humans arrive, we shall return for them.' It looked down at Mary and Alan. 'You will accompany me to meet them,' it informed them. 'I hope you will have better fortune convincing them to be wise.'

Mary looked at Alan, hopelessly. They were now all that was left of Radio Crossbones. Somehow, that name now seemed terribly appropriate.

Lethbridge-Stewart returned to his office and put a call through to Sergeant Maddox. 'Ah, Maddox, let me know when you hear anything from the RAF recon flight. In the meantime, put a call through to General Hamilton's office for me. I'll take it here.' She acknowledged, and he replaced the phone for the moment.

Well, this was it; the first official mission for the Fifth. Heavens knew, they weren't really ready for it. He'd have preferred a few more months of recruiting and training, but needs must and all that. He was confident of his top officers, and they were confident of at least some of their men. He could only pray that they were right. They had to prove themselves, both to Whitehall and to the men who were funding them. But this was what Lethbridge-Stewarts were bred for, wasn't it? To take command and forge ahead when others hesitated.

The phone rang, and he scooped it up. 'Lethbridge-Stewart?'

'Hello, Alistair.'

He stiffened slightly. Once again it was Sally making a social call. This couldn't keep going on. 'Ah, hello, Sally,' he said, lamely.

'You don't sound happy to hear from me.'

There was much Lethbridge-Stewart could have said to that, but instead he chose the safest course. Now was not a time for domestic strife.

'It's not that. It's just that I was expecting to talk to General Hamilton.'

'Oh. Well, he's on the road right now, so he's temporarily unavailable. He's on his way in, though, and should be here in an hour or so. I'll let him know you called. Is there any message for him?'

He considered. Her question was perfectly valid, after all she was Hamilton's secretary, but Lethbridge-Stewart wasn't entirely sure he wanted Sally to know what was going on. She would probably just start worrying.

'I'll take that as a no,' she said, engaging her ersatz cheery tone once more, as he hesitated.

'Yes, well, right then,' he said. Why was it that he never did quite seem to know what to say to her? It never used to this awkward, until he had taken up his post in Edinburgh, that is. 'Bit of a flap on here, so I'd better be off.'

'Take care, Alistair.'

'Always,' he promised. 'Probably nothing, you know,

but, well, we can't take chances. Ah, I'll talk to you later.' He almost slammed the phone down.

Well, that could have gone better.

He wished Sally wasn't Hamilton's secretary.

Still, at least she hadn't brought up her transfer again, since he still hadn't broached the subject with the general. And, to be honest, he wasn't at all certain that he *wanted* to bring it up.

Fond as he was of Sally, he wasn't at all certain it would be good for morale for him to wangle a transfer for his misses. How would *that* look to his men? He had to set a good example. He knew that certain generals were already frowning upon him because of the engagement, despite Hamilton's best effort to assure them that Lethbridge-Stewart had a lid on it. Besides, he wasn't at all sure how he would feel having her so close to him. He hoped it wouldn't affect the performance of his duty, but he was smart enough to know that was far from certain.

Courting someone in the Armed Forces seemed like such a good idea before March. But now? Now he wasn't so sure.

Thank goodness there was action in the offing. That, at least, he was confident he could handle!

Anne was on the phone also. To her pleasant surprise, she got through to Brinstead almost immediately. 'Professor Brinstead? It's Anne Travers. I hope you remember me?'

She could almost hear the cogs turning in his mind. 'Travers? Yes, of course, hard to forget a mind like yours. How's that father of yours?'

A good question. 'Fallen off the face of the Earth again,'

she admitted. 'I haven't heard from him in weeks. I should probably check in with Alun, see if he's heard from Father.'

'Typical of the man. Well, I assume you've not called just to talk to another old crank. What's on your mind?'

She plunged straight in. 'How's the bathysphere coming along?'

There was a short pause. 'Ah, yes, well... The university's balking at paying the bills to test it. It's sitting in a warehouse on the Hull docks at the moment, I'm afraid. And that damned Froggie is gallivanting all over the world and he's even on TV in the States! Can you imagine it? You'd think a university would be more interested in exploration, but no, it's always what they call the bottom line. No sense of national pride.'

'But it's ready to go?'

'Very nearly. I could have her in the water in half a day if I had the money.' Brinstead paused, and Anne smiled. He was never slow. 'Do *you* have the funding?'

'Not myself,' she answered, laughing. 'But I think I can get it for you, if you really can be ready in half a day.'

'Ten hours, tops,' he vowed. He sounded lively now. 'You really have the money?'

'I have *access* to some. Ministry of Defence. There's a job I'm on that is in dire need of a bathysphere. Timing is very important. I'd need your... What was its name again?'

'*Tethys.*'

'Right! Well, we need her in Peterhead as fast as possible. If I can get a vessel there quickly, can you finish prepping her on the way up here?'

'Of course,' he promised. She could hear the excitement in his voice. 'To get her in the water and exploring...' He broke off. 'What is there to explore in Peterhead?'

'I don't know,' she admitted. 'But that's the fun part, isn't it? But it could be rather dangerous.'

'Progress often is. Anyway, it'll be one in the eye for Cousteau, so it's worth a bit of a risk. I'll just pop over to the docks, you give me a call there when you've arranged transport.' He gave her the number and then rang off, no doubt scooting right out of his door.

Anne hoped she hadn't exceeded her authority, but she was pretty sure the brigadier would go along with it. Now if there was just a ship close enough to divert to Hull. She headed off to find Lethbridge-Stewart.

He was in his office, on the phone, and waved to her to wait as he finished the call. Some routine to do with transportation, getting more of his trained troops into the field, and it was finished in a minute.

'Sorry about that,' he apologised, putting down the phone. 'Blasted phone calls, such a nuisance. Politics and administration, two things I swore to never get involved in.' Lethbridge-Stewart offered a smile, which Anne returned. 'Now, what can I do for you?'

'Pick the phone up again, I'm afraid. Brinstead's all set to go, provided we can transport the bathysphere up to Peterhead.'

'I'll get onto it right away.'

'And is there any chance you can lay on transport for me to Hull?' she asked. 'If I can get there, I can travel back with him and help him prep the vessel for a dive.'

'I'm sure I can scrounge up a helo somewhere,' Lethbridge-Stewart said. 'Anything else?'

'No, I'll just pop off and pack a few things. I'll be ready to go as soon as you get the helicopter lined up.' She started to leave.

'Just a moment.' Lethbridge-Stewart pulled open one of the desk drawers. He rummaged around and then handed her a form. 'Better get the professor to sign this.'

'What is it?'

'Official Secrets Act.' He caught the look in her eye. 'Yes, I know your *knowledge must be free and shared* speech off by heart by now, Miss Travers. But in this case, we're dealing with a missing sub at the very least and possibly much worse. I don't want the gutter press getting even a whiff of this.'

Anne glared at the paperwork. 'He's not going to like this,' she warned.

'Then *get* him to like it, Miss Travers. I'm adamant on this matter.'

'I'll do my best. But this may not be something you can quietly sweep under the rug this time, you know. We were lucky last time that everything happened in a TV studio and we could keep it all under wraps. But this is out in the open, you can't control the seas, Brigadier.'

'Then I'll just have to do *my* best, won't I?' he replied. 'You really don't need to remind me of the headaches we're facing.'

She couldn't help feeling sympathetic. Lethbridge-Stewart could be obstinate and opinionated, but she knew he was genuinely doing his best to protect the country. 'No,' she agreed. 'I'm sure I don't.' She waved the papers at him. 'Packing. Off now.' As she left, she heard the brigadier sigh and pick up the phone again.

*

Samson surveyed his squad as they assembled in the side yard of Edinburgh Castle. He had a Land Rover and a lorry at the ready, and the small squad – just ten men – stowed their gear aboard. He turned to Bishop. 'How are we doing?'

'Just about set,' he said. 'I took the liberty of adding a couple of inflatables to the gear. We were told to be ready for anything, and we will be beside the seaside, so to speak.'

Samson grinned. 'Good idea. Did you tell the men to pack their buckets and spades, too, just in case?'

'I knew I forgot something.'

'Do them good to improvise.' Samson felt a wince of pain as he saw Evans ambling across to him. 'What is it, Evans?'

'I don't recall volunteering for this mission,' the Welshman complained.

'I don't recall asking you to, either,' Samson replied. 'This is the Army, Evans, we give orders, not ask for volunteers. And lazy and dodgy as you are, you're a driver and I need a driver for that lorry. So stop feeling sorry for yourself and do your job.'

'Oh, all right.' Evans slouched off.

Bishop sighed. 'I'd place him on charges, but what's the use? He actually enjoys being on jankers, and it gets him out of doing real work. It's more punishment to him this way.'

'He'll do his job,' Samson said, hoping he was right. 'Although can't see him remaining with 1 Battalion for much longer.'

'Salisbury then?'

Samson smiled. 'The reserves they call themselves, Bill.'

Bishop grinned, and they both turned back to the lorry. Evans swung himself up into the cab and started the engine.

'Okay, Sergeant,' Bishop said. 'We'd better get moving. Give the tourists something to take pictures of, eh? The Army off on manoeuvres.' He slipped into the passenger seat of the Land Rover, and Samson took the driver's side.

As the Land Rover pulled out, Bishop reached back and waved for Evans to follow. With a throaty roar, the truck fell in line behind them, and they started off.

Chorley sat in the bow of the small boat, holding on for grim life as it ploughed through the waves. Thankfully, the old sailor's boat turned out to have an outboard motor; Chorley had been picturing a tiny sailing ship, which would have taken forever. Glancing back, he saw that Peterhead had already disappeared over the horizon. The boat rose and fell, and he was splattered with spray from time to time. There was a strong tang of salt in the air, of course, and the cry of gulls could be heard even over the engine. Luckily, Chorley was not prone to motion sickness, otherwise he'd probably be leaning over the side by now.

'How long to the island?' He yelled to be heard over the noise of the engine and the howl of the wind.

The old man, hunched over the tiller, his ever-present pipe jammed tight in his mouth, didn't speak, but he pointed to a small smudge on the horizon. Evidently that was Strommach. The journalist had no idea how far off that might be, but he realised it couldn't be a long trip.

It *seemed* long, of course – whenever you were waiting for something to happen, minutes grew into hours somehow – but eventually he made out details. The island was low-lying, smallish – probably just a mile or so across at the widest point – and with an off-centre hill rising up from the sea to maybe a couple of hundred feet. There were no signs of life, save for a few circling gulls. As the small boat drew nearer, Chorley could start making out details. There was a dock jutting into a small bay, and there were about a dozen fishing smacks moored there. But there was still no sign of life, or buildings.

The old fisherman steered the boat toward the dock, scowling as he did so.

'Where are the people?' Chorley asked. 'And where's the village?'

'Up yonder,' the old man offered, pointing with the stem of his pipe. 'Wrecked.'

For an ancient mariner, he certainly had good eyesight. Chorley's glasses had misted over from the spray. He wiped them and replaced them, and was able to make out what the fisherman meant. There were no houses, but there were small piles of rubble. It was as if some maniac had run a bulldozer straight through the town.

'But where are the people?' Chorley asked again.

'Buried?'

That was a grisly thought; had the houses been collapsed on the villagers? That would be awful, but what a story it would make! 'You'd better put me ashore,' he said.

'Not staying,' the old man informed him.

'What?' Chorley looked at him. 'You can't just abandon me here.'

'Back in the morning. Be here–' he gestured at the end of the dock '–or else.' He held out a hand for payment.

Chorley gave him half the promised amount. 'You'll get

the rest when you pick me up,' he said.

'Fair enough.' The mariner steered in next to the dock. 'Up you go.'

Without grace, Chorley scrambled onto the dock. Without a word, the old man gunned the boat's engine, turned it and started to head off without a backward glance. Chorley hoped he really would be back in the morning. He had a rucksack with some food and a thermos of tea, along with his camera and notepad, but that was it. He wouldn't be able to survive here alone for long.

Still, no point in worrying about that right now; he had a story to cover. The young boy back in Peterhead had said something about machines coming from the sea, so there ought to be some evidence of that.

Chorley started walking along the dock, toward where the ruins were, looking all around as he went. Yes! He could see on the beach that there were deep, wide ruts, showing that something had emerged from the ocean, crawled up the beach to the village and back again. He carefully took a couple of pictures, and his excitement was mounting. He'd been right; there was a real story in this. But *what*? Machines from the sea, attacking an isolated island village, wrecking it completely... But who would do such a thing, and why?

The Ruskies, maybe? God knew what those sneaky Commies were up to. Maybe this was a test of some kind, some new weapon? Russian subs had been spotted in the North Sea plenty of times; were some of them carrying a new weapon to unleash against England and NATO? If so, he needed some kind of evidence. He started toward the ruins. Whatever had done that, a few pictures of ravaged houses would help sell the story.

Then he stopped, puzzled. There were plants growing everywhere, and he meant *everywhere*. In the rubble, in the streets, on the hillside. They were spaced some eighteen inches apart, and they were all about a foot across. He'd never seen anything quite like them, but he was no expert in botany. In fact, he loathed plants. Whenever he'd been given them as misguided gifts, he managed to kill them within a week. He had whatever the opposite of a green thumb was. He leaned in close to one to take a picture; somebody he knew would be able to identify them. And maybe even tell him why anybody would want to plant them like this, all over the place.

It didn't make any sense. The villagers would hardly have planted them, but the young man had claimed that the village had been attacked only last night. He was no expert, but surely these plants had to have been growing longer than overnight?

The plant he was photographing was a foot or so across. There was a central sort of bulbous growth, and it was fringed with extremely dark green leaves that were quivering slightly. It was an ugly-looking thing, certainly nothing you'd find in a florist's shop.

It suddenly sprang to life, making him jump back, which was probably the only thing that saved his life. A single tendril shot out of the central bulge, unravelling at an incredible speed, striking like a whip exactly where his face had been seconds before. Chorley fell on his backside and back-peddled quickly. The tendril writhed about, striking out, and instantly several other plants sprang to life, firing off tendrils of their own. They writhed about, questing, and one of them touched his leg.

Instantly, it whirled about his ankle, tightening, making him cry out in pain. It started to withdraw, dragging him with amazing strength towards the plant.

The bulbous area was showing signs of life, pulsing and writhing in its turn. *Dear God!* He scrambled in his pocket and found his Swiss Army knife. He had to drop his camera to use both hands to pry open the blade, and hacked at the tendril that was pulling him, slashing at the vegetable fibres. It spasmed, but didn't release him. Panicking, he slashed and slashed, and then felt with relief the tendril snap in two. Quickly, he scrambled to his feet and backed off, scooping up his camera on the way. He held the knife out, protecting himself against any further attacks.

The plants were all in a frenzy now, as if they somehow knew he'd attacked and damaged one of their kind. One that was waving the stump of its tendril futilely in the air, still menacing him.

Chorley retreated back onto the dock. There were no plants here, of course, since there wasn't any soil for them to root in. So he was safe. Probably.

But for how long? If those things had really grown to this size overnight, how big would they be in the morning, when (hopefully) his ride would return?

He had a horrible image of a plant big enough for those tendrils to hunt him down.

CHAPTER NINE

Release Me

Mary looked from the burned vessel up to the stoical Ymir. 'Are you happy now?' she asked, her voice flat. She was cold inside, her emotions shut down by the death she had witnessed.

'I do not understand.'

'I'm sure you don't,' she agreed. She gestured at the ship. 'You've killed everyone on board except Al and me. Are you satiated now? Or are we next?'

'Ah.' The Ymir inclined its head slightly. 'You are under the misapprehension that I rejoice in the deaths of others.'

'Don't you?'

'No.' The Ymir stared down at her. 'If anything, I regret it. I regret the waste, when there is so much need for workers. But others have arrived. You will speak with them and ensure that they will co-operate. I sincerely wish to harm no other human being, unless they should make it necessary for me to do so.'

'A kindly killer?' Mary sneered. 'You'll pardon me if I find it hard to swallow.'

'All that matters is the work,' the Ymir informed her. 'If you can get the other humans to acquiesce, then you will preserve their lives, at least for the time being. If not, we shall be forced to kill them and feed them to the

Grandfathers.'

'For the time being?' Alan pounced on those words. 'And when the work is done?'

'The human race will no longer rule this world. We shall.'

Alan snorted. 'And you expect us to *help* you to take over our world?'

'You will work, or you will die,' the Ymir stated flatly. 'Those are your choices. Those are the choices given to all humans we acquire.'

'Well, I for one–' Alan started to yell, but Mary grabbed his arm.

'Al, *think*! You've seen it kill, and you know it will kill again, without anything more than *regret*. At the moment we don't have any option. If we stay alive, then we may have a chance to do something. If we die, we die.' Also – though she didn't want to say this in front of the Ymir, of course – she might be able to learn what the creatures were up to. With knowledge came the possibility of counteracting their plans. As long as it thought she was co-operating, the Ymir seemed to be willing to talk to her. And, unlike human beings, it was devastatingly honest. It might be that it didn't even know the meaning of *lying*.

But she did. That might not be much of a weapon against these terrible monsters, but it was all she had right now. She had to convince it she'd go along with its plans. Unfortunately, that meant she'd have to make Alan believe her, too. And that would be very hard. She could already see the disappointment in his face. And that might deepen into disgust. To have her friend feel that way about her twisted her inside, but it was more important to learn from the alien than to not disappoint Al.

'I would never have taken you for a coward, Mary,' he said, distaste evident in his voice.

'It's not cowardice to want to stay alive,' she told him. 'It's just common sense. Just go along with me for now, and we'll talk about it later.' *When the Ymir aren't listening.*

'Whatever you say,' he agreed, numbly.

'You will prepare yourselves,' the Ymir said.

Before Mary could ask for what, it scooped the pair of them up, one in each arm. She gave a shocked gasp as her head whirled, and then it started off with long strides through the dark cavern. She'd managed to hang onto her torch, and the beam wobbled and shook as the Ymir strode along.

It was a beauty, Anne had to admit. She stood beside Brinstead, who was hopping from foot to foot, wincing and crying out as the crane from *Dorset* lifted his bathysphere into the air from its cradle and then swung it aboard. It was generally spherical, of course – the optimum shape to resist pressure – with a pair of portholes facing forward and a smaller one in the bottom so you could look straight down. There were two extendable clawed arms and an array of lights (currently dark, of course). The whole sphere was painted a rather garish yellow – to make it easy to spot in the water – and the name TETHYS painted in black above the front portholes. It was about sixteen feet around, but would be considerably smaller inside, Anne was certain, as there had to be a fair amount of armour around the work space. Brinstead hadn't allowed her inside it yet, but she'd check it out the moment *Dorset* was underway.

She loved it, so far.

She couldn't exactly say the same about its inventor. She'd studied under Brinstead for a term. He was an expert in marine biology and in adaptation to the life aquatic, and he certainly knew his stuff. But that had been five years ago. He'd always been... well, *overly-focused* was a kind way of putting it, if you didn't want to come right out and call him a fanatic. He was utterly obsessed with his competition, with Cousteau (who obviously knew of Brinstead, but apparently didn't value him), and that obsession had grown worse in those five years. He was now a committed Francophobe, avoiding and loathing anything that had emerged from France since Napoleon. His every conversation was punctuated with this irrational distaste, which made conversation difficult. It was no surprise to Anne why he had never managed to get any serious funding.

And, as she'd suspected, he reacted to signing the Official Secrets Act the way Christopher Lee's Dracula would react to a request to kiss a cross. 'How can you ask me to do that?' he cried.

'Because if you don't, you won't get your funding to do these sea trials,' she said, patiently.

'I'm surprised at you, Travers,' he growled. 'I always thought you were the *make love not war* type. Didn't you drop out of university to become a Flower Child or something?'

'Not exactly.' She wasn't going to get side-tracked into talking about her personal philosophy. She waved the form. 'Are you going to sign this, or shall I have them unload the *Tethys* again?' She really hoped she was reading him right, because at the moment she needed the bathysphere more than he needed the funding. She really didn't know what she'd do if he called her bluff. 'I could always give Cousteau a call,' she mused.

Brinstead snatched the papers from her hand and scrawled his signature across the bottom before thrusting them back at her. 'How can you live with yourself?' he growled.

Anne considered his question seriously for a moment. 'Surprisingly well,' she confessed. 'I would never have thought it six months ago, but I honestly think I'm making a difference. And the group of people I'm working with are truly doing their best to protect this country, if not the world.'

'That's overly dramatic,' he sniffed, scornfully. 'As you know, I think *Tethys* is a gigantic leap ahead of the Frogs, but *saving the world* is a bit over the top, don't you think?'

Anne smiled cheerily at him. 'You know, I do so hope you're right.'

The walk lasted barely two minutes. Mary was wondering just how large the cavern was when she saw lights ahead. They quickly resolved themselves into the most bizarre sight she never could have imagined.

There was… well, a *flying saucer*, she supposed it had to be. It was huge, some of it lost in the shadows cast by the lights. At least a quarter of a mile long, and a hundred feet tall. Unlike in the popular press, it wasn't really a saucer shape, not round at all, in fact. It looked like a huge torpedo or bomb, but with pods and protuberances all over its surface. There were portholes (did they call them *portholes* in space ships?), and a huge access door that had opened up in the side, with a wide ramp leading down to the scuffed dirt. At least a dozen more Ymir were moving about, all –

as far as she could tell – absolutely identical to the one carrying her and Alan.

Gathered around the main ship were half a dozen smaller craft. These looked like huge metal slugs, and they were glowing, which provided most of the light hereabouts. They were about forty feet long each and twenty tall at the rear.

Most incongruous of all, there was a submarine lying off to one side.

What the hell was going on here?

'The Navy's here,' Alan said, happily. 'They'll sort this bunch out.'

'I think submarines work better when they're immersed in water,' Mary murmured back. 'This one's high and dry.'

The Ymir, apparently, had sharp little ears. 'That craft belongs to your warrior clan?' it asked.

'Yes,' Alan said, cheerfully. 'Now you'll see what the human race can do.'

'Now isn't the time for patriotic cheering, Al,' Mary growled. 'I don't see any signs of life on that sub.'

'The inhabitants of the vessel have all been stunned,' the Ymir informed them. 'As they awaken, you will inform them that they are to work for us or die.'

'I'll do nothing to help you,' Alan vowed.

'You have the same choice,' the Ymir said. 'Work for us or die.'

'Al!' Mary grabbed his arm. 'Your wife and kids, remember them. You owe it to them to live. *Please*, do as they say. At least for now.' He gave her a defiant look, and she felt like punching the idiot. 'Al, *please*, stay alive for me. I can't do this alone.'

128

That made him waver. 'All right,' he finally said. 'I'll do as I'm asked, for now.'

'Good.' The Ymir didn't seem at all bothered by Alan's attitude. 'Your first task is to help with the land humans.'

'Land humans?' Mary was confused. 'What land humans?'

'Those.' The Ymir gestured toward the metal slugs. As he did so, panels opened in the side of each. Slowly, hesitantly, small clumps of people emerged, all clearly terrified. 'They are to be workers; you will inform them.'

'What have you done to them?' Mary asked, shocked. There had to be almost two hundred of these people; men, women and children. Young and old, hale and infirm. 'They can't possibly all work.'

'Those that do not work will be fed to the Grandfathers,' the Ymir said. 'You will make clear to them this option. Separate all who will work from those that will not or cannot.'

'That's inhuman,' Mary growled.

'We are not human,' the Ymir pointed out. 'Inform them now, else we will start culling them.'

'No, no!' Mary said, urgently. 'Don't hurt them! I'll do it.'

Without even pausing to see if Alan was following her, she hurried across the chamber to the closest knot of terrified people. They were clearly locals, none too prosperous. Most of the men were dressed in thick sweaters and heavy duty trousers. The women wore homespun clothing, some of it patched several times. The children – babies howling, younger kids snotty-nosed and snivelling in fear – were generally a ragamuffin bunch.

'Listen to me!' she called, as loudly as she could. 'Listen to me! Please, try and calm down! Listen to me!' To her surprise, dozens of faces turned to look at her. They actually did seem to be calming down a bit, and they were looking at her like she was some sort of authority figure, and not just another scared and tired-looking woman who'd been through a terrifying experience.

'We're all in danger here,' she said, trying to sound as if she *was* an authority figure. 'But we can and will survive it if you all keep your heads.' She gestured at the looming Ymir. 'We have been taken prisoners by these alien creatures. They insist that we have to work for them.'

'Doing what?' one of the older men asked.

'I don't know, yet,' Mary admitted. 'But if we *don't* agree, they say they will kill us. So, please, for your children's sake, for your wives' sakes, for your loved ones' sakes, agree.'

'They're beasties from the pits o'hell,' one old woman cried. 'We cannae trust them!'

'I don't know how much we can trust them,' Mary answered her. 'And I think they're from space, not hell. But I do know that they will keep their promise and kill anyone who refuses to do as they command. I've seen them kill, and it's not something I want to see again.'

'Why are ye workin' for them?' one man called out.

'I'm not working for *them*,' Mary snapped. 'I'm trying to save *your* lives! Please, believe me, I've seen what they can do.'

'I'm no' sure I want to listen ta a traitor,' the man insisted.

'Then you're an idiot!' Alan had indeed followed Mary, and he stood beside her now. 'She's not a traitor, she's trying to help. Those monsters, wherever they are from, are killers. The only thing keeping your babies and children alive right now is that they're giving Mary a chance to convince you. Do you *want* your children to die? If you like, I can ask them to give you a demonstration.' He glared at a woman cuddling a squalling infant. 'You want your kid to be the first to die?' He made as if to move forward.

'No!' the woman screamed, clutching the child even harder, making it howl even louder.

A man moved in front of her. 'Ye'll no take our bairns,' he vowed.

'The only way you'll save them is to do what the Ymir say,' Mary snapped. 'So, I ask you, will you calm down and listen?'

The man looked dubious, but he finally nodded. 'Aye.' He agreed. 'For the sake o' the wee ones, we'll listen.'

'Thank you.' Mary looked around, feeling what she knew was only a moment of relief. 'Look, I know you're scared. Hell, I'm terrified myself! But you have to control that fear for now, for the sake of your families. Gather together, and try to stay calm. I'll see if I can talk to the Ymir and learn what is to be done. But, please, do try and remain calm, and do try and do as you're told. It's the only way that we may live through this.'

'You go back to big, tall and rocky,' Alan said softly. 'I'll stay with these people and try to keep them orderly. See if you can get some concessions from it.'

'Thanks for the help, Al,' Mary said, truly grateful he was with her. 'I couldn't do this without you.'

Somehow, he managed a grin. 'Always selling yourself short,' he said. 'You do just fine, love. Now, go talk to the monster from outer space.'

Grateful for his support, and relieved that the captives appeared to be calming down a bit, Mary walked back to her Ymir. 'All right,' she told it. 'I think I can keep them in order, and agree to work for you. But what is it you want them to do?'

'You appear to be efficient,' the Ymir answered. 'You are required to speak. You will speak for us to them, and speak for them to us. That is your task. Is it acceptable?'

'Yes, for God's sake, yes!' Mary snapped. 'But what is it you want *them* to do?'

'You will be informed. There is a further task for you to perform first.' The Ymir gestured toward the stranded submarine. 'The humans inside that vessel are awake. You will inform them that they are captives and must also work for us.'

'You've got to be joking,' Mary said. 'They're sailors, they won't listen to me.'

'If they will not listen to you, then you will have failed in your function. You are required to work or die. What is your decision?'

Mary swallowed. She knew the Ymir was stating a fact, but what could she do? These were men of action, not scared and helpless villagers. They were hardly likely to surrender without a fight. 'I can try,' she said. 'But I can't promise they'll do as you wish.'

'They will work or die; there is no other option for them,' the Ymir stated. 'Speak to them.'

'Okay.' Mary glanced over at the villagers; Al seemed to have them all gathered together. Aside from a few crying babies, they were sullenly silent. They were probably still suspicious of her, but there wasn't much she could do about that. If she was to save everyone's lives, she had to appear to the Ymir to be co-operating fully. Which meant trying to talk to the men on that sub.

Bishop had to resist the urge to whistle happily as the two vehicles pulled up in the Peterhead docks. The prospect of action at last! Not that he resented his administration duties he'd been on, but he was more of a doer, and this was far more in his line. To his surprise, though, a couple of policemen barred his way, and gestured for him to park to one side. He'd not been expecting any sort of official welcome, so he hopped out of the Land Rover as Samson parked it and crossed to the Bobbies.

'What's going on?' he asked.

'If you're here for those kids, you just missed 'em.'

'What kids?'

The policeman blinked. 'They're not why you're here?'

'First I've heard about kids,' Bishop admitted. 'Why don't you tell me about them?'

'From Strommach,' the policeman said. Seeing Bishop's blank stare, he added, 'Not heard of that, either, eh?'

'I guess I'm not really up on the local gossip.'

'It's an island,' the policeman said, helpfully pointing off to sea. 'A couple of miles out. Two kids showed up in a fishing boat this morning, babbling about everyone being kidnapped by monsters from under the sea. Sounds a bit fishy, so we sent 'em off to hospital to be checked out, if you know what I mean.' He made a screwing motion with his finger next to his temple. 'Kids these days. I thought you were here to investigate their silly story.'

Every instinct Bishop possessed was tingling. 'Perhaps I am,' he said softly. He glanced around as Samson reached him. 'Get the inflatables out and readied,' he ordered. 'I think I'd better give the brigadier a call.'

Mary crossed the gap to the sub, and then yelped as a stony hand gripped and lifted her, placing her down on the conning tower. She regained her balance and glared at the Ymir. 'I wish you'd tell me when you're going to do that.' It didn't bother to answer her, and simply stood there, waiting. Well, there wasn't any point in hanging around. She didn't know what else to do, so she crossed to the hatch, and then slipped off one of her shoes. Holding the toe, she banged the heel hard against the hatch several times. 'Oi in there!' she yelled, having no idea if anybody could even hear her.

She heard muffled sounds from below the hatch, so she slipped her shoe back on and waited. After a moment, the wheel in the centre of the hatch started to turn, and then the lid popped up.

A gun emerged first, waving about. She only hoped they'd ask questions first and fire later. She swallowed nervously and waited. Slowly a head and then arms and shoulders emerged. She didn't have a clue as to ranks in the submarine service, but this was a fairly good-looking youngish man in his late twenties, and he looked startled.

'Bloody hell,' he said.

'Yeah, I probably look it,' she agreed.

'What's going on?' he asked. 'Where's the sea?'

'The tide's out,' Mary told him. '*Way* out. As for what's going on... Well, you're like the rest of us. You've been

134

captured by a bunch of alien stone giants called the Ymir. They want you all to surrender and come on out of there.'

'Aliens?' he echoed. 'Aliens from outer space?'

'Yeah, that's where they generally come from.'

The sailor stared at her. 'I'd say you were nuts,' he said. 'Except there's no sea.'

'Come on out,' she suggested. 'You'll see I'm not nuts; though, honestly, I'd really prefer it if I was.'

The sailor glanced downwards. 'I'm going up top, sir,' he called down. 'Hang on.' Then he popped up out of the hatch, which promptly closed behind him.

'What's that about?' she asked him.

'Standard security,' he replied, and then straightened up and looked over the side of the sub. 'Bloody hell.'

'Yeah, you said that already,' Mary informed him. She watched as he took in the view – the spaceship, the metal slugs, the captives – and the Ymir looming over the side of the submarine. 'Right, you can see you're stuck here with the rest of us.' She pointed at the stone giant. 'That's an Ymir, and, right now, it's in charge around here. Over there are some Scottish villagers the Ymir have caught for workers. I'm from Radio Crossbones, which is over there somewhere in the darkness, just as stranded as you are. The Ymir want you all to surrender and come out of there.'

'The captain's not going to agree to that,' the man said firmly.

'He's not got a lot of choice,' Mary stated. 'You've got no idea what these Ymir can do when they get started.'

'They won't stand up to bullets,' the sailor promised, hefting his gun.

'Actually, yes, they will. They're made of *stone*, bullets

just bounce off them. It's been tried.'

'Then we'll use heavier artillery,' he said.

Mary pointed to the villagers. 'They have hostages. Are you really going to try and start a war with innocent kids and mums around?'

The sailor looked uncertain. 'That's not my decision,' he finally said. 'That's up to Captain Browne.'

'Fine. Then pop back down your rabbit hole and let the captain know what he's up against, and urge him to make the right decision.' Mary glanced at the Ymir. 'Trust me, these aliens aren't really into being patient, and they're lethal if you don't do what they say.'

'Right.' He bent and rapped three times on the hatch with the butt of his gun. The hatch opened up again. As he started onto the ladder, he looked back at her. 'You want to come down here? You'd be a lot safer.'

'Believe me, none of us are safe right now,' Mary told him. 'And I'd better hang around up here. If I disappear from view, the Ymir are likely to get jumpy. Just get your captain to agree.'

He looked dubious. 'I'll try,' he promised. He vanished down the tube, and the hatch slammed shut behind him.

'What is happening?' the Ymir asked. It sounded vaguely annoyed. 'Why are they not coming out?'

'They have to make a decision,' Mary said. 'Only their captain can do that.'

'Time is growing short,' the alien said. 'They must do as they are instructed. Now.'

'Give them time to talk,' Mary begged.

'I do not have much more time!' The Ymir sounded really annoyed now; the first true emotion it had demonstrated since she had met it. 'I cannot tolerate this abominable cold much longer. The decision will be made immediately.'

Cold...? Of course! Mary was starting to understand. The Ymir's ability to release heat was because it had a high internal temperature. It wasn't a weapon as such, merely the way it was. And the stone-like skin of the alien kept the heat inside, but only for a limited time. Normal Earth temperatures were far too low for it.

And that explained why it needed humans as workers. Whatever the Ymir were planning, they needed hands that could work in normal conditions.

The Ymir gave a call; a low, resonant sound that make her teeth ache, and the metal beneath her vibrated. Evidently, this was the Ymir's own language, for three more Ymir strode to join her alien. There was no way to distinguish any of them from the others, though humans probably all looked alike to these creatures, too.

'Inform them they must emerge. Now!' the Ymir snapped.

Mary smacked the heel of her shoe down on the hatch three times. A moment later it popped open and a different sailor peered out. 'Tell your captain that the monsters from outer space want him out here now,' she said with forced politeness.

'He's not to be disturbed, miss,' the sailor said. 'He's in a briefing.'

'I think he's going to be *very* disturbed,' Mary muttered, as the Ymir gestured.

Its three companions stepped forward and each laid its hands on the metal shell of the submarine. The metal construction of the sub conducted the heat beautifully.

Mary swallowed. It was going to happen all over again, only this time she was standing directly on the soon-to-be melted sub.

CHAPTER TEN

English Country Garden

L ethbridge-Stewart was in the communications room again. It galled him just how much of his time was taken up with simply talking to people when he'd much rather be leading the charge into action himself. But he had his men in place, and he had to trust them to do their jobs right.

'Mayhem One, this is Madhouse,' he said into the microphone.

'Madhouse,' Bishop's voice replied. 'This is Mayhem One. We're preparing to head out to Strommach to investigate. Two of the locals have been taken to Peterhead General Hospital for evaluation. The local authorities think they're touched in the head for reporting some kind of amphibious assault on the island.'

'Mayhem One, understood.' Lethbridge-Stewart considered his options. 'Stay in contact and report in as soon as you have the island in sight. I'll have a couple of men swing by the hospital to talk to those locals and prevent the story from spreading. Madhouse, out.' He glanced over at Douglas. 'Dougie, get a couple of good men to that hospital.'

'Right away,' Douglas agreed. 'You think there's anything to this story?'

Lethbridge-Stewart turned to the situation map.

Maddox's girls had it up to date, of course, and Strommach had been highlighted. 'The island's only a few miles from where that pirate radio ship went down,' he said thoughtfully. 'Everything seems to be happening in that small area of the ocean. Maybe there's nothing to it, but Bishop is doing the right thing in the situation, I think.'

'He's a good man; he's been well-trained,' Douglas said, approvingly.

'I trust *all* of our men will turn out to be good men.' Lethbridge-Stewart pointed his swagger stick to the position of Hull, which had a small ship placed close by. 'Miss Travers is on her way with the *Tethys*, though she's not likely to arrive before this evening at the earliest.'

'Do you think it's a good idea to let her go down to investigate?'

Lethbridge-Stewart had been wondering exactly that himself. 'I don't see that we have any choice,' he admitted. 'We need intel very badly, and there's really no other way of getting it. Besides, Miss Travers is a very capable woman, as she's proven on more than one occasion. Hamilton has managed to convince the Admiralty to keep *Kraken* in the area, so we'll have a little back-up at least. And with both the Army and Navy involved, the Air Force is chomping at the bit to get in on the action, even if they don't know what it is yet. If we call for help, they'll be standing by to give it.'

'You think we'll need it?' Dougie asked quietly.

'God knows; I hope not. But I feel better that it's available. I sincerely hope that this is all a bunch of coincidences building up to nothing.'

'But you don't believe that?'

'No, Colonel, I think this is the real thing.'

Mary could feel the plating beneath her growing uncomfortably warm. She could only imagine what it must be like inside the sub.

'Hey!' she yelled at her Ymir. 'I'm baking here!'

Once again, it scooped her up, holding her a few feet in the air. She could feel the heat radiating upward, and hear the yells of the men inside the vessel.

'Your captain had better get a move on,' she called to the sailor in the hatch. 'If he doesn't, you're all going to be cooked. Trust me, these things don't play games.'

The sailor nodded and vanished, yelping as he did so. Mary could picture the burns his hands must be getting.

'I think they've got the point,' she snapped to the Ymir. 'You can stop now.'

'We will stop when they emerge,' it replied.

A moment later, amid intensified howls and cries, she heard feet on the ladder. On both the fore and aft decks, hatchways opened up, and steam issued forth. Sailors poured from all of the exits, clambering onto the decks.

All were armed, many of them with machine guns.

Mary knew this wasn't going to end well. And she realised that she might well get caught in the shooting. She scrunched down as best she could in the Ymir's massive hand, praying that she'd be safe.

Gunfire erupted all around her, and she heard bullets ricocheting off stone bodies. The screams of dying men followed, and the stench of burning flesh made her want to gag. She didn't dare look, but she knew what was happening. The Ymir were lashing out with their internal heat, destroying all resistance. She wanted to scream in rage, in frustration, at the futility of it all. Gunfire wasn't going to harm the Ymir, all it was doing was getting helpless sailors slaughtered.

She heard a desperate voice calling out for cease fire, and the other noises stopped, replaced by the sound of guns and rifles clattering to the decks. She slowly straightened up to peer through stone fingers at the scene below.

It was as bad as she had feared. There were at least a dozen bodies, charred and smoking on the deck below her. The Ymir loomed over the sub, none of them in the slightest bit injured. A man in uniform stood atop the conning tower, his head bowed; clearly Captain Browne.

One by one, the remaining sailors emerged from the hatches and lined up on deck. The men tried to avoid looking at their cooked friends. The captain straightened up, haunted and defeated.

'I surrender my ship to you,' he said quietly.

'It is well,' her Ymir said. 'You will all join the other human captives and prepare yourselves to work. The dead humans will be removed and taken to the Grandfathers for disposal. This human…' The Ymir held Mary aloft, and she had to grab one of his fingers to steady herself. '…Speaks for us. You will listen and obey all commands it passes along. That is all.'

Indeed it was. The Ymir had clearly won this encounter.

The two inflatables were on their way, bouncing up and down as they ploughed through the waves. Bishop was steering the one he and Samson were in, along with Evans and two of the squad. Samson would almost have enjoyed the trip if Evans didn't keep breaking into *A Life on the Ocean*

Waves every couple of minutes. It didn't help that he didn't know the lyrics and couldn't keep to the tune, either. Samson had decided it wasn't worth telling him to shut up, and instead studied the waterproof map he had.

From the look of things, Strommach was a tiny island, hardly worth noticing in the normal course of events. Just a cluster of houses for the local fishermen and nothing much else. If there really was anything to the youngsters' story, it was a perfect site for an enemy incursion. If the two teens hadn't managed to get away, nobody would have checked the place out for weeks, probably.

Samson wasn't entirely certain what their story was, exactly. Everyone he'd spoken to at the docks had agreed that the youngsters had claimed that the village had been attacked and destroyed, but after that the stories varied wildly from everyone being murdered gruesomely to everyone being taken captive to everyone becoming blood-crazed zombies.

Well, they'd find out in about twenty minutes which, if any, of the tales were true. To be on the safe side, Samson had ordered all of their ordinance brought with them. Maybe a bazooka was overkill, maybe it was just wishful thinking, but he preferred being ready for anything just at this minute.

'That's it!' Bishop called, pointing.

Samson scanned the indicated area and saw a small brownish smudge against the grey of the sea. 'Not long now.'

The old feeling of excitement was building up inside him. Samson wasn't exactly a danger junkie, he was far too level-headed for that, and that kind of an attitude could get you killed very quickly, but the thrill of impending action was a high he anticipated and enjoyed. It was what had lured him into stunt work for the films, the adrenaline rush, but also the careful checking that all contingencies had been planned for.

Of course, going into an unknown situation, there was no way of knowing whether all possible contingencies *had* been planned for.

The inflatables drew closer and closer to the rocky little island. According to the map there was a jetty jutting out in the small bay, and he hoped that was still intact after the destruction of the town. If not, they'd have to land directly in the bay. Most of the island was ringed with cliffs, and they had no climbing equipment with them.

He brushed the spray from his eyes, and used his glasses to scan the bay as they approached. As he'd hoped, he could see the jetty, which looked intact. There were several fishing boats still moored to it, though one or two of them looked as if something had ploughed right through them, leaving them looking like beached whales.

He saw movement. He blinked, wiped his face again, and then rechecked. Yes, there was a lone figure on the jetty, waving its hands. Another survivor, it appeared. Maybe he'd get some better intel in a few minutes. He gestured for Bishop to head for the end of the jetty, and the inflatable changed heading slightly. As they approached, Samson scanned the island again. He couldn't see a single building standing, but there were the broken teeth of rubble. And, everywhere, there was a dark greenish colouration that he couldn't understand.

He turned the glasses back on the lone figure, who appeared to be doing some kind of a Highland fling, and the man came into focus. Samson couldn't help an amazed grin. 'Well, I'll be blowed,' he muttered.

'Something wrong?' Bishop asked, curiously.

'There's someone there.'

Bishop peered closer. 'Oh, joy. Here we are, out in the middle of nowhere, and we run into somebody we know.'

They drew close to the jetty, and the man leaned down to greet them. It was his turn to stare in amazement. 'Bishop!' he exclaimed. 'What are you doing here?'

'My job, Mr Chorley,' Bishop told the journalist, trying not to smile at Samson's groan of irritation. 'And what are *you* doing here?'

'*My* job,' Chorley grunted. 'But I *am* glad to see you again. I was supposed to be picked up by a fisherman, but he never showed up. It's been a rough time here, I can tell you. Those things are after me. They know I'm here, somehow.'

Samson scrambled up to join the journalist. Both inflatables were tied up against the jetty and his squad rapidly joined them, weapons at the ready.

'*Who* knows you're here, Chorley?' Samson glanced around, but could see no other people.

'You!' Chorley shook his head. 'So, Colonel Lethbridge-Stewart recruited you after all.'

'Never mind that, man. Where are they? Are they hiding? Is this an ambush?'

'Hiding? No.' Chorley gestured back at the rubble that had once been a small village. 'There they are, in plain sight.'

Samson was wondering if Chorley was quite sane. His previous experience of Chorley left that a viable option. He looked in the indicated direction and could see nothing but a bunch of knee-high plants. Well, that explained the green colouration he'd seen; these things were literally everywhere. They grew in the rubble, in the gardens, on the muddy streets… That was a bit odd, come to think of it. But there were no other people – or even monsters from outer space – in sight. Could Chorley see something he couldn't?

'There's nothing there, Chorley,' Samson said, gently.

'Of course there's something there!' Chorley glared at Samson and pointed again 'All over the damned place!'

Light finally dawned. 'You mean the *plants*?'

'Those damned things *want* me. They know I'm here and they want me.'

'They're just plants, Chorley,' Samson said, patiently. 'Plants don't *want* anything beyond a patch of dirt and some sunshine.' The fella really had gone around the bend, and showed no signs of wanting to return.

'You don't know these plants, Ware,' the reporter growled. '*These* plants aren't normal. And they're hungry for meat.'

'What makes you think that?'

'I saw them attack a dog,' Chorley said, grimly. 'Several of them caught it, ripped it to shreds and then ate it. It was… horrible. Thank God you've come for me! Now we've got to get out of here.'

'We didn't come for you, Chorley. I had no idea you were here until five minutes ago. We're here to check out the island, and we won't be leaving until we do.'

Chorley grabbed his arms. 'No, you don't understand; we can't stay here! We've got to leave!'

Samson glanced around. Hanging back, as usual, was Evans. 'Evans,' he called.

The private looked behind himself, then tapped his chest. 'Me?'

'Yes, you!' Samson snapped. 'How many Evanses are there on this island? Take Mr Chorley here into one of the boats and stay with him.'

'Gladly,' Evans answered, honestly. He hurried forward and took Chorley's arm. 'Come along, then,' he said, gently. 'Let's go and have a fag, shall we?'

Chorley looked torn. 'You? You were in the Underground.' He sighed and went with Evans, calling back over his shoulder. 'You'll be sorry.'

Samson hoped the man was wrong. 'Right,' he said to the men, 'let's take a look, shall we? Come on, and stay alert.' He wasn't at all sure that Chorley was right, but it would be stupid to assume he was completely wrong. 'Don't get too close to any of these plants.'

Bishop and Samson led the way forward, their pistols in their hands. Samson scanned the area ahead for any signs of movement, but all he could see were leaves on the plants rustling in the wind. He'd never seen anything quite like these plants, but, then, he was no expert. Plants were what you gave a girl on a date as far as he was concerned. He could recognise roses, and tulips from Amsterdam, and a handful of other common flowers, but that was it. The plants before them, however, were dark green and leathery, with broad, thick leaves. The centre was rounded like a football.

Wait a minute… If the leaves were so thick and heavy, how come the light breeze was making them move?

'Bill…' he began.

The closest plant exploded. The 'football' opened and several thick, wiry tendrils shot out. One touched his ankle, and then whipped around it and tightened. With a powerful jerk, it ripped his feet from under him and he fell heavily. He was dimly aware of other plants jumping into motion around him, but his focus was on his ankle, caught in a powerful grip.

The tendril started to contract, dragging him across the ground with astonishing strength. He still had a grip on his pistol, and he fired twice at the heart of the plant. It produced no apparent effect. Well, he should hardly have expected it to, should he?

Then Bishop stepped in. He slammed a foot down on the tendril hauling Samson along, and whipped out his knife. In two blows, he cut through the tendril and grabbed Samson's arms, hauling him clear.

Samson's ankle was in agony. The plant material had fallen free, leaving pain where it had been attached.

'Fall back!' Bishop called out, as he dragged Samson out of range of the thrashing tendrils.

The squad retreated, but Samson could see that Manning had fallen and was being dragged by the plants. His face was purple, a tendril wrapped about his throat. He was spasming.

'Bill,' Samson said, gesturing. 'I'll be fine; Manning won't.'

Bishop eyed the situation. 'I don't think we can get to him,' he said. 'Those damned things have dragged him too far in.'

Samson managed to prop himself up on one elbow, and looked back. Bishop was right, Manning was in a thicket of the plants, and there were more and more tendrils wrapped about his now-still body. What they needed here was a flame thrower, or a damned good weed-killer.

The plants started to rip Manning's body apart.

There was nothing to be done, not even an attempt to recover the body. It would just be putting more men at risk. Guns were useless against plants; there weren't any vital spots to hit.

'Back to the boats,' Bishop ordered, with a heavy heart. Samson knew how he felt. His first command and he'd lost a man, unable to even recover the body.

Samson struggled to stand, but could put no weight on that ankle. Bishop moved smoothly to support him. 'We'd better get back,' Samson said, dully. 'We've got to report this to base, and we can't contact them from out here.'

As the boats fired up and moved away from the jetty, Samson caught sight of Chorley in the other boat. The journalist looked as down and defeated as he felt. And Samson could almost have sworn he could hear the plants eating poor Manning.

Samson lowered his head. First round to those plants, maybe, but the Corps wasn't beaten yet.

CHAPTER ELEVEN

Stop Stop Stop

Lethbridge-Stewart had always unconsciously assumed that all admirals were stout gentlemen, faces reddened by years of drinking rum, bearded and either irascible or jovial. Admiral Hennessey fit none of his preconceptions; he was a tall, thin, clean-shaven man approaching sixty, with an utterly unreadable face. And his preferred tipple turned out to be Scotch. The two of them had small glasses while awaiting the arrival of Air Marshal McMillan. When the flyer arrived, Lethbridge-Stewart wasn't too surprised to discover no accompanying handlebar moustache. The three of them sat around the table in Lethbridge-Stewart's outer office. Since Bishop was absent, he roped in Hawke as his temporary aide.

'Bad business,' McMillan opined. 'You've lost a sub, eh, Reggie? They'll probably take it out of your salary.' The two men clearly knew one another well, and were not exactly on friendly terms; this didn't bode well. Lethbridge-Stewart needed co-operation here, not antagonism.

'Gentlemen,' he said, briskly. 'I thought I'd bring you up to date on what we're doing about the situation and see if we can't all help one another here.'

'I don't understand what the damned army is doing in this business anyway,' Hennessey growled. 'It should be a strictly naval operation. And I expected Hamilton here, not some underling.'

The crack annoyed Lethbridge-Stewart, but he tried not to allow his anger to grow. 'I'm here because the Fifth has experience of these matters in the past, and we're taking steps to deal with this event.'

'Dammit, man, I have jurisdiction here,' Hennessey complained.

'With due respect, sir–'

'I have long since learned that when somebody begins a sentence *with due respect*, then that's the last thing I'll get.'

'*With due respect*,' Lethbridge-Stewart said, pointedly, 'I am confident that you and your forces are more than capable of dealing with the usual run of things. This, however, is not within your usual frame of reference.'

'It's a missing – presumably sunk – ship and a missing – presumably sunk – submarine. How is that not my *usual run of things*?'

'Because I believe both events were caused by non-human interference,' Lethbridge-Stewart stated.

'Non-human...' McMillan scowled. 'You talking bug-eyed monsters here, man?'

'I'm not at all certain of the shape of their eyes,' Lethbridge-Stewart said slowly, 'but the *monsters* part may be accurate, yes.'

'You've been watching too much *Doctor Omega*,' Hennessey snapped.

'I rarely have the time to watch television,' Lethbridge-Stewart replied drily. 'And you're both senior enough to know the particulars of the London Event.'

'Certainly,' McMillan agreed.

'Of course,' Hennessey added.

'And if you have the clearance, I suggest you talk to Air Vice-Marshal Gilmore.'

McMillan eyed Lethbridge-Stewart for a moment. 'What the devil has old Chunky got to do with anything?'

'Talk to him and you'll see.'

'Very well, I will,' McMillan said, glancing at Hennessey. 'Regardless, the last thing we need is somebody yelling *aliens* at everything that we can't immediately explain. There are other answers you know.'

'I understand that,' Lethbridge-Stewart agreed. 'But in this case, *aliens* appear to fit the facts. There are other events beyond missing vessels tied into this case. I have a squad up in Peterhead at the moment. They've just returned from a recce on Strommach, a small island off the coast. It's been infested with some kind of killer plants.'

'Killer plants?' Hennessey asked, with a snort.

'Yes, sir. One of my men is dead as a result of this vegetation.' He had known this would be a hard sell, but he had no choice but to press on. 'A small island off the coast near Peterhead, just a handful of miles from where the sinkings happened. It's difficult to believe the two events are not connected. Everyone living on Strommach has disappeared, with the exception of two young people. They tell of metallic ships emerging from the sea and kidnapping the entire population of the island and then seeding it with these plants. My men investigated, and the plants have grown tremendously fast and are carnivorous.'

'Well, what do you plan to do about it?' McMillan asked. His previous mocking tone had vanished completely.

'I'm having a large supply of DN6 shipped to them,'

Lethbridge-Stewart replied. 'They will return to the island and spray the entire place.'

'DN6?' Hennessey scowled. 'I seem to recall reading about that stuff a couple of months ago. Isn't it a pesticide that indiscriminately kills every living thing?'

'That's the one.'

'Isn't that something of an overkill?'

'Frankly, Admiral, that entire island has been infected with what I can only assume is an alien life form inimical to terrestrial life. I don't think *anything* is overkill in this case,' Lethbridge-Stewart stressed. 'We need to sterilise the island. There's no telling how soon those plants may reach maturity and start reproducing. The prevailing winds could carry seeds or spores or whatever to the mainland, and then it would be almost impossible to contain.'

'Quite right, man,' McMillan agreed. 'Or I could send in a couple of jets from Buchan to napalm the whole place. Might be simpler and a lot more effective.'

Lethbridge-Stewart knew full well the effectiveness, and indiscriminate nature, of Napalm from his time in Korea, and he sided with Churchill and his views on the use of it. However, Strommach was now clear of civilians... He turned his mind from it and focused on another point. 'I thought Buchan is just a radar monitoring installation?'

McMillan gave a tight smile. 'Ostensibly, yes.'

'Ah. Quite.' Lethbridge-Stewart considered the matter. McMillan seemed awfully keen on the idea, and allowing it to go ahead might make for better relations with the Air Force... And there was a certain finality to Napalm, but still its use did not sit well with him. 'Very well,' he agreed. 'I'll put a hold on the spraying, keep it on the back burner, just in case.'

'Trust me, there won't be any need,' McMillan said, smiling. 'Once my lads are through with that island, it'll be nothing but bare rock.'

'Excellent.' Lethbridge-Stewart turned to the admiral. 'I have to admit we would like a little help from the Navy also.'

'In what way?' Hennessey asked, suspiciously.

'If you've a vcsscl you could station by the island to prevent access, it would help. I don't really expect tourists, but it would be embarrassing, not to mention disastrous, if any should turn up while the RAF were strafing the place.'

'Fair enough,' the admiral agreed. 'I'd prefer *Kraken* to stay in the area anyway, so I'll have them posted there for the next day or so. Is that all?'

'For the moment, yes. Shall we say that the bomb run is scheduled for oh-seven-hundred tomorrow? In the meantime, we have a second operation underway.'

'My,' McMillan drawled, 'you *have* been busy.'

'Just doing my job.'

'Don't get your feathers ruffled. Well, what else should we know about?'

'Doctor Travers, Head of Scientific Research for the Fifth, is *en route* to the sinking site. She has commandeered a bathysphere and intends to make a dive in the morning.'

'Given that a ship and a sub have both been lost in the area, isn't that a trifle… unwise?' McMillan asked.

'We need reliable intel on what is happening there,' Lethbridge-Stewart pointed out. 'The only way to get it is to look. Miss Travers is aware of the risks and finds them acceptable.'

'Fair enough,' McMillan agreed. 'Let me know when the dive starts, and I'll bung a couple of aircraft up, just in case.'

'A couple of those non-existent fighters from Buchan, no doubt,' Hennessey said drily.

'No doubt.'

The admiral turned to Lethbridge-Stewart. 'Well, Brigadier, I have to say you appear to have matters well in hand. When Hamilton contacted me about the Fifth, I have to confess I had my reservations. But you appear to be running a tight ship here, and I approve.' He glanced at his watch. 'Would you have any objections to my observing events in the morning?'

Lethbridge-Stewart felt some relief; he'd been warned by Sally that Hennessey was a tough man to impress, and was glad that he'd turned out to be amenable to reason. 'I'd be happy to have you with me, sir,' he replied. 'Your advice could prove to be invaluable.' He nodded at McMillan. 'You're welcome to attend, too, sir.'

The air marshal cracked a smile. 'Wouldn't miss it for the world, old boy,' he drawled. 'If we *are* up against bug-eyed monsters, then I think the RAF will be all we need to have a crack at them, eh? And I can observe the bomb run just as well from here as Buchan.' He looked at Hennessy. 'Well, Reggie, fancy a bite at the club?'

'That I do.'

The two of them left the room together.

Lethbridge-Stewart felt a trifle peeved that he hadn't been invited to join them. Still, he was rather out of their league, and he did have a lot of work to do.

'Hawke,' he said. 'Get me Bishop on the line, will you?

I think I'd better warn him the plans have changed for the morning.'

'Of course, sir.' She saluted and left the room.

He gave her a couple of minutes to organise the link and then joined her in the communications room. As he had expected, she was ready and handed him a mike.

'Madhouse to Mayhem One,' he called.

'Mayhem One here,' Bishop's voice answered.

'Spraying operations are on hold. The RAF want a crack at the place first, so they're doing a bomb run instead at oh-seven-hundred.'

'Understood, sir. I'll hold off on the spraying, then, and see if that's effective first. Oh, incidentally, I ran into an old friend on Strommach.'

'How jolly for you, Lieutenant,' Lethbridge-Stewart said.

'It was Mr Chorley, sir.'

Damnation! 'I don't suppose I need to ask what he was doing there, do I?'

'The usual, yes, sir.'

'May I ask what you've done with him?'

Lethbridge-Stewart could almost hear the grin on Bishop's face. 'He's in the local jail, sir.'

'In jail?'

'Well, he *was* trespassing...'

Lethbridge-Stewart managed to restrain an urge to smile. 'Quite right, Lieutenant Bishop, quite right. And how much does Mr Chorley know?'

'About the island? Pretty much everything, sir. He managed to get those kids' story, and he saw the plants in action. But he won't be telling what he knows for a couple of days. Should give you time to concoct a believable story.'

'Indeed. Thank you.' Well, that was another complication Lethbridge-Stewart hadn't foreseen and didn't need. The local press could be stonewalled fairly simply, but Chorley was an entirely different matter. He could become a problem.

The *Tethys* really was remarkable. Anne had been in submersibles before, but nothing quite as sophisticated as this. The interior space wasn't much bigger than a wardrobe – and not a large one at that – but there were two couches, both aligned to look out of the forward-facing portholes. All of the controls and instruments were on panels around the glass and easily reached from either couch. At the back of the couches were the air bottles, all attached firmly to the inner shell wall.

'Not a lot of room,' she commented to Professor Brinstead.

'It's not meant for luxury tours,' he snapped. 'Oh, and do make sure you pee before we leave. There are no toilet facilities.'

'Charmed,' she said, amused. 'How long can we stay submerged?'

'There's air for twelve hours. The batteries will last only eight; I need to upgrade them. If I had the funding, I could afford to buy from NASA or the British Rocket Group.'

'If this test dive works,' Anne said to him, 'then I think you'll get plenty of interest, and better funding.'

'Can't come soon enough.' Brinstead pulled out one of the charts he had stored under a couch and spread it as best he could on top of the other couch. 'The seabed at the point we're going down is only about half a mile, so we should be down to that depth in less than an hour. That should give us plenty of time to look around.' He scowled. 'My only concern is whether these Navy boys can operate my winches properly; I'd hate to be stuck on the seabed.'

Anne winced. That problem had never occurred to her. 'They're well-trained lads,' she said, trying to sound confident. 'I'm sure they'll be up to operating a few controls.'

'They'd better be,' Brinstead warned her. 'If they aren't, we'll be dead this time tomorrow.'

That was a cheery thought.

Mary collapsed, exhausted. When the Ymir had said they would put people to work, it hadn't been kidding. Everyone had been given tasks and there had been no respite for hours. The creatures had assembled various mechanical and electrical units in their spaceship's airlock, and the humans were ordered to move all of these out into the cavern to a specific spot about half a mile from the ship. Most of the units required two or three people to carry them, and some even more. An Ymir watched over the work, but didn't help. It wasn't the same Ymir Mary had been speaking with, but she couldn't make out any physical differences from the first one.

For some reason she had been appointed in the Ymir minds as the leader of the humans – probably simply because she was the first one they had communicated with – and all instructions to their captives were relayed through her. She was getting some very dark looks from a handful of the submariners, as if she were some sort of quisling. That was annoying, but there was nothing she could do about it.

Thankfully Captain Browne understood that she was simply trying to keep everyone alive for as long as possible.

At least the Ymir didn't seem to mind them conversing as they worked, so she could talk with the experienced naval officer as they struggled with the units they were moving.

'The Navy must know you're gone,' she said quietly. 'Won't they send another sub to investigate?'

'There will be an investigation, certainly,' Browne agreed. 'But I don't know how much good it will do us. Do you have any idea where we even are?'

'Not a clue,' Mary admitted. 'I woke up in this cavern. I've seen no entrances or exits. But I do have a few thoughts. Look at the ground we're walking on; it's totally flat in most directions, and there are just the odd boulders and rocks sticking up. It can't be a natural cavern.' She pointed upward. 'The light just peters out overhead, so I don't even know how high the ceiling is. And I've seen no signs of supports for that ceiling. It should just collapse on us, but it doesn't. I think we're in some kind of space the Ymir have hollowed out specifically for this mission of theirs.'

'It does seem to be the only sensible conclusion,' Browne agreed. 'To be able to achieve that, though. They must have amazing technology.'

'They came to this planet through interstellar space,' Mary pointed out. 'We've barely reached Mars, so that's an entirely new level of technology to us right there; who knows what else they're capable of?'

'Quite.' Browne eyed the unit they were hauling along with Logistics Officer Nation. 'Do you have any idea what their ultimate aim is?'

Mary shook her head. 'I'm afraid all I know is the cliché

part of it, they aim to take over our planet. Theirs seems to have suffered some sort of a catastrophe, and they need a new home.'

'That doesn't bode well for us,' the captain muttered. 'And do they plan on turning the human race into some sort of slave species?'

'I don't know.' Mary thought for a moment. 'That first Ymir I met seemed to be a chatty sort, though this new one is the strong, silent type. If the first one turns up again, I can try and pry some more information from it. Though God knows how I'll be able to tell if it's actually the same one or not.'

'And this equipment we're moving; do you have any idea what it's for?'

Mary laughed, rather bitterly. 'I'm just a disc jockey, Captain,' she informed him. 'I can tell you all about the Top Thirty, and I'm full of useless information about The Beatles or Dusty Springfield. But my knowledge of science only goes as far as A-Level, I'm afraid.'

'Quite,' Browne said, sighing.

'Excuse me, sir,' Lieutenant Nation said. 'But I've an idea what some of it might do.'

'Really, Nation? Good man. Fill us in, then.'

Nation gave Mary a pointed glare. He was obviously one of those who mistrusted her. Thankfully, Browne caught on.

'Miss Wilde is one of us, Lieutenant; you can speak freely in front of her.'

'If you say so, Captain,' the young man agreed, clearly unconvinced.

'Look, sailor,' Mary snapped. 'If I'm actually a spy for

those Ymir, then I already know what this stuff's for, don't I? So you can't be giving any secrets away, can you? As it is, I'm on your side, you twit, and I'd like to know what we're being forced to do.'

That seemed to sink in, at least, but Nation pointedly addressed his commanding officer and didn't even glance in her direction. 'Well, sir, I'm a sonar man, as you know, and some of this stuff is clearly some kind of sonar equipment. Like nothing I've seen, of course, but the general outline is clear enough. And other bits seem like they're for power units. For lots of power.'

Mary scowled. 'So they're after something underground, then?'

'That's what it looks like, sir,' Nation said, still looking at Browne.

Mary couldn't understand it. 'But what can there possibly be here that they're interested in? I mean, I'm assuming we're not too far from where we were captured, and that was off the Scottish coast.'

'The only thing that comes to mind is oil,' Browne said, slowly. 'There are extensive oil fields out in the North Sea that we've just started to tap.'

'But what the hell would aliens want with oil?' Mary objected. 'That bloody spaceship of theirs can't be powered by an internal combustion engine, can it?'

'No,' the captain agreed. 'It would need to be an awful lot more powerful than that. But, of course, we have atomic power stations ourselves and we still use oil. You can't power cars with atomic fuel, for example. They may have a need for oil. And it *is* a finite resource. You said their world was no longer suitable for them; maybe they're here to drain our planet of the resources they need, starting with the oil.'

'Feels like I'm in some kind of B-movie.' Mary sighed. There was a certain logic to that, but she was unconvinced. 'I think they've more in mind than just drilling for oil,' she said. 'Though what that more might be, I don't have a clue.'

They had reached the assigned site for the unit they were hauling, and they laid it down carefully and took a breather. Other groups were still working, though, and a steady stream of equipment was being brought over.

Their Ymir watcher moved in and loomed over them. 'You will return to work,' it ordered.

Mary glared at it, too annoyed to be wary of what she said. 'Look you,' she yelled at it. 'We've been working for a couple of hours now; we need a break, a rest. And we need food and water. If you don't allow that, we'll collapse and be no use to you at all.'

The stone giant appeared to consider this request. Mary was hopeful. Finally it looked down at them. 'Your request is allowed,' it agreed. 'You will assemble by the ship. Food and water will be brought to you, and you will be allowed a short rest interval. Then you will recommence work.' It went back to ignoring them.

'Well done, Miss Wilde,' Browne said. 'It seems that these creatures aren't entirely devoid of feeling.'

'I think they're simply looking after their slaves,' Mary admitted. 'Nothing more than that. But did you notice something?'

'What?'

'When I asked for relief, he seemed to be thinking. Then he agreed and said we'd be supplied. But he didn't contact anyone on the ship or anything, so how could he know that?'

Browne grinned. 'Well observed,' he said, approvingly. 'These Ymir must have some sort of non-verbal means of communication.'

'Great,' Mary muttered. 'Not only are they bigger and stronger than us, they're also telepathic. I wonder what other good news we'll discover about them.'

'At least you've managed to get us all a break,' Browne said. 'And I can tell you that I for one am hungry and thirsty. And bone weary, of course.' He managed a smile. 'I'm far more used to giving orders than taking them.'

Mary and her companions made their way back to the spaceship, informing the other work parties on the way of the impending break. By the time they reached the area outside the ship's airlock, there were large baskets awaiting them. Some had stone jars that contained water. The remaining baskets contained some kind of fruit.

One of the sailors tried the water and spat it out. 'Salt,' he complained, wiping his mouth.

Mary glared at the Ymir. 'We can't drink salt water,' she complained. 'We need pure water.'

'That is illogical,' the alien said. 'The vast majority of the water on your planet is salt. You must be able to live on it.'

'I don't care whether it makes sense to you or not,' Mary snapped. 'We need pure water. Can you supply it?'

The Ymir paused. 'It is not sensible, but we are able to produce it, yes. It will be a short while. You are a curious species.'

While they were waiting, Mary picked up one of the fruit and examined it. It was greenish yellow, and very large – bigger than any melon she'd ever seen – about three feet across and lozenge-shaped. At one end was a scar where it had obviously been broken off some kind of stalk. Mary looked up at the Ymir, who had accompanied the parties back to the ship.

'What's this?'

'It is fruit,' the Ymir replied. 'Is that not obvious?'

'It's nothing like any fruit I've seen before.'

'It is from the Grandfathers,' the Ymir replied. 'Do your not Grandfathers provide something similar for you?'

'Both of my grandfathers are dead,' Mary replied.

The Ymir was silent a moment. 'Then how is it you are still alive?' it asked.

'Why shouldn't I be?' As usual, the Ymir didn't seem to be making any sense.

'Without the Grandfathers, we would all perish,' the alien stated. 'You must be a strange species if you can survive without them.'

'Yeah, that's us, the strange human race,' Mary agreed. She eyed the fruit. 'Is this safe to eat?'

'It is what I eat,' the Ymir replied.

Mary nodded. 'And what a big boy – or girl – you've grown up to be,' she said. 'But I think we're rather different from you, and what sustains you might not do the same for us.'

Alan had joined her. He reached out and picked up one of the fruit. 'Then I guess somebody's just going to have to try this, aren't they?' He pulled a penknife from his pocket, and managed to saw out a slice.

'Al...' Mary said, pleadingly, worried for him. 'I don't know that this is a good idea.'

'Somebody has to try it, love,' he said, gently. 'They

don't seem keen on giving us anything else to eat.'

'It is all we eat,' the Ymir said. 'You will consume it also.'

'See?' Alan said. He raised the slice to his mouth.

Mary grabbed his hand, stopping him. 'Al... It could kill you.'

He gave her a brave smile. 'Mary, love, these people are hungry. They need to eat. One of us has to try it, and I've elected myself. It's as simple as that.'

'Let me do it,' she said, screwing together all of her remaining courage.

Alan shook his head. 'They need you,' he informed her gently. 'You're keeping them together. We can't spare you. Me, I'm a radio producer without a show. Who'd miss me?'

'*I* would!'

'That's sweet of you to say so.' Before she could stop him, he took a bite from the fruit and chewed. 'Hey, you know, this doesn't taste at all bad. It's like grapefruit with a hint of bacon in it.' He grinned at her. 'I could get to like this.'

'Al, you idiot!' Mary breathed a sigh of relief. 'Well, it didn't kill you instantly, thank God. But how long should we wait until we're sure it's safe?' She looked to Captain Browne for advice.

'Hard to say,' he grunted. 'Some poisons take a long time to kick in.' He patted Alan's shoulder. 'You're a brave man.'

'I don't feel brave, just hungry. I think I'll have a little more.' Alan took another bite and chewed.

Nation piped up. 'We've got rations on the old *Venom*, sir,' he pointed out.

'Quite right,' the captain agreed, brightly. He looked up at the Ymir. 'We have food that we can eat on our ship; will you allow some of us to fetch it?'

The Ymir stared back. 'You will not be permitted to enter your vessel of war.'

Mary raised an eyebrow ironically. 'I don't think they trust you, Captain. But there's food on *Crossbones*, and no weapons.' She looked up at the Ymir. 'How about that as an option?'

Before the alien could reply, Alan gave a strangled gasp. Mary whirled around, her heart beating furiously in terror.

There were flecks of foam at Alan's lips, and he was struggling for breath. Abruptly, his eyes spasmed, and he collapsed. Mary and Nation caught him before he hit the ground and gently lowered him. Mary was shaking, and she was forced to wipe her eyes with the back of her hand. Alan's breathing was sharp and shallow.

'Help him!' she screamed at the Ymir.

'I can do nothing,' the creature replied. 'You beings are alien to me. I do not know your physiology.'

'We've got a doctor,' Browne snarled. He looked around. 'Cleary!' A man came running over from one of the other groups. 'Do what you can, man.'

Cleary knelt beside Alan, who was trembling and shaking now. 'I need my equipment!'

'You will not be permitted to enter your vessel of war,' the Ymir repeated.

Browne looked at Mary. 'Is there a medical kit on your ship?'

'What? I don't know. Probably. But I wouldn't know where it was.' Mary couldn't focus. The only thing she could see right now was that her friend was sick, probably dying.

'This is… unexpected,' the Ymir announced. 'It would appear that your people cannot safely consume the gift of the Grandfathers. You must not be permitted to perish before your work is accomplished. You will therefore be allowed to collect food from your surface vessel. You may also bring these medical supplies. Choose among yourselves for those who will go.' A second Ymir appeared in the spaceship's airlock and stepped out. 'You will be accompanied, and watched.'

Browne stood up. 'I'll go,' he announced. He patted Mary gently on the shoulder. 'Be brave, young lady. I'll send someone back as soon as we find any medical supplies. Cleary will do everything he can for your friend.'

Mary nodded, numbly. She placed her hand over Al's and squeezed her eyes shut.

CHAPTER TWELVE

Flash! Bang! Wallop!

The morning dawned bright and clear, and everyone showed up in plenty of time. Air Marshal McMillan greeted Lethbridge-Stewart as he strode into the Dolerite Base communications room at precisely oh-six-thirty. Lethbridge-Stewart smiled to himself; no doubt the air marshal had checked to make sure things were running smoothly before he put in his appearance. Lethbridge-Stewart didn't blame the man, he'd have done precisely the same thing himself.

'I spoke to Gilmore last night,' McMillan said, taking Lethbridge-Stewart aside. 'He told me certain things, but it was clear he was not at liberty to discuss everything. Cosmic Hobo, eh?'

'Quite, sir,' Lethbridge-Stewart said. 'All true, unfortunately.'

McMillan tapped his nose. 'Need-to-know, and all that. Well, I shan't pry further, but needless to say you have my complete support.'

'Thank you, Air Marshal.' Lethbridge-Stewart looked over as Maddox called him. 'Shall we?'

'After you, Brigadier, after you.'

Maddox and her efficient girls had the board ready. The position of the naval vessel carrying the *Tethys* was marked.

They had arrived on site close to midnight, and Miss Travers had reported in an hour ago that she and Brinstead were readying the bathysphere for their descent. The small ship representing *Kraken* was in place by Strommach. There was also a small model airplane shown in position at RAF Buchan, and McMillan's eyes lit up.

'There's actually a flight of three, Brigadier,' he said. 'And they'll be the new Phantoms out of RAF Leuchars. Been dying to see what they can do, to be honest.'

Lethbridge-Stewart looked at Maddox. She gave a virtually imperceptible nod to show him that she'd actually known that – but, obviously, didn't want the RAF to know she could intercept their signals – and gestured for one of the operatives to move the plane further south to the Leuchars position.

McMillan rubbed his hands together. 'Should be educational,' he said. 'Nice to get a chance to see what the hardware can do, eh?'

The door opened again, and Admiral Hennessey strode in. He glanced at the large clock on the wall. 'Still time,' he said, cheerily. 'All set, Monty?'

'My lads are rarin' to go,' McMillan replied, cheerily. 'Those lads of yours on *Kraken* should have a ringside seat for this.'

Lethbridge-Stewart said nothing. He could only hope that his two colleagues weren't being overly optimistic. Things rarely went quite as planned. 'Any news from Lieutenant Bishop?' he asked Maddox, quietly.

'They reported in twenty minutes ago, sir,' Maddox answered. 'Their supply of DN6 has arrived, and they're transferring it now.'

169

'Back-up plan, eh?' McMillan asked. 'Well, your lads won't need that; my boys will fix this, you'll see.'

'I sincerely hope so, sir,' Lethbridge-Stewart admitted. 'But I do always prefer to have a second string to my bow.'

'Quite right, too,' Hennessey agreed, approvingly. 'Plan B, what?'

'Yes, sir.' Lethbridge-Stewart glanced at the clock; two minutes to go. Maddox had the Air Force on the monitors, and they were droning on through their usual technical preparations. All three of the new US-made Phantoms were fuelled, loaded for bear and their pilots sounded eager for things to get started. No doubt dying to put their new planes through their paces. Well, he couldn't blame them.

'Did you hear from Doctor Travers?' he asked Maddox.

'They're in position also, sir,' the sergeant replied. 'She and the professor are doing the last-minute checks. She expects the dive to commence within the hour.'

That was... well, *good news* wasn't quite accurate. Pleasing, yes. Maybe now they'd find out what had happened to *Venom* and that ship, but worrying at the same time. Miss Travers was going into an uncontrolled environment, and there was no telling what sort of danger she might face. He had total respect for her judgment when matters scientific arose, but he still couldn't get used to the idea of allowing a woman to go into danger. Another reason – if he needed one – to not have Sally here. Thank goodness all of the women under his direct command had nice, safe jobs, like Maddox here! But Anne Travers was a bit of a wild card. Yes, she followed his orders – for the most part – but she was also fiercely independent when she felt the call for it. And she felt that call far too often for his liking.

He'd have felt much better about this if a couple of his men could have accompanied her. Or if that ruddy submersible was at least armed in some way.

'This is it,' McMillan announced cheerfully. Lethbridge-Stewart stopped his introspection and paid close attention.

The control tower at Leuchars gave clearance to the Phantoms, and a moment later reported that they were on their way.

Now it was just the usual; wait.

'Come on, Evans,' Samson called. 'Get the lead out.'

The Welshman glared at him and lugged the metal spray container with effort. His face was flushed, and he was grunting. Admittedly, each of the DN6 tanks weighed fifty pounds, but even so the driver was overdoing his fatigue.

'It's not easy, you know,' Evans complained, between grunts. 'I'm a driver, not a flippin' mule.'

'There are people who'd argue that point, Evans,' Samson assured him. 'And as I understand it, you're a *private* now, seconded to the Fifth, not the Engineer Corps, so I suggest you act like it! The rest of the lads are doing fine. Stop complaining and get on with it.'

'I notice you're not doing any of the hard work yourself,' Evans complained.

Samson grinned. 'That's because I'm the brains, and you're the brawn. Well, loosely speaking, you are.' He glanced at their new transportation.

The Navy were in a generous sort of mood, and they'd provided a motor torpedo boat and crew. Lethbridge-Stewart must have sweet-talked the admiral a bit to get even this help. Mind you, this was a Vosper Type II, a real World

War II vintage model. It must have been in mothballs somewhere and hauled out just for this mission. Still, Samson knew it was a reliable craft, and it could transport his men and the canisters of the weed killer with ease. The squad had already loaded about half of the stuff (though Evans was still struggling with his first can), and they'd be ready to go in half an hour, if the order was given. The RAF had their crack at the problem first.

Samson glanced at his watch. It was just about time for...

There they were! Flashing past in formation were the Phantoms, heading out to sea, leaving just an echo of their passage and contrails behind them.

Samson grinned. 'Right, lads, let's get ready in case we have to finish the job the fly boys have started. That means you, too, Evans!'

Anne checked the connections to the *Tethys* for the final time. It was resting in the crane's cradle that would lower it over the side of the ship in a matter of minutes. The cradle had been attached to the ship's deck; securely, she prayed. The Navy crew stood by, eagerly watching what was going on. Well, it was a break from their normal routine, and she couldn't blame their excitement. If she was being honest, she was excited herself. A descent in a bathysphere! No matter what they found under the waves, it was going to be quite an experience.

Everything seemed safe and secure, so she made her way to the ladder that was propped temporarily against the *Tethys*. A couple of sailors stood by, ready to remove it once she was aboard.

There was a roaring overhead, and three jets shot by. They were the RAF, on their way to – hopefully – bomb the hell out of those carnivorous plants on Strommach. It was turning out to be quite an eventful day.

Anne hurried up the ladder and clambered onto the hatchway. The sailors hurried the ladder away, as she swung her legs up and into the opening.

Professor Brinstead looked up, a broad grin on his wiry face. 'I hope you did a pit stop, as I told you,' he said. 'It's a long way to the next petrol station.'

'I'm ready and rarin' to go,' Anne assured him, slipping down inside. She gripped the hatch and swung it shut. She turned the wheel, locking it into place. A green light lit up on the panel to show that it was secure. She took her place on the right-hand couch beside him. The controls were all illuminated, and a soft glow permeated the tiny cabin. She slipped on the headset that Brinstead indicated for her. He had an identical one on his own head.

'*Tethys* to Mother,' he said into the mic. 'We're ready to go.'

'Mother to Baby, acknowledged.'

Brinstead gave Anne another broad grin. 'Here we go.'

Captain McKenzie stood on the bridge of HMS *Kraken*, Mellors beside him. Both had binoculars and were waiting impatiently as the clock ticked onward. McKenzie had been on the bridge since dawn, watching the sun come up behind Strommach, blood-red, as if some prophet of doom. *Kraken* was on station a mile from the island, but hadn't seen any attempts by other boats to approach the small island since they had arrived. Still, if those tales of killer plants were anything near accurate, it was best to err on the side of caution.

'Should be arriving any minute if they're on time, sir,' Mellors reported, glancing at the chronometer.

'Oh, they'll be on time,' McKenzie grunted. 'Top brass are watching, after all, so they'll be punctual to the second.' Mellors gave a polite chuckle. 'And we have a ringside seat.'

'Here they come, sir,' the radar operator called out. 'Three aircraft, bearing 270, coming in fast.'

'Thank you, radar,' McKenzie acknowledged. A couple of seconds later, he saw the three aircraft – strung in a line – pass over the ship. He and Mellors raised their binoculars and watched.

The trio swooped down over Strommach. McKenzie could make out several smaller shapes detaching from the lead aircraft and falling towards the land below. Then that plane was gone, and the second and third came in, all releasing their deadly cargo before the first Napalm bombs struck. The aircraft were receding dots when the first explosions began.

Bright flashes were followed by rising smoke, and then the noise hit. Everything on the island was lost in flames and heavy smoke, and the explosions echoed across the waters. The noise and light died out, but a huge cloud hung over the island.

'Take us in,' McKenzie ordered. They needed to be much closer to be able to see the effects of the bombing.

Mary had spent a horribly restless night watching over Al. She'd dozed a bit, spelled by Doctor Cleary, but she was far too anxious for her friend to be able to get any real rest. She kept waking, to hear his raspy breathing. He was still alive, but unresponsive. At least he wasn't coughing up gunk any more.

She glanced at her watch. It said it was shortly after seven, but it was impossible to know if that was am or pm. The only light in here was artificial, after all. She nodded at Doctor Cleary, silently thanking him for looking after Al. The sailor nodded back, and settled down to try and get some rest of his own. Mary took a swig of water to rinse out her mouth, and then checked on Al.

His pulse was fast and erratic, but strong enough. That was probably a good sign. But he showed no signs of waking, which probably wasn't.

There was movement by the alien spaceship, and one of the imposing Ymir emerged. Maybe one of those she'd already met, maybe a new one, who could tell? When you'd seen one giant, stony alien, you'd seen them all. Mary knew she was reacting rather irrationally, and tried to clamp down on it.

'The rest period is over,' the alien stated. 'You will all return to work.' It moved to loom over Mary. 'Is that human unable to work?'

'He's sick,' Mary snarled. 'Your fruit poisoned him.'

'Is that human unable to work?' the Ymir repeated.

'Of course he can't work!'

'Then he is non-functional and will be terminated.' The Ymir bent down.

Mary stood up and protected Al. 'He's *sick*. He needs care, not murdering.'

'There is no point in caring for a damaged worker,' the Ymir stated. 'It is not functional, and will be disposed of.'

'Over my dead body,' Mary snapped.

'If you wish it,' the Ymir agreed. 'Though you are functional and are useful to us. It is illogical for you to be destroyed.'

'We humans aren't always logical,' Mary informed it.

Captain Browne gripped her arm. 'There's no sense in losing your life over this,' he said, gently. 'We can't fight these creatures.'

'I won't just allow them to kill Al,' Mary answered. 'He's my friend, and he's sick.'

'There is—' the Ymir began. Then it screamed, and clutched at its head.

At the same instant, Al sat bolt-upright and screamed, his eyes still closed, his body stiff.

'What the hell?' Browne muttered.

Mary didn't know what was happening. The Ymir staggered.

'The podlings are under attack,' it gasped. 'The humans have attacked them.'

Mary didn't know who it was addressing, but she was too busy trying to see to Al. His body was stiff and cool to the touch, but his muscles were locked and rigid. He was screaming, but nothing else.

'What's happening to him?' Mary asked Doctor Cleary, who had joined her.

'I don't know,' he admitted. 'This man's completely unconscious.'

Mary couldn't understand it. Al had started screaming the exact same second as the Ymir. And the Ymir communicated with their own kind telepathically. Al had eaten some of the Ymir fruit, had he somehow become linked telepathically to the aliens? Was that even possible? It had to be. It was the only thing that made sense of the madness that was happening.

The Ymir seemed to have stabilised. It reeled a little, but regained some of its composure. It looked down at the humans. 'There has been an attack,' it stated.

'I hope it hurt!' Mary snarled.

'Why did the human scream?' the alien asked.

'I don't know.'

The Ymir considered for a moment. 'The Grandfathers are interested in knowing the answer,' it stated. 'He will be brought to them.'

Those often-mentioned Grandfathers! Mary was full of curiosity, mixed with apprehension about her friend. 'I'm going with him,' she said firmly.

Again, the Ymir paused. 'Very well,' it agreed. 'The Grandfathers will meet with you also. You may be able to offer them some explanation for what has occurred.'

Mary nodded in satisfaction. She only hoped that she would not regret this decision.

Kraken had halved the distance to Strommach by the time the smoke finally began to clear over the small island. Tongues of fire still licked at the ground, and even without binoculars Captain McKenzie could see that there were craters where the bombs had struck. He ordered the ship to move parallel to the land, and trained his binoculars on the island.

Destruction had occurred, certainly, but the plants were still there. Some had been uprooted and some even destroyed in the explosions, but the vast majority of the plants looked completely unchanged after the passage of the fire.

'Report in,' he ordered the radio operator. 'Tell Command that the plants appear undamaged. Somehow they've weathered the firestorm.'

'Now what, sir?' Mellors asked him, as the radio operator obeyed.

'No idea, Number One,' McKenzie admitted. 'Thankfully, it's not our decision to make. That's for the brass to decide. But I wouldn't like to be in their shoes.'

Lethbridge-Stewart slapped his swagger stick into his gloved palm. *Blast!* The Napalm had proved to be ineffective after all, somehow. What kind of plants must these things be to have survived such an attack?

Admiral Hennessey glanced over at Lethbridge-Stewart. 'Well,' he said, 'it looks like it's a good thing you insisted on a second string to your bow. Better order your men in now, Brigadier.'

'Indeed, sir,' Lethbridge-Stewart agreed. He turned to Maddox. 'Get me Mayhem One, Sergeant.'

'Ready on line, sir,' she reported. He felt satisfaction at that. Good woman, anticipated everything.

'Madhouse to Mayhem One,' he said into the microphone she handed him. 'Come in, Mayhem One.'

'Mayhem One,' came Bishop's voice.

'Mayhem One, the order is *go*. I say again, the order is go.'

'Understood, sir. Mayhem One out.'

Anne heard the report of the failed attack as the *Tethys*

dropped below the surface of the North Sea. Well, there was nothing she could do about that. She had her own mission. Lethbridge-Stewart would want her to focus in on that and leave the rest to him. So be it.

She couldn't repress the excitement she felt. She'd done a little scuba diving during her time in the States and quite enjoyed it, but that had been in only about forty feet of water that was mostly clear. It had been fun watching the fish and checking out the seabed. But here... well, the North Sea was hardly the Pacific Ocean, it was dark and oppressive, and if there were fish about, they were invisible in the gloom. The seabed here was half a mile down. At their current rate of descent, it would take almost an hour to reach it.

Brinstead appeared to be reading her mind. 'There's no point in switching on the external lights yet,' he said. 'There won't be anything worthwhile to see this close to the surface, and it would simply drain the batteries faster.'

'I understand,' she said, admittedly slightly disappointed. Descending without light was like taking a very slow lift down into the basement of a building, all you had to look at was whatever you'd brought with you. In this case, lots of controls, a rather rumpled scientist and very dark portholes. Maybe she should have brought a book along.

The Ymir had recovered fairly well from whatever it was that had affected it. It reached down and lifted Alan in its right hand, and Mary in its left. It then headed for the spaceship.

Mary had a moment of panic. 'Hang on!' she yelled. 'I don't know if it was you or another of your kind, but

179

somebody told me that your body temperature is a lot higher than ours.'

'It was another one of us,' the Ymir said. 'But the words are true.'

'Then won't we humans burn up when we enter your ship?' she asked, anxiously.

'Normally, yes,' the Ymir said. 'But the Grandfathers wish to communicate with you. A safe passageway has been prepared for you; you will not burn up.'

Well, *that* was a relief! Though she couldn't say she was exactly looking forward to meeting these mysterious Grandfathers. She wondered if there would be any way to tell them from the Ymir she'd met; after all, if you were made essentially of stone, *how* could you age? But mostly she worried about Al. Despite the screaming, it didn't appear that he'd actually come out of his coma, or whatever he was in. His breathing was shallow and rushed, and he still looked flushed and sick. But it had been over twelve hours since he'd eaten the alien fruit, and he was still alive. That had to be a good sign, right?

The chances were that she wouldn't last more than a few days herself the way the Ymir were working her. She had to wonder, had she done anything with her life to justify her existence? Her mind returned to her earlier conversation with Al, before the Ymir had attacked *Crossbones*.

So she played music for teens on the radio; what kind of an achievement was that? She got fan letters – that had surprised her! – from kids who told her how much they loved her chatter, and the songs that she played. They were comforting, and made her feel like she was doing something to help a bit. Then came the letters from the creeps who offered – or threatened – all kinds of sick things to her. Those made her want to crawl into a hole and never come out again.

She didn't even have a boyfriend. Oh, she'd courted plenty, but never anyone seriously, and hardly ever the same guy twice. She only liked about half a dozen people, truth be told, and the rest she could take or leave. Did that make her a shallow, uncaring person? Or just someone who was happy enough to be alone without feeling insecure? Al was probably the best friend she had, besides a couple of girls in London she'd cheerfully abandoned to take the job with Radio Crossbones. Al always treated her seriously, and had never made even the gentlest of passes at her. He was devoted to his family, and the thought of cheating with anybody would never have crossed his mind. *He* was the one who deserved to live, and here he was, suffering, and she was unable to help her friend.

Did anyone even know or care that they were gone? Their listeners would just turn the dial to Radio Caroline or maybe even BBC Radio One, and their lives would continue without Mary Wilde or the rest of the crew. Al's family would care, of course, but what could they know? Just that his ship had vanished, and he was gone, presumed dead. They must be going through sheer hell right now, poor things. But if she didn't survive this, would anybody really care?

Her parents, yes. She had always been a troubled rebel to them. Mum had just wanted her to get married and raise a brood of kids, but that had never appealed to Mary. She'd grown up with brothers and sisters – older and younger than her – and *that* was quite enough children for anyone's lifetime! And Mum had never understood her love of American pop and the Mersey Sound. To her music was *Desert Island Discs* or *Music While You Work*. Dad... well, as long as he had his Davenport's, his ciggies and the paper, he didn't much care what she did, just as long as it didn't cost him anything. They'd miss her, but her loss wouldn't be an irreparable hole in their lives.

Mary wrenched herself out of this mood, she was acting like this was the march to the scaffold (and not the pop group, either!). She didn't *know* that. The Ymir had said that the Grandfathers wished to talk with her and Al. Nothing about killing them. Of course, it was unlikely that the Grandfathers would value human life any more than the Ymir did, so that didn't mean that she was in any way safe. Perhaps this would be nothing more than some alien equivalent of afternoon tea.

Yeah, *right*!

She tried to pay attention to where she was being taken, but they had simply entered the ship through the airlock and then walked down a long corridor. There were doorways off to the side, but they were all closed, and probably a good job, since Mary felt sure they would be at the ship's ambient temperature, and likely a couple of hundred degrees too warm for her to survive. For an alien vessel, this was one boring ship. There were no intricate machines, or robots, or anything really science fiction-like. Just grey metal corridors and blank-faced doors.

Finally, though, the corridor came to an end at a pair of double doors, made of the same blank metal. There was an area of coloured plates beside the door, each segment about four inches square. Using one large fingertip, the Ymir pressed a beige-coloured button, and the doors hissed apart. The Ymir then strode into the room.

Mary almost gagged. The room was immense; perhaps fifty feet tall and at least a couple of hundred feet across. The lighting was subdued, but everything was quite clear.

It was a greenhouse, but the kind dreamed up in Edgar Allan Poe's fevered imagination. There was a strong stench of soil and other foetid smells. The reason for this was quite clear; there were several dead bodies in the room. She vaguely recognised one of them as a sailor from *Crossbones*. There were a number of Ymir in here, working. That work included ripping apart one of the bodies and feeding it to…

The room was filled with huge plants. The closest ones were between twelve and twenty feet across. They looked a little like water lilies, with large, flat leaves spread about the base and a bulbous central section that stood some six feet tall. Tendrils twitched around the central core. Several shoots had those fat, obscene fruits hanging from them. The plants were mostly a mottled dark green in colour, though there were tinges of yellow around the central opening.

The Ymir that had ripped the body apart took a section of it and threw it toward the plants. A tendril snapped out and caught the bloody mess and then whipped it back and deposited it in the bulbous opening. The Ymir repeated the action with the rest of the grisly remains, and other plants snatched up their share of the grim feast.

Mary wanted to be sick. So *this* was why the Ymir were so obsessed with the dead humans; they were simply food for their greenhouse plants.

Were these gardeners the Grandfathers? But the workers ignored the Ymir that carried Mary and Al, so it didn't seem likely. Was this just some unsubtle warning to Mary? Co-operate or end up being fed to the plants? That thought revolted her. Dying was bad enough, but to then have her body torn apart and thrown to a bunch of carnivorous daisies…

She looked up at her Ymir. 'Where are the Grandfathers we are supposed to be meeting?'

It looked down at her. 'Look around you,' it replied. 'They are here, and they are waiting.'

But there was nothing here except…

Oh, dear God! Realisation suddenly hit her.

The *plants* were the Grandfathers.

— CHAPTER THIRTEEN —

I Get Around

A nne had pictured descending into the depths as being an endless journey of wonder, of seeing fabulous sights, and of uncovering the secret of the sinkings. Playing the role of a modern day Professor Pierre Aronnax in her own version of *20,000 Leagues Under the Sea*. Instead, all she had discovered so far was that Brinstead scratched a lot. With nothing to be seen outside the *Tethys*, this exploration was dull.

It did give her a chance to think, though. She added up what they knew about this situation so far, and it didn't amount to very much. A pirate radio ship vanished in mid-transmission. A submarine in the same place vanished without warning. *Something* invaded a small island and kidnapped virtually the entire population and replaced them with carnivorous plants. The events were clearly interconnected, but the connections weren't available to her.

Her experiences since returning to the UK back in February had shown her that there were forces outside normal human experience. It seemed more than likely that this was some new incursion by an extra-human agency, but even that was by no means certain. The possibility that this was in some way a Russian plot had to be considered, even if it made no apparent sense. It was like attempting to do a thousand-piece jigsaw with only twenty-five pieces that didn't even connect together.

She glanced at Brinstead, who was happily muttering away to himself, pleased as punch with the way his invention was working. And she had to admit the *Tethys* seemed to be doing just fine. There were no leaks, and the instrument panel showed that everything was working perfectly.

Time for a check-in, then. She picked up the microphone that connected them to the ship. '*Tethys* to Mother,' she called. 'Come in, Mother.'

'Mother here,' came the steady voice on the radio.

'Everything seems fine so far,' she stated. 'Nothing to report. Will check in again in thirty minutes.'

'Acknowledged. Mother out.'

And that was her work finished for another half-hour. She *really* wished she'd brought a book with her. Or even some of those dratted reports that Lethbridge-Stewart insisted she fill out on a regular basis.

Finally, though, Brinstead grinned at her. 'Time for some light, eh?' he said.

'Yes please!'

The professor chuckled, and threw the switches that turned on the exterior light bars. Instantly the blackness evaporated, and was replaced by–

Greyness.

It wasn't much of an improvement, really. There was still nothing to see, only now there was a grey nothing instead of a black nothing. As her eyes adjusted to the fresh level of lighting, though, she started picking out minute details. Particulate matter, suspended in the waters and stirred by their passage drifted past the portholes. She'd been hoping for fish of some kind – any kind! – but these were probably microscopic brine shrimp and other krill mixed with shards of vegetable matter. Far too tiny to make anything out, they resembled dust motes dancing in sunbeams. Technically, it was a step forward, but it was still virtually as dull as seeing nothing.

And so it went.

She reported in again on the half-hour as she'd promised, and then went back to staring at the tiny particles drifting in the grey water. They were descending slowly and steadily, and Brinstead seemed to be very pleased with their progress, and even happier with the behaviour of the bathysphere. Anne had to admit that it was fulfilling all of his promises. There was no doubt that the *Tethys* would be a great tool in underwater exploration once this mission was over.

'The seabed should only be a couple of hundred feet below us now,' he finally informed her. He was as happy as a child on Christmas morning. Well, he was finally getting to prove that he knew what he was talking about, and she could understand the great satisfaction in that. 'Let's take a look and see what we can see, eh?' He moved the controls that altered the orientation of the light bars. They slowly moved from horizontal to vertical, and illuminated straight down.

Anne looked eagerly through the lower porthole, but there was still only greyness to see, at least for the moment.

'Still a little high, I suppose,' Brinstead commented. He rubbed his hands together. 'Ha! I'd like to see Cousteau's face if he could watch us now.'

He'd probably be as bored as I am, Anne thought. Then she considered that was probably not true; he'd more likely be as excited as the professor. Two peas in a very small pod.

She continued to stare. Gradually she could make small details out in the depths.

She grabbed the mic. 'Mother, please slow descent,' she said, certain she had caught sight of something interesting.

'The plants are the Grandfathers,' Mary said slowly, after running that notion through her head a few times. Saying it out loud did not make it more believable.

'Of course,' the Ymir agreed. 'Are not yours?'

'No,' Mary replied. 'We don't have those kinds of grandfathers.'

The Ymir sounded amazed. 'Truly, alien species are most peculiar.'

Mary stared at the horrible vegetation. They had been fed their revolting diet of flesh and were presumably digesting it. She'd heard of plants like the Venus fly trap; they caught and devoured flies and other small insects. These Grandfathers were clearly some sort of gross alien equivalent.

Al stirred. His eyes opened, though they were cloudy and unfocused. His body was twisted and hunched, as though he were somehow unused to how it should be. His mouth opened, and after a moment he slurred, 'I hear you.'

Mary stared at him in concern. The Ymir placed them both down on the metal rim that surrounded the immense space filled by the Grandfathers. Al slouched against the wall for support, and she knelt beside him. 'Who?' she asked, anxiously. 'Al, who can you hear?'

His arm came up, stiff, like the arm of a puppet, and he gestured vaguely toward the centre of the room. 'Them,' he said, vaguely. 'They're in my head. I hear them talking, talking, talking...' His voice faded out.

She looked up at the Ymir. 'What's happening?'

The Ymir looked at the plants. 'He is in contact with the Grandfathers,' it stated.

'How?' Mary tried to listen, but she heard no voices in her own mind.

'He is a part of them now, as are we all,' the Ymir said.

The seabed took shape, finally giving Anne something to look at. It was rugged and uneven, of course, with rocks and gravel scattered about, and fish. Plenty of fish darting out of the light in swift, silvery flashes. Scavengers of the debris that fell down through the water, and nervous of light they never normally knew. There were crabs making their ungainly way across the sea floor. There were even plants and seaweed.

There were no wrecked ships, though. There was nothing here that hadn't been in place for a million years or more. Well, it was hardly likely that the *Tethys* would drop right on top of the missing ship or sub on the first attempt.

'Stop the descent,' Brinstead ordered, and she relayed this to the ship above. A moment later, they were hanging suspended, perhaps sixty feet above the seabed. 'Right,' the professor decided. 'Tell them to slowly start the search pattern.'

After a short delay, they were moving again, but this time in an easterly direction rather than a vertical one. The naval ship would make a slow circle of the rough area where the sub had vanished. If they saw nothing, then it would widen the search. Now was the time to look out for anything at all out of the ordinary.

She and Brinstead scanned all about the *Tethys*. From time to time details would emerge on the seabed, but never anything relevant. There was the odd bit of junk that had fallen – or more likely been discarded – from passing ships. Bottles, cans, sometimes an oil drum or something similar. All were partially buried in the sand and had clearly been there for some time. Fish or prawns would occasionally amble in and out of the junk in their never-ending quest for food. But there was nothing that could have definitely come from either ship or submarine.

Time passed slowly. Now and then Brinstead would have the ship haul them up or lower them a dozen feet or so to avoid large rocks or to peer into small ravines. Other than that, nothing much happened. Anne understood, of course, that they might completely miss both vessels. They could be as little as a quarter of a mile from either or both and not even see them in this gloom. Their search pattern was as good as it could be, but it could never be perfect.

And then–

'Hold it!' Anne yelled into the mic. The ship came to a halt, and she and Brinstead stared out of the forward portholes.

At the limits of their vision, there was a glint of reflected light.

'Ahead slowly,' Anne called out.

Now Mary understood. Al had eaten some of the fruit, fruit which she could see growing on the Grandfathers. The Ymir subsisted on the same fruits, and they were obviously in telepathic communication with the Grandfathers. Now Al could hear their voices, too.

She grabbed his arm and shook him. 'Al,' she snapped. 'Al! Fight it! You're human, not an Ymir!'

The unfocused eyes turned in her vague direction. 'Mary?'

'That's right,' she said, encouragingly. 'It's Mary. Listen to *me*, not to *them*.'

'I can hear them, Mary,' he said, dreamily. 'They're in my head. I can hear the Grandfathers now. They're talking to me.'

'Don't listen to them, Al,' she begged.

'They're in my head,' he repeated. 'I can hear them.'

He was like a perfect idiot. Mary didn't know what to do. Her friend was slipping away from her, like sand trickling through her fingers. She had to get him to hang on somehow, but she didn't know how.

'I understand,' he said, but obviously not to her. 'I hear you.'

'Al,' she growled. 'Al! What are they saying to you?'

He smiled, vague and getting vaguer. 'They have come a long way,' he said. 'A long way, a long time. They need soil to root in, to grow. They need air to breath, and food to eat. They need a new home for their Grandchildren, one that is warm and pleasant and spacious.'

'That's *our* world, Al,' Mary informed him. 'They want to take it away from us.'

'Yes,' he agreed, happily. 'Earth... It is infested with potential food, but it is too cold. So cold... It must be warmed.'

'Al,' Mary said, barely able to keep the tremble from her voice. 'That *food* is the human race!'

'Yes,' he admitted. 'Yes. There are many nutrients in the human bodies, more, even, than in the Ymir. The humans are an… interesting race. And now we can talk to them, talk through them.'

'Al,' she begged. 'Stay with me, Al! Don't listen to the Grandfathers! Stay with me! Stay human!'

The *Tethys* started forward again at a crawl, and Anne screwed her eyelids to try and peer further. The reflected light increased and grew in size. 'What is that?' she asked Brinstead.

'I'm not sure,' he admitted, looking as intently as she was. 'It's almost like a mirror, which makes no sense at all.'

The reflection was quite intense, almost as if a light was being shone at them. Brinstead wiggled their own lights, and the reflection wiggled in time with this action. It was obviously their own illumination, then, being returned to them. But from what? Anne knew that the Navy had a reputation for cleaning their ships, but she really didn't think that extended to polishing their subs. And she knew that a commercial freighter-turned-pirate-radio-station would have a pretty grimy exterior.

'Move the lights slowly toward the vertical,' she requested of Brinstead. He obeyed slowly, and she could see that the reflected glow receded slightly the higher the light went. Realisation dawned on her. 'That's a *dome*,' she said, softly. 'A highly reflective dome. Some kind of metal, most likely, to withstand the water pressure at this depth.'

'I think you're right,' Brinstead agreed, puzzled. 'But

what's it doing *here*?'

'Just sitting, by the looks of it,' she replied. She was lost in awe.

'I mean, who could have built it?' Brinstead asked. 'It's like something out of Jules Verne or some American science fiction movie. And how could anyone build it without being noticed?'

'I don't know. But it's quite beautiful. And it must be a mile or more across, judging from the bit of the curvature we can see.' Anne remembered the mic in her hand again and switched it on. 'Mother, there's a dome down here of some sort; clearly artificial. It's huge; about a mile or so across, and probably a few hundred feet at the highest point. We can't see all of it – hell, we can't see much of it – but it's quite something.'

'Mother here,' came the reply. 'Any sign of life?'

'Not at the dome – just fish and such.'

'Any sign of an entrance?'

'Not yet,' she reported. 'We're just approaching it now – it's just a few hundred feet away from us. Anchor, this is *beautiful*. It must be made of some sort of highly-polished metal. It's reflecting a lot of light. You should see this...' Anne stopped herself, remembering that nobody knew that Dolerite Base was able to eavesdrop. 'Um, I mean, make sure Brigadier Lethbridge-Stewart is aware of this development, please.'

'Understood,' the ship answered. 'We're relaying the message to the Madhouse.'

'Obviously, this must be part of what you're looking for,' Brinstead said. 'I mean, it's in the same spot as the sinkings, isn't it?'

That rang an alarm bell in Anne's mind. 'Mother,' she called, quickly. 'Winch us up. *Now!*'

'What are you doing?' Brinstead asked. 'We haven't finished exploring–'

Anne gestured at the dome. 'That thing *must* have something to do with the sub's vanishing, and we're here on its doorstep, dangling like a lure on a line...'

'You think we'll be next?' Finally, the professor started to get the picture.

'I think it's more than likely, yes. We've found what we were after. As much as it pains me to say this, it's time to get out of the way and let the military take over.'

The *Tethys* was ascending, horribly slowly, but it was already too late.

As she stared at the dome, Anne saw a flash of motion, and then impossibly long tentacles whipped out and grabbed hold of the bathysphere. As they tightened, the upward motion stopped with a jerk.

'Anchor, we're under some sort of attack!' Anne reported frantically. 'Tentacles of some kind. They've grabbed us and they're dragging us back!'

She could hear the groan of the cables attached to the *Tethys* complaining under the strain. There was a final jerk on the bathysphere, and then the horrible sound of the cables snapping. The bathysphere sank immediately, fast...

Anne felt her head go light, and for a moment wondered if that was what it was like to be in space... and then nothing.

In the CC, Lethbridge-Stewart heard every transmission. As the radio link to the *Tethys* went dead, McMillan turned to him.

'It sounds like she's gone, Brigadier.'

Lethbridge-Stewart nodded, feeling slightly numb. He was used to sending soldiers into dangerous situations, aware that some might well not return. But Miss Travers was not a soldier, even though she was a part of his staff. 'How far away is *Kraken*?'

'I can have her there within the hour,' Hennessey said, quite gently. 'If there's anything to be found...'

'There won't be,' Lethbridge-Stewart said. 'There was nothing left of the ship, or the sub. But at least, thanks to Miss Travers, we know what likely happened to them. They were attacked from this dome under the sea. Now we know where it is, we can deal with it.'

McMillan nodded. 'I can have the Phantoms back in the air in no time at all, Brigadier,' he promised. 'We can bomb that place out of existence. That will solve the problem.'

'I'm not certain yet that bombing is the best solution,' Lethbridge-Stewart said. 'For a start, we don't *know* that it would be effective. For another thing, we don't know that Miss Travers, or the people from the ship and sub are dead. For all we know they could be taken *inside* that dome... Certainly it's prudent to assume that's where the tentacles were dragging the bathysphere.'

'Prisoners?' Hennessey nodded. 'It seems probable. And what of the inhabitants of Strommach? I read those reports. Dead or captive?'

Lethbridge-Stewart thought for a moment, his eyes lingering on the map. 'I think the wisest course of action is to assume the best. That whatever intelligence is behind these attacks has taken captives. In which case, we need to get inside that dome.'

'Perhaps the humans can be of use,' Alan mused. 'If they can speak with us, and we with them... Perhaps annihilation is not required?'

'What?' Mary stared at him. 'Al, what's this about annihilation?'

He was clearly losing all sense of reality. He was speaking to her and to the Grandfathers as if they were the same, and he was speaking as both himself and the Grandfathers also. He was losing his identity. But he had also lost all inhibitions, and was quite happy to answer her questions.

'This world is to be used. The soil is good, and we can grow and thrive here. Once it is warmer, this will be a fine home.'

'Annihilation, Al,' she said, shaking him. 'What about annihilation?'

'That is the plan. That *was* the plan.' He seemed confused. 'The infestation of this world is – was – to be cleared and consumed. But if we can communicate with them, is there a need to replace them? Can they not act as the Ymir do? Do we even need the Ymir any longer? Can they be replaced?'

Oh, God! Mary finally understood.

She looked up at the looming Ymir. That was what must have happened to these stone giants in the distant past. The Grandfathers had connected with their minds, and the two races had grown together.

And now the Grandfathers were thinking of adding the human race to the mix.

CHAPTER FOURTEEN

Bits and Pieces

S amson heard the news with concern. He'd grown rather
fond of Anne over the past month or so; she was
brilliant, amusing and extremely pretty, which was a
combination he couldn't help but like. Now she was
missing, possibly dead, and he had to bury any feelings he
had for her. He had a job to do, and this was no time to get
side-tracked by emotional responses. Right now he had to
focus solely on Strommach.

He saw no need to pass the news on to his squad; he
knew that Bill was also fond of Anne – more than fond, if
Samson was any judge of such things – but there was no
need to distract the man. So he simply acknowledged the
news from Lethbridge-Stewart and reported that they would
be arriving at Strommach in about twenty minutes.

It was time to get ready. This DN6 was dangerous stuff;
they had environmental suits along for the men who would
be handling it. He recalled vaguely hearing about it a couple
of months ago, and he'd checked with Anne. Naturally,
she'd known all the facts and passed them along to him.

It had been developed as simply a pesticide, but had been
banned when it was discovered that it killed all insects and
plants indiscriminately. The firm involved had been engaged
in some shady manipulation that had led a financier to kill

the inventor; the killer had been jailed and all supplies of DN6 had been confiscated and stockpiled, thankfully, close enough for Lethbridge-Stewart to successfully requisition the stuff. And now it was to be used on Strommach.

Samson had assigned six men to spray it. He found them suiting up, along with a surprise seventh. 'What's this, Evans?' he asked, puzzled. 'I thought you didn't believe in volunteering?'

'Well, you see, it's a bit different this time, innit?' Evans said. 'Those disgusting plants… We've got to destroy them all, haven't we? We don't need them eating people, we don't.' He gave Samson a pathetic look. 'You won't tell me to stay behind, will you?'

Samson grinned. 'Far be it from me to deny you your first show of initiative, Evans. Go with my blessing, old son.'

Evans grinned crookedly. 'Thank you, sir.'

Sir? That was a first! Well, it was good to see that Evans was finally attempting to pull his weight.

'Right,' Samson said to all seven of the men. 'That stuff's lethal, so make damned certain you don't get any of it on your skin. If you do, down tools and hurry back to the boat. It takes a while for the skin to absorb it, so we should be able to clean it off before it sickens or kills you. But be very, very careful with it. Second, make sure that you cover every last inch of your assigned areas. Those plants are growing at a tremendous rate, and if we miss even one pod, it could reseed the whole island. Third, we're not certain that even DN6 will work on those plants. If it's clear that it isn't, stop spraying and return to the ship immediately. You've already seen how nasty those things are, and I'd really not like to lose any of you. The paperwork involved in filling out death benefits is bloody awful.' That got a couple of chuckles, at least. 'Well, enough rabbiting on from me; carry on, men.'

He returned to the cockpit, where the MTB's captain and Bishop were waiting. Bishop gestured ahead, and Samson saw Strommach growing in front of the boat.

'Be there soon,' Bishop announced over the roar of the engines.

'Good. The men are getting suited up. Evans volunteered.'

'Evans volunteered?' Bishop laughed. 'Two words I thought I'd never hear together.'

'Me either,' Samson confessed. 'But he seems to have it in for those alien plants.' He grinned. 'It probably helps that they can't fire back.'

Bishop smiled too, but it didn't last. He frowned, eyes on Strommach. 'What are the chances that this will work?'

'You tell me. You were around when the brig investigated the fallout.'

Bishop nodded in thought. 'DN6 can kill anything that's native to this planet, but there's no telling just how alien those plants are. For all we know, it might be like giving them nerve tonic. But ours not to reason why...'

'I suppose we'll find out soon enough,' Samson agreed.

The Vosper was drawing closer to the island now, so the captain had it slow down slightly. He brought it in toward the jetty, and joined them in surveying the scene.

Through binoculars, one thing was immediately apparent, the plants were growing at an amazing rate. They were all about six feet across now, their leaves overlapping so that virtually no soil or rubble was apparent. Aside from the plants, the island seemed eerily devoid of life. Even the birds were staying away, and Samson suspected that everything else had been devoured.

The MTB slowly pulled in to the jetty, and the engines were idled. A couple of the sailors leaped across and tied the Vosper up, then lowered a small gangplank. Bishop nodded to his squad members in their suits, the tanks of DN6 strapped to their backs, sprayers at the ready.

'Off you go, lads,' he said. 'And good luck.' They saluted, and set off down the gangplank. Bishop turned back to the captain. 'How's the prevailing wind?'

'Onshore,' he replied. 'Should keep any fumes well away from us.'

Bishop nodded, and patted the box Samson had over his shoulder on a strap. 'Keep your gas masks close, though. The first sign of a wind shift, and I want everyone to don them. It's only a precaution, but that's nasty stuff.'

'Don't worry,' the captain assured him. 'My men have all been warned.' He patted his own box. 'Nobody's taking any chances.'

'Good.' Bishop turned his attention back to his men.

The front man was approaching the first of the plants now, and brought the spray gun up into position. The plants knew they were there, and they were twitching, clearly eager for fresh food. If the soldiers went any further, those plants would erupt.

The first of his suited men turned on the nozzle of his sprayer, and a faintly-visible spray hissed out, enveloping the closest of the plants.

Mary was emotionally exhausted. It was all too much for her to take in: to be right at the heart of an alien invasion, and with her best friend possessed by the minds – *minds!* – of alien plants and losing himself in them. She just wanted to scream and retreat. She had never felt so scared and alone in her life. But the desire to do something, *anything*, to stop what was happening drove her on. She listened to Al, still speaking with the voice of the Grandfathers. They appeared to be debating among themselves.

'More humans must be fed,' Alan said in a soft, whispery tone. 'When they eat our fruit, we have an entry point. But is it stable? Can we trust it?' With every question his inflection changed subtly, an indication of the multiple entities talking. 'This human seems to be adjusting well. We have access to his mind, and he to ours. I never imagined that the humans could be communicated with. Perhaps domestication is possible, then. But what of our ongoing plans? Without action, the Ymir will be unable to live on this planet. The podlings are doing well; they enjoy the soil, and the food here is good. It has more flavour than the Ymir. Perhaps the Ymir have become expendable? But they are connected with us and would know any decision we make.'

Mary shuddered. Plants with intelligence. It seemed so impossible, and yet it was clearly the case here. She couldn't imagine how they could possibly think, but there was no arguing with what she was seeing and hearing. The big problem was that they had such an alien way of thinking. She doubted that there was any way of reasoning with them, but she had to try.

'We humans don't wish to be *domesticated*,' she snapped. 'We value our independence.'

'That is illogical,' Alan informed her. 'Your species will become a part of us, or else it will be destroyed. There is no other option. But can we trust such a joining? Will the humans not struggle and fight it? This one we have touched fights us even now. Yes, but he is not succeeding, is he? And these humans know many things alien to our technology. If they became a part of us, their knowledge could become useful.' Poor Al's head was bobbing back and forth like a bird's toy as he conversed with himself.

Mary shuddered. It was horribly creepy to watch.

But he had said that he was fighting this connection. Perhaps there was a way to draw him back, to make him just Al again. Not for the first time, Mary wished she knew a lot more about science than she did. Even if Al was still in there, she didn't have a clue how to get him out again.

'Should we proceed with the plan against the humans?' The discussion continued. 'Or should we investigate the possibility of joining with them? But the plans have been made and are being executed. To pause now would be counter-productive. There is no proof that the humans might even be valuable to us. This one knows a smattering of science, but hardly enough to—'

Alan and the all of the Ymir screamed in unison. It was a sudden and brutal sound that made Mary wince. She backed off hastily, unsure what was happening, or why. The Grandfathers were thrashing about also, probably screaming in their own inaudible vegetable fashion.

She forced herself to approach Alan again, and to reach out to touch him. His eyes were blank, and he was screaming.

'Al! Al!' She shook him. 'What is it? What is happening?'

Al's screams gradually diminished, and she could see a spark of the man she knew in his haunted eyes. 'The humans,' he managed to gasp. 'They are killing the podlings. The podlings are dying in agony. I hear their cries as they perish.' He threw back his head and screamed and screamed.

Bishop's voice came through the speakers. 'Mayhem One to Madhouse; the plan is working. Repeat; the plan is working. The plants are dying. Repeat; the plants are dying.'

Lethbridge-Stewart allowed himself the tightest of smiles. 'Mayhem One, that's excellent news. Continue the spraying until they're all dead. Madhouse out.' He looked up at Hennessey and McMillan. 'The operation appears to be proceeding well,' he informed them. 'The alien plants are dying.'

'Bang-on,' McMillan said, grinning. 'Now what?'

Lethbridge-Stewart gave another tight smile. 'Well, if I were the enemy, I'd want to know how the defoliation was being accomplished. That means a recce team.'

'You think that these... whatever they are... will counter-attack?' Hennessey asked.

'I think they're more likely to take a look first. They'll want to try and obtain a sample of whatever is killing those plants. We're disrupting their scheme, so they will have to discover how to combat it.'

'Sounds reasonable to me,' McMillan agreed. 'So we have to plan a counter-counterstrike?'

'Already under way,' Lethbridge-Stewart said. 'Whatever comes next will probably involve those metallic machines that initially attacked Strommach.'

McMillan grinned. 'And we can bomb the daylights out of them,' he said, approvingly. 'I can have Phantoms in the air in fifteen minutes.'

'No, sir, not just yet. This time I want them to make another successful raid on Strommach.'

Mary retreated until her back was against the immense room's wall. She huddled against it for scant comfort as the Ymir and Al howled and screamed. Finally, they began to calm down, and the Grandfathers slowed their wild thrashings. Al gasped for air, and then began talking to himself again.

'The humans did this! They have killed all of the podlings. We must retaliate. We must wipe out the humans. *Now!*' Alan's head shook. 'No, we must discover what weapons they have that can be used against us. Samples must be procured and analysed. Then they can be countered. And *then* we can wipe out the vermin. The great plan must be sped up. The captives must be worked harder.'

Mary moved forward. 'No!' she cried. 'You can't work us any harder. Everyone is already exhausted.'

Alan looked right through her. 'Then further workers must be obtained to replace the failing humans. There are surface vessels in the area that have humans on them, and there are humans on the island. They must be obtained when the samples are taken. They can be worked. But now the great plan must be sped up. Fresh humans have arrived, and they can be put to work.' Now Alan's eyes focused on Mary. 'You will be returned. You will work, and you will make the other humans work. The plan must proceed immediately.'

'What plan? Al, what plan?' Mary hoped she was getting through to her friend, but it was so hard to tell. She didn't know how much of him was still in there.

'The oil fields,' he gasped, as if fighting something inside himself. 'Mary, it's the oil fields! They… *You* will return to work *now*. Instruct the newly arrived humans to help. This soil room is too cold. We need the warmth returned.'

The Ymir stirred again, reaching for Mary and Al. 'You must go now,' it stated, its words echoed hollowly by Alan. 'The temperature will be returned to ambient level in here. If you do not go, you will perish.'

'Believe me,' Mary said, 'I'll be happy to go. This place really creeps me out.'

She was glad when the door to the greenhouse hissed shut behind them and the Ymir took its long strides down the corridor leading to the cavern beyond. She never thought she'd be happy to return there.

But… more humans?

Anne groaned as she awoke. She felt wretched, reminding her of the late nights and morning-afters back in her university days. She managed to open her eyes to gloom. There was a low level of lighting from the few instruments on the control panel that were still lit. And there was an even vaguer light through the portholes. She could make out indistinct shapes that looked like rocky ground. Had the *Tethys* hit the seabed?

No, that didn't make much sense. She could recall those tentacles grabbing and pulling on the bathysphere, and then something had made her black out. She hadn't fainted, that much she was sure of. Somehow there had to have been something connected to the attack that had stunned her.

And Professor Brinstead, of course. He'd half-fallen off his couch, and was starting to wake up himself. She helped the dazed scientist back to a more comfortable position.

'What has happened?' he asked, confused and dishevelled.

'We were attacked.'

'Yes, I recall that,' he said. He looked around and peered through the lower porthole. 'But where are we now?'

'I don't know,' Anne answered. 'On the seabed, perhaps? That looks like rocks out there.'

'It seems fortuitous that we landed upright. And that the *Tethys* wasn't breached, or we'd be drowned by now.' Brinstead checked his panel. 'That's odd.'

'What is?'

'The pressure outside isn't registering. The gauges show normal atmospheric pressure.' He scowled. 'Are we ashore somewhere, and it's night outside?'

That was certainly odd. 'Do we still have power for the lights?' Anne asked. They were all out though they had been lit when they were attacked.

'Batteries are virtually drained,' Brinstead said. 'They shouldn't be, but they are. If we use the lights, we won't have enough power to keep the air circulating for very long.'

'And if we don't use them, we may never know where we are,' Anne pointed out. 'If we *are* washed ashore somewhere, we won't need the air circulators, will we? We can just open the hatch.'

'And if we're not, we'll asphyxiate faster.'

'I'm willing to take that chance if you are,' Anne said. She was a scientist first and foremost, and, above all, she wanted to *know*.

'Very well,' Brinstead agreed, and snapped on the switch that controlled the light bars.

Instantly, a large area was illuminated. The first thing that Anne saw was a submarine, flat on the ground, just as they were. '*Venom*,' she breathed, softly. It had to be.

She jumped at the sudden loud banging on the hatch above their heads.

'I do believe there's somebody out there,' Brinstead said.

'As long as it's not a door-to-door salesman,' Anne muttered. She stood on her couch and twisted the wheel to free the hatch. As she started to swing it up, somebody on the outside helped her, and then there was a pretty – though rather grimy – face peering back at her.

'Will you turn off those bloody lights?' the woman snapped. 'They nearly blinded me.'

'Sorry.' Anne glanced down at Brinstead, who promptly complied. She looked back at the woman in the opening. 'Who are you?' she asked.

'Mary Wilde.'

Anne remembered seeing the name. 'You were on Radio Crossbones.'

'Glad to see you know me.'

So the missing ship was probably here also. Wherever *here* was. 'Where *are* we?'

Mary gave her a wan smile. 'Welcome to hell.'

— CHAPTER FIFTEEN —

Wishin' and Hopin'

To her surprise, Mary felt a little better now that there was another woman with her. The two of them toiled together, helping to drag the Ymir's equipment from the spaceship to the indicated site. Mary had never met anyone like Anne before – well, the circles she travelled in didn't usually include scientists and the military! – and the other woman somehow inspired confidence.

She was also a non-stop source of questions. Mary told her everything she'd managed to learn so far, and – despite the terrible working conditions – Anne seemed to be more excited than depressed. The scientist simply delighted in learning anything new. She'd even regarded the Ymir with fascination instead of fear.

'Silicon-based life forms,' she said, as much to herself as to Mary. 'Well, that makes sense. Silicon is one of the most common elements in the universe. Carbon chains wouldn't form too easily under extreme heat, so any life-forms on their world must be based on sturdier elements.' Then she frowned. 'But these Grandfathers you've told me about, they're *plants*... Fascinating. But silicon *might* explain how they can think.'

'How come?' Mary asked, her knowledge of science still at a classroom level compared to Anne's.

'Silicon chips are used to make computers,' Anne explained. 'If the silicon in the Grandfathers were to evolve just right, maybe the plants have some form of intelligence... Oh, how I'd love to be able to dissect one of the Grandfathers!'

'They're more likely to dissect *you*,' Mary pointed out. 'They eat the dead.'

'Yes,' Anne said cheerfully. 'It's a lovely system they've got set up. The Grandfathers produce fruit which the Ymir eat, the only thing they eat, apparently. And the Grandfathers then consume the dead bodies of the Ymir and anything else they run across. It's a lovely system, self-sustaining and quite beautiful.'

Mary shuddered. 'You didn't see them feeding the bodies of people you know to those bloody plants.'

'No,' Anne agreed, contritely. 'And I'm sorry if I sound callous. It's simply that this is a wonderful example of symbiosis: two species living together for mutual benefit. On Earth, it's never evolved to such a high degree. As a scientist, I find it absolutely fascinating.'

'Well, I'm glad one of us can enjoy it,' Mary said, drily. Anne's enthusiasm was really quite amusing, actually. At any other time, Mary might enjoy it. But under the current circumstances, it might get on her nerves if the other woman kept it up.

'This friend of yours,' Anne prompted.

'Al?'

'Right. He ate some of the Grandfather fruit and is now in mental contact with them?'

'Yeah.' Mary shuddered. 'It's really creepy. It's like he's lost inside his own brain.'

'That must be horrible,' Anne said, without much conviction. 'Where is he now? I'd love to speak with him. He can probably fill in a lot of the blanks.'

'I don't know,' Mary admitted, worried. 'When I was brought back from the ship to talk to you, he was taken off somewhere. I haven't seen him.'

'Oh well.' Anne shrugged. 'It sounds as if they were as surprised by what happened to him as we are. You know, we might be the first alien species the Ymir and Grandfathers have run across.'

'Well, they're not exactly friendly about it, are they?'

'No.' Anne mused for a while. 'I wonder why they chose Earth?'

'What?'

'Well, think about it for a minute. They need a world much warmer than this, but one that should be able to support life. Venus sounds ideal for them; it's hot and lethal for us, but it would be like a seaside resort for the Ymir. I wonder why they picked the Earth instead?'

'I haven't the vaguest idea,' Mary confessed. 'Maybe the rent was too high there. Look, what difference does it make? They're here now, and they have some plan that involves this machinery and the North Sea oil fields.'

'Oh, that part's obvious.'

Mary was getting a bit annoyed now. 'Not to me,' she pointed out. 'I never got further than Boyle's Law in school.'

'Sorry, I keep forgetting. Okay, as simply as I can manage. Venus ought to be a twin world of Earth. Most scientists thought it would be until recently. People expected a jungle world or maybe even a world of oceans. The Soviet *Venera* probes are showing that it's actually a boiling hell, and that the reason is carbon dioxide.'

'But there's carbon dioxide on Earth,' Mary said. She vaguely recalled seeing some mention of the Russian probes in the papers, but she hadn't bothered reading about them.

'There's considerably more on Venus. And it traps the heat from sunlight, causing the temperature to rise. Here on Earth the level of carbon dioxide is too low for that to happen. But if there was a large release of the gas into the atmosphere, our world would start heating up. Given enough time, or a lot of carbon dioxide freed all at once, and we'd turn into a twin of Venus. Incidentally killing all life as we know it. But not as the Ymir know it. They'd be happy as anything.'

'I'm still not getting it,' Mary admitted. 'How will what we're doing affect the carbon dioxide in any way?'

'The reason there isn't much carbon dioxide in the atmosphere on Earth is because plants absorb it,' Anne said patiently. 'They take it in, and oxygen is formed as a side effect. One that keeps life on this planet possible. All life on Earth is formed from carbon atoms. When something – plant or animal – dies, there's a chance it can get buried. In that case, given time and pressure, the organic molecules of life transform into oil.'

'The North Sea fields,' Mary said, starting to see the picture.

'Among others. There are vast fields of oil underground and underwater all over the world. We're using dribs and drabs of it as fuel, mostly in engines, because it burns so nicely. But when it burns, it frees carbon dioxide. We humans use so little of it overall that it's mostly absorbed back again by the plants still alive. But if we were to increase our use of it, more would be released than could be reabsorbed, and this planet would be in serious trouble.'

'And that's what the Ymir are planning?'

'It makes sense. If they reached the oil field under the North Sea and ignited it in one sudden burst, trillions of tons of carbon dioxide would be released into the atmosphere all at once.' Anne shook her head. 'There's no way the flora of our planet could cope with that. And they undoubtedly would follow up the initial attack with ones on the Middle Eastern oil fields, causing even further carbon dioxide poisoning...' Her voice trailed off as something occurred to her. 'Arthur's Seat!'

Now Mary really was lost. 'Arthur's...?'

'Seat,' Anne said with a nod. 'In the centre of Edinburgh, it's formed by an extinct volcano system from the Carboniferous age. Edinburgh, including the castle, is on an extinct volcano!'

'So?'

'If the Ymir detonate a bomb in the oil field, it could set off a fault, and that could restart some volcanos. Even if people somehow survived the oil explosion, they'd probably perish in renewed volcanic activity. And volcanos produce carbon dioxide as well. It would be one massive cycle of hell.' Anne stared at Mary in shock. 'We're looking at the possible total extinction not merely of the human race, but of *all* terrestrial life. All that would be left is a world that only the Ymir and Grandfathers could inhabit.'

Mary could comprehend *that*. 'Isn't there anything we can do about it?'

'Us? No, we're helpless here, forced to obey the Ymir. I do, however, have a friend who can probably do something, *if* he has any idea what is happening. And I don't see how he could have, because I'm only just starting to see the true scope of the problem myself. And, besides...'

'What?'

'He's occupying a base in Edinburgh, right on top of that sleeping volcano.'

Lethbridge-Stewart stared at the large operational map in front of him.

One of Maddox's girls had removed the *Tethys* marker and placed it on the edge of the board. *Kraken* was on station just off Strommach. The MTB that had carried Bishop's squad was on Strommach. The Radio Crossbones ship's last position – a few miles from Strommach – was marked, as was the lost sub. All in a single, concentrated area.

It all came down to Strommach. And Bishop had reported in that the island was now almost completely clear of those carnivorous plants. DN6 had certainly lived up to its deadly reputation.

'Well, Brigadier,' Admiral Hennessey growled, 'what do you think?'

'The key, gentlemen, is Strommach,' Lethbridge-Stewart stated. 'We've wiped out the plants that were seeded there. Our unknown adversaries will be forced to investigate. The last time they came ashore, they took human captives.'

'For what purpose?' McMillan asked.

'Who can say? Experimentation, perhaps?' Lethbridge-Stewart shook his head. 'Or there may be another reason. But from both sinkings, the only bodies we recovered were the divers who were outside *Venom* at the time. No bodies from the sub itself, and none from the radio station. If the purpose of the attacks had been simply to sink both vessels, we would undoubtedly have found bodies. Since we haven't, therefore, the unknowns are clearly kidnapping the people involved.'

'So what?' Hennessey demanded. 'How can that possibly help us?'

'It seems logical to assume that the next time these creatures emerge from the sea they will also take any captives they may find.'

'Then you'd better get your men off that dratted island,' McMillan said.

'On the contrary, sir, I believe we should put *more* men ashore.'

'But they'll only be captured...' McMillan started, and then realisation hit him. 'And taken to where the other captives are.'

'Precisely.' Lethbridge-Stewart smiled grimly. 'Thus giving us a chance to rescue the captives they already hold, and put a stop to whatever our foes might be up to.' He turned to the admiral. 'I think you had better pull *Kraken* out of the area, sir. We don't want to give them another ship, do we?'

'No, by Jove,' Hennessey agreed. 'Damned expensive, these ships. And the *Tethys'* home ship, as well.'

Sergeant Maddox joined them. 'I have a dedicated line to *Kraken* open, sir,' she murmured. The admiral hurried off to withdraw his men.

McMillan stared at the map. 'You may need tactical support,' he suggested.

'Indeed, sir,' Lethbridge-Stewart agreed. 'I'd be most grateful if you could arrange to have a flight of your

Phantoms ready if needed. These attacks seem to take place mostly at night, so I suspect we have several hours before we see any action, which should give me time to set my plan into motion.'

'A squad of your men on the island?'

'Quite. With concealed weapons, and disguised to look like civilians. With a little luck, that should fool the enemy. Maddox, can you get me some sort of small radio transmitter?' Lethbridge-Stewart asked her. 'We're going to need to be able to contact base, and alert the air marshal in case we need, so that he can order in a strike.'

'We don't have anything small and powerful enough to reach here from Strommach,' Maddox said. 'But if you can set up a relay box on the island itself, sir…?'

'Good idea, Sergeant. Get onto it. We'll need it ASAP.'

She saluted and hurried off.

'You've got an efficient staff, Brigadier,' McMillan said, approvingly. 'But what's this *we* I heard? You're not thinking of going on this mission, are you?'

'Indeed I am, sir,' Lethbridge-Stewart replied. 'Whatever situation we face will need instant decisions, and I don't want any delay from the team having to contact Dolerite Base for instructions. I'll leave Colonel Douglas here to handle things; he's a good man. But I will be leading the assault team myself.'

The Ymir had allowed the exhausted humans a chance to rest, eat and drink. The Ymir themselves seemed tireless, and they really didn't seem to understand why humans needed the breaks. But even they could see that working their captives to death would be counter-productive.

The food wasn't bad, considering it was mostly canned and cold. The Ymir didn't want time wasted in cooking it. The water was certainly welcome, as was the rest. Anne's muscles were aching quite badly from the physical labour. She was used to more cerebral pursuits. But the part about the break she liked the most was that Al had rejoined them.

He was eating the strange fruit from the Grandfathers. He was happy enough to allow Anne to examine it, but without equipment she could make very little from it. It looked fibrous, but with a high content of moisture. That bothered her, though Mary couldn't understand why.

'It can't be water,' Anne pointed out. 'The Grandfathers and the Ymir live in an ambient temperature a couple of hundred degrees above what we're used to. If this was water and an Ymir bit into the fruit, it would instantly boil.'

'Maybe it does, and instantly cooks the fruit?' Mary suggested.

Anne regarded her with fresh respect. 'You know, I hadn't considered that. It's possible, I suppose, but...' She peered at the slice again. 'It looks like some sort of a complex liquid, though. I wish I could just analyse it. It might tell me quite a lot. There must be chemicals dissolved in it that help with telepathic communication. God, I'd kill to be able to break it down... Can you just imagine what it would be like if we could synthesize those compounds?'

'Yes,' Mary said, angrily. 'Anyone who took them would be as crazy as he is.' She pointed to Al, who was twisted and talking discordantly to himself.

'No, it's only affected him like that because he wasn't prepared for it,' Anne argued. 'He's suffering from sensory overload; too much information coming in too fast for him to process it. Eventually his mind may get used to it, and his own personality could re-emerge.'

'May! Could!' Mary glared at Anne. 'Don't you understand, he's my *friend*, and look how he's suffering!'

'I know it must be hard for you to see him like this,' Anne said gently, touching the other woman's arm. 'But he's providing us with an incredible opportunity to gain insight into the minds of the aliens.'

'I don't care what insights you can gain!' Mary snapped. 'I just want my friend back.'

'If there is a way, I promise you I'll take it,' Anne said. She could understand and empathise with the poor girl; it had to be harrowing for her to see Al in this twisted shape. 'But, for the sake of the rest of us, I have to use this opportunity. If I can just *understand*, then I may be able to get them to free us.'

'And what good would that do?' Mary asked. 'These Ymir would still carry on with their plan to make the Earth unlivable for us.'

'Perhaps not,' Anne said. 'Something Al said gives me hope.' She turned back to the gibbering man. 'Al!' she snapped. 'Al! Are you still in there?'

His head turned toward her. The eyes were hooded and blank, but perhaps he was paying attention. It was just that he had so much else going on in his head that it had to be hard for him to concentrate on just one thing.

Anne turned to Mary. 'He's your friend,' she urged. 'Talk to him. We have to get him to answer us.'

Mary gave her a filthy look, obviously disapproving of Anne's tactics. Anne slapped her gently on the arm, and nodded toward Al. Finally, Mary complied.

'Al,' she said gently, taking his hand. 'Al, can you hear me?'

His face clouded, as he struggled to speak. Finally, though, he managed to say, 'What's happening, Mary? I feel so sick.'

'Al,' Anne said, moving forward slightly. 'My name is Anne Travers, and I'm trying to help. You can hear the Grandfathers, can't you?'

'I can't shut them out,' he whined. 'In my head, in my thoughts, in my eyes... I see terrible, cold things.'

'They can speak to you,' Anne said, sympathetically. 'But can *you* speak to *them*? Can you talk with the Grandfathers, Al?'

'Yes,' he said, hesitantly. 'But I don't like the way they think. So cold, so alien.'

'Al, I need you to ask them a question for me.' Anne touched his hand gently. It felt so cold, but there was sweat on his forehead. 'Can you do that? Can you ask them a question for me?'

'I don't want to,' he whined, pulling himself into a foetal position. 'It *hurts* when I think with them.'

'I know. But this is very important, for Mary and for the rest of us. Can you do it for us?'

His head twisted and he looked at her. Finally, he nodded. 'For Mary...'

'Good man!' Anne approved. 'Now, Al, ask the Grandfathers. Can they join with the humans? Instead of changing the world, can they simply join with the humans instead?'

Mary looked appalled. 'Anne! What are you doing? If they *can* do that, instead of killing us all, they'll be making slaves of us!'

'Shut up!' Anne snapped at her. She turned back to Al. 'Can you ask them that, Al?'

'I'll try.' His face went blank again.

Mary looked as if she was about to explode with anger. Anne grabbed her arm and dragged her away, hopefully out of Al's hearing.

'I'd rather be dead than a mindless slave!' Mary snarled. 'What the hell do you think you're doing, putting ideas into their... well, whatever plants have instead of heads!'

'Keep your voice down,' Anne ordered. 'Yes, I'm giving them something to consider. And yes, I'd rather be dead than a mindless slave. But the Grandfathers don't know that! And they seem to operate by some sort of consensus system, rather than having any one individual in charge. You've heard Al's voices. They debate *everything*. I've just given them something new to consider. With luck, it should take them quite a while to reach a decision. And until they do, they'll have to keep us alive. That buys us time.'

'Time for what?' Mary asked, but she sounded a lot less belligerent now.

'I told you, I have friends, and they aren't going to be sitting around and doing nothing. If I know Lethbridge-Stewart, he's already on the move. What I mostly have to do is to get him as much time as possible.' Anne smiled. 'And there's always a chance that the Grandfathers will delay using their bomb while they debate.'

'And if they *don't* take long?' Mary asked. 'What then?'

Anne sighed, and gestured to the machinery they had moved. 'They'll be ready to start drilling in a couple of hours. I can't be certain because that's alien technology, and

219

I've been mostly shifting it rather than studying it, but… It looks like some sort of laser-based drilling system, very powerful. It'll cut through the bedrock here like butter. Once they start drilling, they'll reach the oil levels in a matter of hours.' She gave Mary a bleak look. 'The countdown to our extinction has already begun.'

— CHAPTER SIXTEEN —

I'm a Believer

Samson regarded the island with a great deal of satisfaction. The men had sprayed DN6 everywhere, laying down the poison in the smallest of gullies. Every last plant had withered, blackened and died. The island was cleansed of alien life.

Evans came over to him and dropped the empty canister of DN6 onto the wooden jetty. He took off his gas mask and hood and wiped his sweating face with the back of his hand. 'There, tidy. Can't wait to get out of this, I can't,' he said. 'Itches something awful, it does.'

'You did a good job, Evans,' Samson said, approvingly. 'We'll make a soldier out of you yet.'

'Maybe,' the Welshman said, dubiously. 'Mind if I go back aboard and get out of these things, sir?' He indicated the protective suit and the bag slung over his shoulders. 'I've got this terrible itch right under–'

'I really don't want to know,' Samson informed him. 'Off you go, but be careful. There could be DN6 on that suit.'

'Trust me, boyo,' Evans said fervently. 'I don't aim to take no chances with this horrible stuff.'

Samson grinned as the private headed below. The rest of the squad tramped aboard to do the same. Samson thanked them as they passed him; a bit of appreciation kept the men happy. And they'd done a very unpleasant job. They'd used up a good deal of the DN6, but there were still some full canisters stacked up below deck.

He joined Bishop, who was calling in to report, and both were surprised when the call was routed to Colonel Douglas. The colonel was glad to hear the report, and then added that he'd been about to call Bishop anyway.

'The brigadier's on his way,' he reported. 'I'm left here minding the store while he's getting to have all the fun.'

'Trust me, there's not a lot of fun to be had around here, sir,' Bishop assured him.

'There will be soon, if the brigadier's read the situation right, and he usually does. He's expecting a raid from our unknowns to investigate what you've been up to.'

'We'll be waiting for them, then,' Bishop promised. 'I've got some good lads with me. And Evans.'

'Orders are not – repeat, *not* – to engage the enemy, Lieutenant,' Douglas said. 'The brigadier hopes to arrive before any attack, but if you *are* attacked, don't fight back. Surrender, and play along with the enemy. But hide some guns about your persons. He's expecting that the enemy will take further captives to where the earlier ones are.'

Once Douglas had signed off Bishop looked at Samson.

'The old Trojan horse ploy, eh?' Samson said.

'That's the idea,' Bishop said. 'But with a little luck, it'll be absolutely brand new to these folks.'

If Lethbridge-Stewart thought the missing people were captives and not dead, he was probably right. Samson had never known anybody who could read a situation as well as Lethbridge-Stewart. And he liked the idea of being a part of a rescue attempt. With any luck, Anne would be a captive and not dead at the bottom of the North Sea.

Work had begun again – the Ymir didn't like long rest breaks – and this time Anne fell in beside Professor Brinstead. 'How are you holding up?' she asked him.

'I'll manage,' he promised her. 'Though my degree isn't for dragging machinery around.' Then, surprisingly, he grinned. 'Here's one in the eye for Cousteau, eh? In all his voyages, he's never found a single alien!'

'Well, that's one way of looking at it.' It wasn't much, but Anne felt cheered up by his odd good humour. 'Look, you're a bit of a technician as well as a scientist; what do you make of this equipment?'

'I should have thought it was obvious,' he said, surprised. 'It's for drilling.'

'I know that. Laser-based, obviously. The aliens are planning on tapping into the North Sea oil reserves and setting them alight with a bomb.'

He blinked. 'Why would they want to do that?'

'To loosen a blanket of carbon dioxide.'

Brinstead considered this. 'Hmm. Might well work, at that. Ah! To raise the ambient temperature.'

'Right. A pleasant summer day to us is like a night in the Arctic for them. This will be their first attack, then they'll move on to other oil fields and repeat the process.'

'A reasonably sound plan,' Brinstead agreed. 'Should work, if they're not interfered with.'

'Well, that's rather my point, Professor,' Anne said. '*How* can we interfere with it? I'm expecting a friend sooner or later, but if it's later, I'd like to have a back-up plan.'

'Hmm again.' He considered the matter for a moment. 'I could really do with some better information, but I'm not averse to a bit of guessing. Nothing I'd dare publish in a paper, you understand.' Anne allowed a small smile before Brinstead continued. 'We're rather far from the main oil fields, which are a considerable distance from here, so dropping a bomb down a hole here normally wouldn't much affect them, let alone set them afire.'

'That's the bit that's been puzzling me,' Anne said. 'I was thinking that they simply set down here by accident, and they made their plans once they'd sized up the situation.'

'Possible, but I doubt it. Everything so far seems planned, reasoned.'

Anne agreed. 'They do seem to be remarkably astute. Not the sort of people – as it were – to rely on chance.'

'Therefore, they're here, in this spot, for a very good reason. And the only one that occurs to me is the volcanic shield.'

'Yes, with those bombs of theirs setting off a volcanic chain reaction.'

Brinstead waved his hand airily, almost dropping his corner of the equipment. 'No, no, no, nothing so simple,' he said. 'Volcanos are produced when molten rock forces its way to the surface under tremendous pressure. When the eruption is over, they leave hollow tubes that can sometimes extend for miles.'

Anne started to grasp what he was getting at. 'And you think they've detected one of these tubes below us? And *that's* what they're trying to reach?'

'Isn't it possible?'

Anne considered it very possible. More so in fact. 'If

they set a large enough bomb off in such a tube, it might be intended specifically to reignite the volcanos. And if they burst open, they would most likely touch off the oil field.'

'Yes, creating a wall of fire from Iceland through Scotland and into Scandinavia. And *that* would certainly have some disastrous effects on the Earth's atmosphere.'

'I'll say.' Anne was appalled. She'd encountered a few aliens now, and read up on events she hadn't been witness to, like the Dominators' plans for Earth, but this... 'That makes it even more imperative that we don't wait for help, but do something ourselves.'

Brinstead peered at her apologetically. 'I'm afraid I have only one solution to offer,' he said. 'And you're not going to like it.'

'What's that, Professor?'

'Set the bomb off prematurely, before it can be dropped into the hole they're going to dig.' He sighed. 'Of course, in that case every last one of us here will perish in the explosion.'

Chorley sighed as a cheerful policeman brought him another of the endless line of cups of tea. He was being treated rather well, if you didn't count the fact that he'd been in jail for over a day now. Taking the cup, he tried to stare down the young copper.

'Look,' he said, reasonably (though he felt far from reasonable). 'Aren't I supposed to be allowed to call my lawyer or someone?'

'I wouldn't know about that, sir,' the youngster replied, keeping an impassive face. 'You're only in for trespass, so I'm not at all sure you need a lawyer.'

'Then why not just let me go?' Chorley asked,

summoning up all of his patience.

'Well, sir, we can't do that until we know whether or not the person whose land you trespassed on wants to press charges or not. And the problem is that we've been unable to locate said person, but we *are* trying, and it shouldn't be that much longer. As soon as we speak to him, we'll know just what to do with you. Till then, just sit there and relax and enjoy your tea, sir.' He looked at him in a kindly fashion. 'Can I get you a newspaper or magazine to read? The *Police Gazette* is a real cracker this week. Or I could probably scrounge up a few copies of *The Beano*, if you'd like.'

'I don't want to *read* anything!' Chorley howled. 'I'm a *journalist*, I want to *write* something!'

'Well, sir,' the policeman said. 'I dare say I could find you a pencil and some paper, if that would make you happy.'

'That *wouldn't* make me happy!' Chorley yelled. His patience had all evaporated. 'What would make me happy is getting out of here.'

'And I'm sure it won't be long, sir,' the policeman answered stoically. 'Just as soon as we locate the land-owner. Enjoy your tea, sir.' He spun about and left the cells.

Chorley thought for a second about throwing the cup across the tiny room and using it to bang on the bars, like in so many bad movies. It would probably release some of his pent-up anger, but little else. These coppers were polite and understanding, and absolutely impervious to logic.

He would bet anything that they were somehow following orders that originated close to that dratted Lethbridge-Stewart.

With a sigh, Chorley sat down on the edge of the bed

and started to sip the scalding hot tea.

Lethbridge-Stewart finally clapped his eyes on Strommach. So much revolving about the place, and it was barely more than a smudge in the ocean, a rocky outcrop from the seabed that had managed to hold its head just above the waters of the North Sea. Even through binoculars, there was little enough to see; bare rock, covered in withered brown, dead plants. A few piles of rubble, and the jetty with the Vosper attached. A few of Samson's men were on the jetty – presumably on watch – but that was it. Hardly the sort of place one would think was the forefront of an alien invasion.

Then again, who'd have expected to find Yeti in the London Underground before *that* had happened?

Admiral Hennessey had come through again with other transport. He and McMillan seemed to be vying among themselves as to who could be the most help at the moment. Lethbridge-Stewart didn't know how Hamilton had persuaded them to be so co-operative, but it was certainly exceedingly helpful. Lethbridge-Stewart had some fifty men from A Company preparing themselves below decks for their mission. Added to the squad that was already on Strommach, that was a small but hopefully effective force.

As the boat drew up close to the jetty, he could see that Samson was ready and waiting for him. Lethbridge-Stewart turned to Bishop, who had met him on the mainland. 'Better get the men assembled on deck, Lieutenant.'

'Aye, sir.' Bishop disappeared below as Lethbridge-Stewart strode to the railing. A couple of the sailors were tying up the vessel, and two more ran out a gangplank, then stood aside for him.

'Welcome to Strommach, Brigadier,' Samson called up to him.

'Thank you, Sergeant Major. I'll be with you in just a mo.' Lethbridge-Stewart looked around as he heard the drumming of boots on the stairs. Bishop led the rest of the troop up onto deck. They were all dressed – roughly – in civvies. Half were dressed vaguely as women, with long skirts, padded sweaters and wigs. The rest were supposed to be fishermen, in thick pants and Arran sweaters. There were no weapons visible, but he knew that they were all armed to the teeth. They wouldn't fool any human being close-up, but Lethbridge-Stewart sincerely hoped that all humans looked alike to alien invaders' eyes. If they even *had* eyes.

'Right, men,' he said. 'Everyone ashore and act natural. When the enemy comes, surrender promptly. Once we're at our destination, I'll issue further orders as the situation seems fit.'

'Right, lads, let's go,' Bishop said. He was now dressed in fisherman's gear. He led the squad off the boat and onto the island, nodding at Samson as he passed. One of the men had brought the relay unit for Maddox's transmitter, and he placed it securely on the jetty.

Lethbridge-Stewart thanked the captain of the boat as he went ashore. Behind him, the sailors unhitched the ship and withdrew the gangplank. Their orders were to withdraw to a safe distance until called.

Samson saluted Lethbridge-Stewart. 'Not in mufti yourself, sir?' he asked, the corners of his mouth twitching.

'No, Samson, I'm not. Don't look good in a skirt, I'm afraid.'

'I'm surprised, a Scotsman like yourself.'

'Only in a hereditary sense. And a kilt is *not* a skirt. Besides...'

'We can't all have the legs for it,' Samson finished with a chuckle. 'We're all set, too, sir. No sign of any intruders so far.'

'They'll be here, Sergeant Major,' Lethbridge-Stewart promised him. 'And this time we're waiting.'

The Ymir ordered another break, and Anne settled down with a sigh beside Mary and Al. It seemed to her that Al looked worse than before. She touched his sweating forehead. 'He's burning up,' she exclaimed.

'I know,' Mary said, sadly. 'I spoke with Doctor Cleary, but there's nothing he can do. He said it must be the effects of the alien fruit. But Al won't touch anything else.'

Anne peered at him intently. His eyes were cloudy and unfocused, his head and hands twitching. 'Al, are you still there?'

'Work is progressing on schedule, despite the frailty of these human captives,' he replied. 'Drilling can commence shortly. Then we can bring out the bomb and prime it.'

'How soon?' Anne asked him, urgently. 'How soon till they bring out the bomb?'

'A pair of hours,' Al said, distantly. 'Fusing and priming is being accomplished now. The transport vessels are being prepared. Ymir crew to standby.'

'Transport vessels?' Anne looked back at Mary.

'Those mechanical slugs,' she said with a grimace.

Anne nodded. Of course. 'What are they going to do with the transport vessels?'

'Investigative team is being assembled,' Al said, jerkily. 'Orders are to proceed to the land mass and discover what happened to the podlings.'

'Right,' Anne said cheerily. 'The humans destroyed all of the podlings.'

'There are more humans on the island,' Al said. 'Instructions to all crews; the humans are *not* to be taken alive.'

'What?' Anne was startled. 'Al, what are their instructions?'

'The humans killed the podlings. They are all dead. The humans are to be all dead also. Instructions are to kill all humans on the island.'

— CHAPTER SEVENTEEN —

Strangers in the Night

Night was descending on Strommach, and there was a chill in the air. There was no shelter on the island, and precious little in the motor torpedo boat. Lethbridge-Stewart had ordered his men to stay on the jetty or on the Vosper; he didn't know how long DN6 lingered after it had been applied, or even if it could be absorbed through clothing. Miss Travers would undoubtedly know, and he felt a great loss not having her to call on. He was surprised how quickly he'd come to depend on her scientific know-how; not that he'd tell her, of course. If his theories were correct, she was still alive and inside that sub-surface dome. With a bit of luck, he and his men would be joining her shortly. Then it would be a matter of improvisation to get everyone out again.

He didn't care for that much. He liked to be able to go into a situation with a definite plan of action, and a viable way to retreat if that was necessary. In this case he'd planned as best he could. Before he'd left Dolerite Base, he'd thoroughly briefed Dougie on his aims and plans. And then Lethbridge-Stewart had left him with specific orders: if Dougie heard nothing by oh-nine-hundred hours tomorrow, he was to liaise with McMillan and send in a strike team of Phantoms to blow the dome to pieces.

Lethbridge-Stewart hoped he'd allowed himself plenty of margin. It would be unfortunate if he couldn't get free by then.

Samson came to stand beside him on the deck of the MTB. 'Deep thoughts, Alistair?' he asked, dropping the rank while they were alone.

Just two old friends talking over their day. Lethbridge-Stewart allowed himself an inner sigh. If only.

'Going over the schedule in my head,' he said instead. 'And hoping that all goes well.'

Samson was quiet for a moment. 'You've done the best you can with the information you've got, Alistair. I'm confident – and the men are confident – that we'll come through this, and achieve our aim. Whatever this enemy is up to, we'll stop them.'

'I only hope you're right,' Lethbridge-Stewart said, feeling warmed by that sentiment.

'Not like we haven't survived tight spots before.'

Lethbridge-Stewart looked at Samson with a raised eyebrow. 'Tight spots that carried with them the fate of our world?'

Samson smiled grimly. 'Well, no.'

'We'll probably find out in the very near future if you're right, Samson,' Lethbridge-Stewart said, offering his own grim smile.

'What?' Anne was stunned. 'No, no, you can't do that.'

'The order has been given and understood,' Al said. 'All humans on the island are to be killed.'

Anne was almost shaking. *Probably* the people on Strommach were Lethbridge-Stewart's men; people she worked with and knew. If so, they would *perhaps* be capable of standing up to the Ymir. But what if they were civilians? She dared not take a chance. She *had* to convince the Grandfathers to change their orders.

She gripped Al's hands, giving him something real to feel. They were cold, almost icy, and seemed to be terribly bony. Clearly he was not in good shape, but there was nothing any of them could do in here to help him.

'Al, listen to me. Those people on the island will die if we can't stop the Grandfathers. Al! Can you hear me? Can you understand?'

'The humans killed the podlings,' Al replied. 'The Ymir will kill the humans. The orders have been given and are understood.'

Mary pushed Anne aside. 'Let me try,' she suggested. 'He knows me better than you; he might listen to me.' She, too, took Al's hands. 'Al, you know who I am, don't you?'

There was a flicker of humanity still in his eyes. 'Mary,' he whispered, his voice like wind through autumn leaves.

'Mary,' she agreed. 'Al, you *must* stop the Grandfathers. You can't let them kill everybody on the island.'

'We need a home,' he slurred. 'The soil here is good. The podlings can live and grow. Not like the last world; not like Venus. The humans must not be allowed to kill them. The humans must be stopped. The order is given. Countdown will commence shortly. The human infestation will be eliminated.'

'Al!' Mary cried, almost weeping. 'Al! Listen to me!'

Anne laid her hand on Mary's shoulder. 'I don't think he can, any more,' she said, gently. 'The Grandfathers are so agitated that I think they're drowning Al out.'

'Isn't there anything we can do, then?' Mary asked.

'Our last chance is logic,' Anne replied. 'Al, listen to me! Tell the Grandfathers that the humans on the island are needed. The humans here doing their great work are tired and weak. This will delay the work. The humans on the island are fresh and strong. If they are not killed, if they are brought here, then they can make the work go faster. Do you understand me, Al? We *need* those humans – alive!'

Al's haunted eyes stared right past her. 'There is truth in what is said,' he announced. 'But the orders have been given. The humans must be punished for killing the podlings. If they are brought here, they can work and *then* die. But if they are killed on the island, their death will be a deterrent for the humans remaining. Yes, but the humans *won't* remain once the bomb is detonated. Therefore no deterrent is needed. All humans will die.' Al's voice faltered. He was trembling. He blinked, slowly, and then looked up at Mary. 'So cold,' he said, softly. 'So cold.'

Was he speaking for himself, or for the Grandfathers? At that moment it was so hard to tell.

Mary hugged her friend. 'I'll keep you warm, Al,' she promised.

'The experiment is ending,' Al said, his voice weaker than ever. 'Humans cannot be assimilated. You damned plants.' He gave a soft sigh, and all movement ceased.

'Al!' Mary called. 'Al!' Now she was the one trembling.

Anne didn't have to check; it was obvious that Al was dead. She gently placed a hand on the woman's shoulder and their eyes met for a moment.

'Alan,' Mary whispered, her voice broken. The tears streamed freely down her face as she held her friend.

There was nothing Anne could say to console her. She knelt and hugged Mary, but the other woman only had attention for Al. Clutching his body, she cried and cried.

The sun's last rays touched the horizon, and day dissolved into night. Lethbridge-Stewart knew empirically that it had been a pretty sunset, the kind that you could enjoy if you had your arm wrapped around the shoulders of a girl you were rather fond of. He thought of Sally for a moment, and wondered if he should have called her before he'd left, just in case. After all, his habit of leading from the front was rather dangerous, and one day might well be his last. But he didn't know any other way of doing things that was as effective, and the job was always more important than the person. Besides which, if he'd called her in case it was the last time he ever spoke to her... well, she'd only get emotional. Women – even women in the military – were like that. And, anyway, she'd only have brought up that dratted transfer again, and he'd been doing his best to avoid that subject. It was for the best that he'd left things as they were.

He was getting maudlin, which wasn't like him, especially when there was a job to be done. He shook the thoughts from his head and concentrated on the situation at hand.

His men were spread out along the jetty and on the Vosper, most of them at ease. Samson was scanning the area with binoculars, though they could hardly be of great help with night descending.

With no trees or buildings left, and the only light coming from below decks, the sky above was remarkably visible.

Thousands of stars speckled the night sky, only a few scattered clouds hiding some. Presumably one of those points of light was home to these beings they were awaiting. On a night like this, though, it wasn't hard to accept the presence of aliens, falling from a star.

He was getting almost poetical again; what was wrong with him? It was probably just the waiting; always the hardest part of any campaign. Once the action began, instinct kicked in and all doubts and worries vanished. But the waiting always took a toll.

'Lights, sir,' Samson reported softly, breaking Lethbridge-Stewart (thankfully!) out of his thoughts. Samson gestured. 'Under the surface, about half a mile out.'

Lethbridge-Stewart nodded. He could see the pale illumination, and could make out that it was approaching them. 'This is it,' he said, just as softly. 'Have the men get ready. Remind them, no firing or other hostile action. And make sure they're ready to panic on cue.'

'Got it, sir.' Samson saluted and faded away.

Lethbridge-Stewart wished he had his swagger stick – it always felt better to have it in hand – but he had to play civilian right now, and he couldn't imagine why a civilian would carry such a thing. Instead, he rhythmically tapped his hand on the MTB railing. Nerves, he knew, but the adrenaline was starting to flow. The enemy was approaching.

The lights moved closer, growing brighter, and then finally broke the water about a hundred feet offshore. There were three of the huge mechanical slugs that the two young islanders had described, the ones that had taken their friends and families. Well, with any luck, it would be payback time very soon.

'Right, lads,' he called out. 'Panic!'

The men and 'women' started to run up and down the jetty, throwing their hands in the air and screaming. To Lethbridge-Stewart it looked like a very bad rep company playing a tiny, out-of-the-way town, but with luck it would seem authentic enough to their enemy. He would have preferred less over-acting, but he was their commander, not a theatre critic.

The slugs crawled onto land and moved quietly into position about the jetty. Lethbridge-Stewart's heart was racing; this was the crucial point, and he really didn't know what might happen next.

Panels opened in the machines, and then mesh nets flew out, targeting the 'villagers'. One of the nets enveloped the entire Vosper. As the mesh fell over him, Lethbridge-Stewart felt a jolt of pain, and then darkness and nothing else.

A pair of the Ymir moved to where the humans were resting. 'Work will recommence,' one of them stated. Wearily, the captives staggered to their feet and started to obey. The Ymir accompanied them to where lengthy conduits and control circuits still needed to be moved. The second Ymir came across to where Anne stood; Mary was still hunched over the body of her friend.

'The body will be fed to the Grandfathers,' the Ymir stated.

Mary didn't even look up. 'Go away, you ghoul,' she snarled. 'Haven't you done enough to him already?'

'The body will be fed to the Grandfathers,' the Ymir repeated. 'It has ceased to function. It has no other purpose.'

'It's *ceased to function* because you bloody well killed

him!' Mary screamed. 'Leave him alone. Leave *me* alone. I've had enough. I'm not doing another damned thing for you.'

'Mary,' Anne said, warningly.

'No!' Mary yelled. 'Enough logic! Enough of playing nicely so I can stay alive. These damned monsters have killed all of my friends. I'm the last person from Crossbones alive. And I've had enough. I won't bow and scrape, and I won't let them take Al.' She looked up at the Ymir looming above them, her dirty face streaked with the path of dead tears. 'You hear me? I'm through. I don't care what you do with me.'

'If you will not work, then you will die,' the Ymir said simply.

'Then kill me. Put me out of my misery. Kill me like you killed all the others.'

'No,' Anne said firmly. 'Mary, I won't let you throw your life away like this.'

'It's *my* life,' Mary snapped. 'It's *my* decision. And I've decided that I've had enough. Anne, I'm not strong and brave. I don't work for the army, or the advancement of science. I'm just a stupid woman who thought, a few years ago, that I could be a disc jockey. Do what Susan and Candy Calvert couldn't. Someone who plays music that doesn't make any difference to the world. Now I don't have a ship, I don't have a job, and my last friend just died in my arms. I'm *tired*. I don't want any more. I just want oblivion. Can't you understand that? Can't you allow me my peace?'

'Of course I understand it,' Anne said. 'You've been through enough to terrify or kill anyone. But you're wrong about music not making a difference. Music can inspire and comfort and help people to heal. And when people are down, or depressed, or simply just tired, well... hearing a cheerful voice and some good music can revive their spirits and lift their souls.' She looked at Mary, hoping she was getting through. 'And you're also wrong about having no friends left; you still have *me*. And I admire you for what you've survived and achieved so far. The world needs women like us, forging their way ahead in a man's world. Don't give up on life. Don't give up on me. And don't throw yourself away just because you're depressed.'

The Ymir reached downward. 'She has expressed a decision to die,' it said. 'Her decision will be accepted.'

'Back off, you!' Anne yelled at it. Rather to her surprise, it did. 'Don't you know what she's been through? Give me a minute, and she'll change her mind.' She ignored it and turned back to Mary. 'I need your help,' she said, simply.

Behind her, the Ymir sounded uncertain. 'You will all perish in a matter of hours anyway,' it stated. 'Why do you care if this one elects to perish now?'

Anne turned her head and glared at it. 'You know, she's right, you *are* ghouls. And you don't *know* that your plan will work. There's always the chance that something might go wrong with it.'

'Nothing will go wrong,' the alien said. 'Everything is prepared. The equipment is almost ready, and then drilling will commence. The bomb is being brought out and will be positioned for detonation. Everything is proceeding as anticipated.'

'Then what difference can it possibly make to you if you kill her or let her live for a few more hours?' Anne asked. 'Unless you simply *enjoy* killing.'

The Ymir considered this. 'There is logic in what you say,' it agreed. 'The human unit will be ignored.' It turned and walked away.

Anne stared at its retreating back in amazement. 'Some days, I even surprise myself,' she murmured.

CHAPTER EIGHTEEN

You're My World

A nne sat down with a hearty sigh as the Ymir ordered a halt to the work for the moment. She was next to a panting Brinstead; the scientist was completely unused to physical labour, and seemed to be on the point of collapse. She sympathized with him, but there wasn't much she could do to help him. Instead, she studied the machinery as best she could.

The single Ymir watchman had guided the captives in connecting the wiring between the devices. The main power cable led back to the spaceship, and everything looked ready for the drilling to commence. The alien looked down at Anne.

'All is prepared, but must be checked. You and the other humans will move back to the holding area while this is done. Interference in any way will result in death.'

'All right,' Anne said, meekly. She aided the professor to his feet, while Captain Browne got his sailors and the exhausted villagers onto their feet. She fell in beside the naval man as they trudged wearily back toward the spaceship. 'I think they're ready to start drilling,' she said. 'It's starting to look like the cavalry isn't coming.'

'Indeed,' Browne agreed. 'But I'm damned if I can think of anything we can do to prevent these Ymir's plan.'

'Well, I deliberately mucked up some of the connections,' Anne confessed. 'But that will only delay them a bit. They're not stupid enough to start up the drill without checking it first. It'll buy us a bit of time, nothing more.' She was thinking furiously. 'Have you seen any of the aliens actually carrying any weapons?'

'They hardly need to; their bodies are weapon enough.'

'Agreed,' Anne said, thoughtfully. 'But there aren't any guns or anything, and the Ymir are pretty slow on their feet. I think it's a combination of their size and the fact that they're virtually freezing to death just standing out here with us. But it means that they couldn't chase us if we started an escape bid.'

'And where would we escape to?' Browne asked. 'We're pretty much sealed in here. And according to you, this place is on the seabed. So even if we found a door, we can't really go anywhere. They've planned this well, and we're trapped.'

Anne grinned. 'But we have a submarine,' she pointed out. 'Is it in working order still?'

'If you don't count the fact that there's no water for her to swim in.'

'Not at the moment,' Anne agreed. She looked up at the blackness overhead. 'I've no idea how thick the walls of this dome are, but they've got to be pretty strong to resist the water pressure outside. But there *is* a weak spot. There's one of those Grandfather plants at the exit. It's pretty huge, but it can't possibly be as strong as a wall of solid rock. If we can detonate something in its face, it should collapse and let the sea in. *That* would float your boat.'

'A lot of *ifs*.' Browne looked at her thoughtfully. 'The Ymir aren't just going to sit around and let us take hostile action against them,' he pointed out.

'No, I'd need to create some sort of a distraction,' Anne agreed. 'And I've a couple of ideas on that score. If I do manage to get their attention, is there any way you can get an explosive near that plant? Torpedoes wouldn't work, obviously, without water. Maybe take one out and transport it over there? But that would take too long, wouldn't it?'

'Torpedoes aren't our only armament, Miss Travers,' the captain said proudly. 'We also have a very fine deck gun.'

'Of course you do, Captain,' she said, grinning. Anne indicated the direction the transport mechanisms had gone. 'It has to be in that direction, but I don't know how far.'

'Radar would have that answer,' he assured her. He considered for a moment. 'All right, get me that distraction, and we'll have a damned good try for an escape. I'll have my men escort these civilians to *Venom*. Plenty of room for them aboard for a short trip. Give me time to alert everyone, though. I'd say at least half an hour.'

'Fine,' Anne agreed. 'I could really do with the rest, anyway.' That was no lie; she was bone-weary. But the prospect of escape was giving her hope and strength.

They reached the area that had been designated as their resting place, and everyone flopped down. Browne started moving around, talking to his men in a low voice. Anne moved to join Mary.

The other woman was still hunched over Al's body, deep in grief and lost in her emotions. Anne shook the woman's shoulders. 'Okay, Mary, time to snap out of it.'

'Leave me alone,' came a mumbled response.

'I can't do that,' Anne said, unapologetically. 'I've got work to do, and I need an assistant. You're it.'

Mary glared at her. 'Go away.'

'I'm sorry, that's the wrong answer.' Anne knew she was being harsh with Mary, but she had no other option at this point. Allowing Mary to wallow in her black mood was doing nobody any good. 'Al's dead,' Anne said, as gently as she could. 'The world's in danger, and we have a plan to save the day. Get off your sorry backside and be prepared to help.'

'Leave me alone.'

'That wasn't a request,' Anne said firmly. Maybe some of Lethbridge-Stewart's attitude was rubbing off on her. 'On your feet, Wilde, and face the future, not the past.'

'I'll be no use to you,' Mary said. 'Leave me here.'

'You'll die.'

'I *want* to die,' Mary growled. 'Don't you understand? I've had enough.'

'You *quitter!*' Anne yelled. 'It's oh so easy to just lie down and play dead until you really *are* dead. And if it was just you and I at stake... well, then, I might indulge you and let you do it. But there are women and children here who will *die* if we don't do something. And in a very short while, the rest of the human race will follow them. I'm not letting that happen, and *you're* not letting that happen. Do you understand me?'

'Stop it!' Mary begged her. 'Leave me alone.'

'Not on your life.' Anne grabbed her shoulders and shook her, hard. 'Is this how you would want Al to see you? Mooning over his body, crying up a river and whatever other trite sayings they have in those songs you play? Is that all his death means to you? Cry, cry, pity poor me? For God's sake, woman, grow a backbone! Stand up and fight back! Don't allow Al's death to have been in vain.' She hoped this was getting through to Mary, because she was running out of clichés.

Mary wiped the snot from her nose on the back of her grubby blouse sleeve and then – with Anne's help – managed to get to her feet. 'If I help you, will you shut up and leave me alone?'

'Possibly,' Anne answered, with a grin. 'But I'm all out of *definitelies*.'

Mary pulled herself together. Anne had to admire the other girl's courage and resolve. 'Right,' Mary finally said, breathing deeply. 'What's your plan?'

'Well, *plan* might be a bit strong a word for it,' Anne admitted. 'I'm making a lot of this up as I go along. The captain's going to take everyone aboard the sub and then shoot at the Grandfather plant that's guarding the entrance to this dome. That should flood this place, and they can use the sub to escape in.'

'I'm noting the use of the word *they* and not *us*,' Mary commented.

'That's because we'll be distracting the Ymir.'

'And how do we do that?' Mary asked. 'I doubt the dance of the seven veils will get their attention.'

'Probably not,' Anne agreed. 'I was thinking more of using their drill.' She indicated the device. The Ymir had discovered her mis-connections and was fixing them. 'If it can cut through rock, it should be able to cut through spaceship.'

'And they're just going to allow you to borrow their

drill?'

'No, they're not good neighbours, are they?' Anne grinned. 'I was thinking of distracting them.'

'That's a lot of distractions,' Mary said. 'And another thing occurs to me. If we're shooting them with their own drill, doesn't that mean that we'll be outside the submarine when this place is flooded?'

'Ah, yes, you have hit on the one tiny flaw in my plan,' Anne admitted. 'The fact that if it works, we're not likely to survive it. But you did say you want to die anyway.'

'Yes, but *you* didn't.' Mary sighed. 'Show me what to do, and you go with the rest of them.'

Anne shook her head. 'You won't be able to do it on your own.' She was trying hard not to think about the fact that her plan would sign her death warrant.

There was a low hum that started to build up. They looked at the drill. 'Looks like they're ready to start work,' Mary observed.

'And there's just the one Ymir,' Anne said. 'Well, as soon as the captain's ready, we'll get to work ourselves, eh?'

There was an ear-splitting whine, and the drill began operating. Even at this distance, the light from the laser was almost blinding. The rock beneath it wasn't simply melting, it was giving off clouds of steam. Anne studied this, worried: could she even get to the drill without being cooked?

And then, at the worst possible moment, the transport vessels returned. She saw them crawling into the lit area, gleaming and impassive. Damnation! That would mean more Ymir, and the net-guns they had used to capture the inhabitants of Strommach. If they tried to escape now, they would be stopped almost immediately.

'Plan's on hold,' she muttered to Mary. 'Complications have arisen.' She felt a twinge of guilt that she was almost relieved that she wouldn't die in the next fifteen minutes.

Probably.

The steel slugs crawled up to the spaceship, and hatches in the sides of the three vessels opened. Each ship disgorged bunches of dazed-looking individuals. Anne felt a wave of relief; her arguments had convinced the Ymir not to kill on sight!

'Those are some of the ugliest women I've ever seen,' Mary muttered.

Anne almost laughed. 'That's because they're my friends.'

'You have some ugly friends, girl,' Mary commented.

Anne ignored her and hurried over to the new arrivals. As she'd hoped, she spotted Lethbridge-Stewart among them, as well as Bill and Samson. The latter looked particularly frumpy in a bulky skirt and blouse. Despite the severity of the situation, Anne almost laughed at that. They were all recovering, and she helped them to sit for a moment to gather their wits.

A second Ymir emerged from one of the vessels and stared down at her. 'You will instruct these captives to assist us. The bomb is to be moved into position shortly.'

'Bomb?' Lethbridge-Stewart's voice slurred a little.

'Catch your breath, Brigadier,' Anne said. 'I'll explain it all when you can concentrate.'

Bill grinned at her. 'Anne,' he said simply.

'Lieutenant,' she said in kind.

He cleared his throat, glancing briefly at his commanding officer. 'You had us worried.'

247

'I did? Then I'm going to bloody terrify you in a minute.'

*

Seeing that they were all slowly recovering from whatever had knocked them out, Anne hastily outlined the Ymir plan. She gestured toward the drill, which was still howling and kicking up rock and thick, black vapours. 'That device will cut through to a fault line in fifteen minutes. They then aim to roll a bomb into the fault and detonate it. This will set off the North Sea oil field, and the blowback will probably fill the volcano system beneath Edinburgh; the city will be destroyed! The Ymir will be gone by then, of course, off to their next target.'

'And we'll all be left behind,' Samson finished. 'Nice.'

'Captain Brown and I did have a sort of plan,' Anne informed them. She explained the details of it, and saw Lethbridge-Stewart's scowl.

'So you were aiming to sacrifice your own life to save everyone,' he said. 'Most commendable, but most foolish.'

'If you can think of a way of doing it without my dying, I'd be *very* happy to give it a try,' Anne said.

Lethbridge-Stewart gave her a tight smile. 'That's the advantage of military training, Miss Travers,' he said. He turned to Samson. 'Unless I'm mistaken you have scuba training, correct?'

'Good memory.'

'So have I,' Bill put in. 'I've dived the islands lots of time.'

'*Mine* was actual training,' Samson said, his tone suggesting a friendly rivalry. 'Not a holiday junket.'

Bill rolled his eyes.

'Boys, boys,' Anne chided, also smiling. She turned back

248

to Lethbridge-Stewart. 'What's the idea?'

'Samson can operate the drill wearing the gear,' he explained. 'Then, once the cavern is flooded, he can swim to the submarine before we depart.'

Anne glanced at Samson critically. 'No offense,' she said, 'but I wouldn't trust you to operate a cathode ray tube unsupervised. Sorry, Brigadier, but it has to be me that does it.'

Lethbridge-Stewart was about to argue when Samson broke in. '*Both* of us, then,' he suggested. 'If you're in a suit as well, I should be able to help you get to the sub, even if you're not used to it.' He looked to Lethbridge-Stewart for support. 'It's a better chance for her than she'd otherwise have.'

'*Both* of us could stay with her,' Bill suggested.

Anne lowered her eyes, not wanting Bill to see what was in them. She wasn't entirely sure herself, for one thing. But Bill's offer touched her. Perhaps she was just getting over-emotional due to the drama of the day.

'Sorry, Lieutenant, I need you with me. Someone has to provide the distraction Miss Travers needs to get to the drill.'

Mary had been listening quietly to all of this, but now she spoke up. 'And how do you plan on doing that?' she asked. 'Speak severely to them?'

'No, Miss,' Lethbridge-Stewart said. 'I was thinking more of good old-fashioned firearms.'

'Brigadier,' Anne chided him. 'The Ymir are virtually made of stone; bullets won't even tickle them.'

'I suppose that was too much to ask,' he agreed. 'Luckily, we've brought grenades along as well. I rather suspect they'll be more effective.'

'And the guns will work against their machinery,' Bill pointed out.

Anne glared at him. 'Don't you dare shoot anything I can use,' she warned him.

'Right, then,' Lethbridge-Stewart said, ignoring her comments. 'Samson, go see Captain Brown about getting a couple of suits for you and Miss Travers. Bishop, ready the men for action. Miss Wilde, please stay back out of danger.' He gave Anne a penetrating look. 'I don't suppose there's much point in asking you to do the same?'

'No, Brigadier, there isn't.' Anne turned to Mary. 'Do as he says,' she said. 'He really is very efficient at what he does. Oh, and I'm afraid you're fired as my assistant.' She abruptly hugged the other woman. 'I'll see you on board the sub, I promise.'

Mary looked a little shaken by this, but eventually she nodded. 'All right,' she agreed. 'But take care of yourself.'

'I promise to try *very* hard.' Anne gave her a watery smile.

Lethbridge-Stewart's arrival had changed Anne's chances greatly. She'd been almost ready to die – well, as ready as anyone could be – because it would save others. Not just the people here, but possibly the entire human race. One life against the whole of humanity... Well, that wasn't really a choice, was it? But now there was a chance she might actually live through this.

The Ymir from the transport vessels had disappeared back into the spaceship again to get warm, leaving only the one operating the drill. Anne looked around. Captain

Browne had finished prepping his men, and they were quietly helping the civilians to their feet. Lethbridge-Stewart and Bill were readying their own men. The ugly 'women' were divesting themselves of their poor disguises, and the 'fishermen' were discarding their thick sweaters. Underneath, all had guns and grenades strapped to their clothing. As ever, Lethbridge-Stewart had arrived prepared for action.

There was movement in the airlock of the spaceship, and then two Ymir appeared, hauling a sledge of some kind. Strapped to this was a device; clearly the Ymir bomb. It was squat and square, with blunted corners, and completely featureless save for a single panel on the top of it. Lethbridge-Stewart motioned his men to hold still as one of the Ymir fiddled with the panel.

A single electronic *beep* echoed through the cavern. Then a second, and a third.

'Countdown has commenced,' the Ymir said, rather unnecessarily. 'Detonation will occur on schedule.' It looked at Anne. 'The humans will transport the bomb to the drill site.'

Anne glanced at Lethbridge-Stewart, who nodded slightly. 'Best to appear to co-operate,' he said, softly. 'If we do, they will probably return to their craft. That will improve our chances.'

Bill nodded, and ordered several of the squad to assist him. They moved to position themselves about the sled, and heaved and pushed until it started to move.

'You will be given further instructions,' the Ymir stated, and then it and its companion returned to the airlock.

Anne let out a sigh of relief. 'I'm going to get a look at

251

that control panel,' she said. 'I'd better try and stop the countdown.'

'Not for the moment, Miss Travers,' Lethbridge-Stewart said, grabbing her arm to stop her. 'They're probably monitoring their bomb from inside the ship. It *is* rather important to them, you know. Wait until the action starts, and they're otherwise occupied.' To Bill and the others, he called, 'Keep going, men, for the time being.'

Anne's heart was racing. This was their only chance to stop the Ymir and the Grandfathers. They couldn't afford to fail. While she had confidence in Lethbridge-Stewart, she wondered if she was being overly optimistic. Even with their armaments, the odds were clearly stacked against them. But what else could they do?

Everything felt so surreal. All of her life to date seemed to focus within this pool of light – the spaceship, the still transport vehicles, the submarine, the drill, the bomb – and a scattered flock of people, waiting for a signal from her or Lethbridge-Stewart. Plus a single member of the alien invaders, grimly intent on its purpose to seal the fate of the world they proposed to steal.

'This is *our* world,' Anne muttered to herself. 'They're not getting it without one hell of a fight.'

CHAPTER NINETEEN

Even the Bad Times Are Good

'Right,' Lethbridge-Stewart decided. 'Renfrew, Hollister; grenades. Take out that big stone chap. Captain Browne, if you please.'

Browne nodded and called to his men. They started to herd the survivors and guide them to the submarine. Out of the corner of her eye, Anne saw Samson sprinting towards the sub, on his way for the diving gear. Mary and Professor Brinstead went along with Browne's men, leaving just the troops with Anne.

The two soldiers stepped forward and each threw a grenade. The Ymir hadn't seen any of this, intent as it was on its work. The grenades both exploded, and for a moment Anne could see only a cloud of dust. As it cleared, the fallen Ymir was visible. It hadn't been killed, but it was missing a large portion of its left leg and one arm. It was attempting to climb upright again when the two men hit it with follow-up grenades.

Well, that would certainly have warned the rest of the Ymir that they were in trouble, since they were linked telepathically. With a bit of luck, the shock of the violent death of this one would slow their response. Anne sprinted for the drill, which had stopped working. She prayed it was only because the Ymir had let go of the controls, and not because it had been damaged by the blasts. Bill and Private Sharp accompanied her.

She scanned the panel quickly, but couldn't see any damage, thankfully. She turned to Bill. 'Give me a boost up, these Ymir are a bit taller than me.'

'Only a bit?' Bill asked.

With his help, Anne was able to climb onto Sharp's shoulders and reach the controls. There were no labels or instruction manuals conveniently marked in English, but the thing didn't seem to be too complicated. A pretty standard hand control, something with a light that had to be the power switch, and a group of other instruments and readouts she hoped she could get away with ignoring. Probably nothing more important than overheating warnings.

She was vaguely aware of further explosions. That had to mean that the Ymir had emerged from their ship and that Lethbridge-Stewart was fighting back. There was nothing she could do to help there, so she focused her attention on the drill.

It was pointing straight downward at the moment, obviously, to excavate the hole for the bomb to drop through. The base rock was still molten and giving off a great deal of heat, but she did her best to ignore it. She felt as if she were perched on the edge of the First Circle of Hell; the Ymir probably considered this a mild spring morning.

'Hurry it up, Anne,' Bill called to her. 'Those alien beasties are starting to counter-attack, and the brigadier could really use some help.'

'I'm doing my best, but this *is* an alien device,' she reminded him. 'It's not the simplest thing in the world to understand, you know.'

'I do know, but we don't have all day.'

She'd make him pay for that later, she vowed. Right now, though... 'Okay,' she said. 'I think I've got it.' She moved what she hoped was the drill release lever. To her tremendous relief, the pointy end of the drill started to swing up to the horizontal. She stopped it and locked it into position, and then started to swivel it about to aim it at the Ymir ship.

Then she saw the extent of the battle. There were half a dozen Ymir now outside the ship, moving in their deliberate, ponderous way toward the soldiers. Despite the fact that they were virtually useless against the alien's skin, most of the men were firing their rifles, and bullets were ricocheting away in all directions; luckily none too close to her. Three or four grenades served to take down a single Ymir, but the troops were running short of them. She could see that a handful of the soldiers were down, burned to death by the Ymir's deadly heat, and she knew that more would die just as horribly if she couldn't help.

The drill swung into position, but it seemed to be so terribly, terribly slow. It made sense, since the Ymir were so ponderous themselves, but it was agonizingly frustrating. It would be a minute or so until the laser drill was in position, and the troops needed help *now*.

There was a booming sound that reverberated throughout the cavern, and one of the Ymir exploded into rocky fragments.

Anne realised what had happened; Captain Browne's men had used the deck gun to help out. Yes!

And now the drill was in position. She locked the

controls and started the firing mechanism. With a crescendo of noise, the beam flashed into life, cutting across the cavern and targeting the airlock of the spaceship. Metal groaned, melted and flowed. Smoke and steam billowed from the airlock as the beam slashed through the metal. Anne grinned happily. There was no way for the Ymir to close their airlock now. The spaceship was going nowhere without extensive repairs, and the aliens would never get the time or opportunity for those.

But there was still the bomb to worry about. Lethbridge-Stewart's men had stopped moving it, of course, once the battle had begun, and it sat there, half-way between the ship and the drill, still bleeping slowly away to itself.

'Bill,' she called down to her companion. 'You'd better take over here, I've got to check out that bomb.'

'Right.' They exchanged positions, Sharp taking Bill's weight this time. 'Stop complaining,' Bill said. He kept the controls locked and gave Anne the thumbs-up sign.

She nodded back and sprinted for the bomb. As she ran, she saw more of the fighting. The troops were now winning the battle with the help from the sub. Captain Browne's men were quite deadly with that deck gun of theirs, and had taken out a couple more of the Ymir. The laser drill, which would have been able to slice through them as effectively as it did the rocks, prevented any more of the aliens from exiting the ship. Everything was looking good for the human race.

And then tendrils whipped out of the darkness, lashing at the sub's deck. One caught one of the sailors operating the gun and whirled him off his feet, screaming. It was the huge Grandfather that served as the entrance to the dome!

Its immense tendrils could reach almost as far as the

ship, and they were lashing out furiously. It didn't matter if they caught anything or anyone, merely their threat was forcing the soldiers to duck for cover.

That could change the whole fight. It might give the Ymir a chance to get out of their ship some other way. But there was nothing that she could do about it. She kept low as she ran, and none of the tendrils came anywhere near her. She reached the bomb, but the control panel was atop it; some ten feet in the air. There was nothing to climb on, so she couldn't even reach it.

She was aware of a dark shape running toward her, and whirled about, half-prepared for an attack. With considerable relief she realised that it was just Samson, dressed in scuba gear, and carrying an extra suit with him. His feet were bare, his flippers tied together and slung over his shoulder.

'Here you go, Anne,' he said, gasping a bit. 'The latest fashion in escape gear.'

'Lovely,' she said. 'But right now I need a boost up. I want a look at the bomb.'

'Sorry, love,' Samson said. 'Suit up first, then I'll help you with the bomb. I don't want you drowned when we break out of here.'

She glared at him, but could see that he was adamant. She took the offered suit with a sigh and looked at it. Skin-tight, of course, no way she'd get it on over her heavy-duty jeans and sweater.

Samson had brought a rather large automatic pistol with him, too, and hunched down to use it on the Ymir.

Well, this was no time to be modest. She shucked her outer clothing, and pulled on the wet suit. It felt horribly rubbery and icky to the skin, but it would undoubtedly save her life. She held off on the flippers and face mask. 'Right, dressed for escape,' she informed him. '*Now* will you boost me up there?'

'With pleasure.' He bent down to allow her to climb on his back, and then stood up so she could balance on his shoulders. That enabled her to get a purchase on the top of the bomb, and she pushed her legs on up to help her scramble atop it.

She rested for just a few seconds, then examined the panel. There were several controls and a number of lights. One was changing each time the bomb beeped, so it was clearly the countdown. Of course, she couldn't read Ymir, at least not yet, and she didn't have time to wait for her translation matrix to kick in. So she had no idea what it said, or just how long it would be before it detonated.

With despair, she realised that there really was nothing she could do. There was no obvious way to defuse the device, and if she started experimenting with the buttons, she was just as likely to set the thing off early as to stop it. She leaned over the edge. 'It's no good, Samson,' she said. 'This thing's too alien for me to understand. I can't stop the countdown without taking really great risks.'

'Then you'd best not touch it,' he agreed. 'What will happen if we just leave it alone?'

'It'll blow up, you idiot, what do you think?' she snapped. Then she added, 'Sorry, my nerves are a bit frazzled.'

'I'm not surprised. And I know it'll blow up, but it'll blow up *here*, and not down the hole, won't it? Would it still set off the oil field, and the volcano?'

Anne thought about that for a second, and then grinned delightedly. 'No, it's nowhere near the oil field, so that will be perfectly safe. Most of the force of the blast will be directed upwards and outwards. Of course, I don't know how powerful an explosion like that might mean, but it won't be any worse than an H-bomb detonation, I shouldn't think.'

'Not wishing to be picky,' Samson said, 'but I'd just as soon not be standing this close to a nuclear bomb going off.'

Anne paled. 'We'd better get out of here, then,' she said. She slipped over the edge, and Samson caught her as she fell. 'Thanks.'

'My pleasure.'

'Okay, back to the drill,' she said.

The battle was slowing down now. All of the Ymir that had managed to get out of the ship were dead or incapacitated, and Lethbridge-Stewart and his men were checking the fallen. The Grandfather plant was still lashing out against the sub, though. The surviving sailors had been joined by others, and they had swung the deck gun around to fire into the heart of the plant.

If they killed the Grandfather, then water would start to flood in.

'Brigadier!' Anne screamed. When he looked up, she gestured. 'Get your men to the sub *now*!'

'Right,' he called back, and started to organise an orderly retreat.

Anne and Samson had reached the drill, and Bill looked down at them. 'Time for you two to go,' Anne informed him.

'About bloody time,' Private Sharp muttered, his voice strained.

Bill hesitated.

'It's time,' Anne stressed. 'We can handle this. Go.'

He looked as if he were about to argue further, but then nodded and released the controls. He jumped down, and Sharp stood straight with a loud groan. 'Stop complaining,' Bill growled. To Anne, he added, 'You be careful.'

She laughed. 'If I was careful, I wouldn't be here. Go.' Trusting he'd do as he was told she turned to Samson, and she said, 'Right, it's heave-ho time again.' He raised her to the controls.

She started the drill in motion again. It moved very slowly as she swung it away from the spaceship. The airlock was a molten mess, and it would definitely prevent the Ymir from taking off. She had a more important target right now.

Lethbridge-Stewart was leading his men in a swift but orderly retreat to the submarine. There were several sailors on deck ready to help them aboard. The deck gun had stopped firing, and she saw that two of the tendrils had wrapped themselves about it, wrenching it into a lopsided mess.

Just as soon as she could, she triggered the drill again. The laser beam fired over the sub's deck and into the heart of the Grandfather lurking in the darkness. Those plants could enjoy heat, but she doubted very strongly that it could withstand this kind of temperature.

As she watched, the last of Lethbridge-Stewart's men and the sailors vanished into the sub, and the hatches were slammed and sealed.

It was just her and Samson now.

No more Ymir had come from the spaceship, and Anne was certain she knew the reason. They were linked telepathically to the Grandfathers, and she was burning a massive, ancient one to death; all of the aliens in the ship had to be suffering right now. Their pain had to be horrendous. She felt a very slight pang of guilt, but it was their own fault. They were here to wipe out the human race and take possession of this planet. But this world was already taken. Loyalty, not merely to the human race but to every living thing on this planet, meant that she had to do precisely what she was doing; wipe out countless intelligent beings. She was trying hard not to think about that but, of course, the harder she tried not to think of it, the more she *did* think of it.

She had no other option; none. She was doing only what had to be done.

Then, over the din of the drill, she heard another sound; a crashing noise. For a second, she couldn't place it, and then she realised what it was; water breaking through the entrance to the dome.

'Down, now!' she yelled, almost falling from Samson's shoulders. She grabbed the rest of her gear. 'Behind the drill,' she instructed. 'It'll protect us for a few seconds.' She pulled on the face mask, and slung the bottle over her shoulders. She was fumbling for her flippers when the crashing waters slammed into the drill, throwing her aside. The flippers vanished in the force of the blow, and she was instantly underwater – cold, dark water – and then flung away from shelter.

Holding what little breath she had left, her cold fingers fumbled with the mouthpiece. At the second attempt she managed to get it into position, and started breathing.

Nothing happened, and she was almost choking for air before she remembered she was supposed to open the valve from the tanks. The surge of air filled her immediately. She tried to get her bearings.

The floodwaters had carried her away from the drill, toward the spaceship. Their force was too strong to fight, and she was slammed heavily against the metal shell of the ship. She almost lost her mouthpiece, and she was so winded from the shock she couldn't move.

Somehow, though, the lights were still operational, and she could see the twisted airlock. To her shock, she could also see an Ymir attempting to exit. It was on its back, trying to pull itself through the gap. Then it saw her and reached out.

The immense hand loomed toward her, and opened. The Ymir was aiming to burn her to death. She couldn't move, still too stunned to get her muscles into operation. But she didn't need to escape. The Ymir had forgotten one thing in its anger.

Water started to bubble as it allowed its body heat to rise. Anne felt the warmth reaching her even though the insulated suit. But she wasn't afraid; she felt nothing but contempt for the stupid alien.

The hand hesitated, and then fell back, helplessly, as the Ymir died.

Anne shook her head. It had forgotten that releasing its own body heat was only a part of lowering its defences. The cold, cold water had sapped it of its much-needed internal warmth. In attempting to kill her, it had frozen to death.

There was a touch on her arm, and she twisted to see

Samson there. He, of course, had managed to get his flippers on as well as the aqualung, so he could swim properly. Her own feet were freezing, but she'd managed to recover sufficiently to be able to swim with him back toward the waiting sub.

The blast of water had knocked the sub to the side somewhat, but it looked otherwise intact. The deck gun hung at a funny angle, but they probably had little use for that now, anyway.

Two further divers appeared, and swam out to help them back to the sub, and Anne gratefully slipped into the airlock. As soon as the water was pumped out sufficiently, she spat out the mouthpiece. Samson grinned at her.

'Made it,' he said.

'Obviously,' she replied. She was so cold she couldn't bring herself to be polite. 'I think my toes have frostbite.'

The submarine was quite crowded, but Lethbridge-Stewart was too concerned to really notice it. He threaded through the exhausted and confused civilians to reach the sub's control room. Captain Browne had kept all but his sailors out of it, but they allowed Lethbridge-Stewart through.

'Are we operational?' he asked the captain.

Browne nodded. 'A few small breaches,' he said. 'But nothing too bad. That brave gal of yours is aboard now, and we're ready to go.'

'Splendid.' Lethbridge-Stewart couldn't help but wonder how much time they had before the Ymir bomb went off, and how badly it might affect them.

'Get us underway, Mr Devon,' Browne ordered.

'Aye, sir.'

There was a flurry of orders given, and Lethbridge-Stewart felt the submarine rising from the bedrock it had been resting on for so long.

'Ahead slow,' Browne ordered. 'Torpedo room?'

'Torpedo room ready,' came back the prompt reply.

'Torpedoes?' Lethbridge-Stewart asked.

'Ready tubes one and two,' Browne ordered. Then he looked grimly at Lethbridge-Stewart. 'Want to make sure the exit is quite clear,' he explained. 'Wouldn't do if we got stuck, would it?'

'Quite,' the brigadier agreed.

'One and two ready, sir,' came the response.

Browne checked their angle. 'Fire.'

The vessel shuddered as the two torpedoes launched. The radar operator called out: 'Impact in five... four... three... two...' A pause. 'Impact confirmed.'

'Radar?' Browne called out.

'In a moment, sir. Looking good. Plenty of room, sir.'

'Right.' The captain turned to his first officer. 'As soon as we're clear, lay on the steam, Number One.'

'Aye, sir.'

The captain moved to the radio operator. 'Get a signal through to Holy Loch,' he ordered. 'Tell them to pull back any ships in this vicinity.'

'Aye, sir.'

Browne turned back to Lethbridge-Stewart. 'We're not out of the woods yet,' he said, grimly.

There was a bit of commotion at the door, and Miss Travers appeared. Her hair was a mess, and she was wearing some seaman's clothes that were several sizes too large, but she appeared to be mostly happy.

'Miss Travers,' Lethbridge-Stewart said. 'So good to see you in one piece.'

'So glad to *be* in one piece,' she responded. 'How are we doing?'

'Going as fast as we can,' he replied. 'Are we going to escape that blast?'

Miss Travers shrugged. 'We'll find out soon enough,' she said, simply. 'Either way, though, the Ymir won't be taking over this planet. At least, not today. And that's something, isn't it?'

Lethbridge-Stewart smiled tightly. 'That's doing our duty,' he agreed. 'If we survive, that's a rather pleasant bonus.'

Thanks to the skill and training of the Royal Navy, Browne managed to get the sub into the lee of Strommach mere moments before the explosion came. Although the seabed shook and the waters crashed, the island protected them from the worst of it.

— EPILOGUE —

'Brazilian pitcher plant?' Harold Chorley stared at Lethbridge-Stewart in incredulity.

'Brazilian pitcher plant,' Lethbridge-Stewart repeated, firmly. 'Very aggressive species, so I'm told.'

'Do you *seriously* expect me to believe that, Colonel?'

'It's *brigadier* now, actually,' Lethbridge-Stewart stated, rather proudly. 'And I'm afraid I can't begin to speculate on what you may or may not believe, Mr Chorley. However, the facts are simple: drug smugglers from South America running from a Royal Navy intercept vessel crashed their ship into the pirate radio station Crossbones, causing the sinking of both vessels. The smugglers had aboard their ship several spores from the pitcher plant which were washed ashore on Strommach. Very aggressive species, grew like weeds, so I'm told.'

Chorley sighed; the *brigadier* was obviously sticking to his silly story. 'So, can I go out to the island and confirm any of this?' he asked, feeling pretty certain he already knew the answer to *that* one.

'I'm sorry, Strommach is off-limits for the time being. The plants, as I mentioned, are very aggressive. They were destroyed by a virulent weed killer before they could infect the mainland. A *lot* of weed killer. It will be quite a while before the island is safe to visit.'

'How convenient,' Chorley drawled.

'Convenient? Hardly.' Lethbridge-Stewart gave him a stern look. 'There are dozens of people from the island who have to be re-housed, and new jobs have to be found for them. Believe me, that's going to be quite a headache for someone.'

It was pointless arguing further; no doubt Lethbridge-Stewart had an explanation for every point he might raise, and Chorley knew when he was beaten. *Brazilian pitcher plants* didn't even start to cover what he'd witnessed, but he had no proof. At least he had *some* sort of story to file on this, so he'd get paid. But he knew, and the brigadier knew that he knew, that this was nowhere near the truth.

But it was obviously all the truth he'd get to print.

'Very well, Brigadier. But there is another question I'd like to ask you.'

Lethbridge-Stewart leaned back and folded his arms. 'Ask away.'

'What happened at Dominex? I have almost a week missing, and I *know* that you know why.'

For the smallest of moments it looked like Lethbridge-Stewart was going to answer truthfully, but instead he stood. 'I'm afraid I have no idea what you're talking about, Mr Chorley. Good day.'

Anne regarded Mary with affection and concern. They were outside *The Auld Hundred* on Rose Street.

'What will you do now?' she asked Mary gently.

The other woman turned haunted eyes to Anne's face. 'I'm going to see Al's family,' she said. 'Tell them about the

Al I knew.'

'And *what* will you tell them? It can't be the truth,' Anne added, apologetically. 'The world isn't ready to hear about this latest invasion attempt.'

'Latest?'

'I'll tell you about it... some other day,' Anne said, evasively. 'Do you have an alternative story for them?'

'Yes.' Mary was still withdrawn. 'The brigadier told me the official story; Brazilian drug runners on the run from the Navy crashed into *Crossbones*, sinking everyone. I'll tell them that Al saved my life by getting me into a boat, but that he died in the rescue attempt. Died a hero.' There was a tear in the corner of her eye. 'That part, at least, is true.'

'I'm sorry you can't tell them the whole truth.'

'I'm not!' Mary said fiercely. 'The truth is that his mind was eroded by some alien parasite from outer space, that it ate Al away from inside his own brain. How could I even *think* of telling them that?' She shook her head. 'No, the lie is a lot more palatable, a lot more comfortable for me, as much as for them.' She gave Anne a bleak look. 'He was the most human, the kindest man I ever knew, and he was lost in the worst way possible.'

Anne understood her pain; she had seen people under the effects of alien mind control herself, and knew how shocking and terrifying that was. Time to change the subject. 'And after that?' she asked. 'Back to the airwaves?'

'Oh. Possibly. The BBC have offered me a job, apparently, hosting a pop show for teens, or something, may even be on TV.'

Anne grinned, happy that something good seemed to be coming from all of this. 'You'd look good on the box,' she said. 'Maybe even *Crackerjack* next, eh?'

'I haven't accepted yet,' Mary said. 'I need time.'

'To sleep on it, eh?'

'Sleep? God, I pray I never sleep again. My dreams are too horrible.'

'It will get better,' Anne promised her, thinking of her own nights following that first Yeti invasion. 'I know it doesn't seem so now, but it *will* get better.'

'I hope so.' Mary managed a wan smile. 'Sorry I'm so down. But, thank you. For everything. Saving me. Saving the world.'

Anne gave her a cheeky grin. 'It's just a job.' Then she hugged the other woman. 'Take care,' she said. 'Let me know how the job works out.' She looked over to where Bill was waiting by Lethbridge-Stewart's staff car. 'Your ride to the station's here. He's another good man, but don't tell him I said so!'

She watched Mary wander off, to be gently led by Bill to the car. She'd asked Bill to do this for her, she doubted Evans would have helped Mary's low spirits any with his endless stream of complaints. Evans had been glad to dodge the extra work, of course, and Bill – bless him! – had been more than willing to help out.

Anne hoped that Mary would be okay. She was a strong woman – she had to be to survive what she did – but even the strongest people had their breaking points. Losing her friend might have been Mary's. She sincerely hoped that Mary would be able to recover from this, but many people would not.

She mentally shook herself. She would check up – quietly – on Mary in a couple of weeks, but there was little she could do to help out. The battle the other woman had to fight was internal, and nobody could help here with that. So, onto other matters.

Anne took the lift down to Dolerite Base, passing through security checks almost without noticing them. She rapped on the door to the conference room and walked in.

Bryden was there, at the table, talking with Professor Brinstead. He glanced up as Anne entered, an almost friendly look on his face. 'Ah, there you are, Doctor Travers. I've just finished offering the professor here full funding for his next bathysphere.'

Brinstead was all smiles. 'Mr Bryden was telling me you gave him a glowing report of *Tethys*,' he said. 'Thank you.'

'My pleasure, Professor,' she said, sincerely. 'It was an extremely efficient vehicle, and the next generation should be even more so.' She looked at Bryden. 'Thank you.'

'Oh, it's not altruism,' he said, laughing. 'I believe I'll make a tidy profit off the professor here. I'm thinking we could dive after lost treasure ships. Do you have any idea how many Spanish galleons were sunk bringing treasure back to Spain?'

Trust Bryden! Anne smiled. 'Happy dives,' she said. 'Now, I've got to get back to work before the brigadier thinks I'm lazy and docks my pay.'

Bryden was on his way down the Royal Mile to where his limousine waited when Evans sidled up to him. 'Ah, there you are, man, I was wondering what had happened to you.'

'I had to wait till you were done down there, didn't I?' Evans said. 'Don't let anyone catch us together, you said.'

'Quite right,' Bryden approved. 'So, do you have something for me?'

Evans glanced around furtively, and then unslung the rucksack from over his shoulder. 'Here you go, then,' he said.

Bryden took the bag and opened it. Nestled in the bottom was an intact pod. He didn't know how the Welshman had managed to sneak it back from Strommach, neither did he care. He smiled happily as he looked at the dormant alien plant, before closing the bag again. He reached into his inside pocket for the envelope of cash that he handed to Evans.

'And here *you* go, then. Stay helpful to me, and there will be more like that.'

Evans greedily accepted the money and stuffed it inside his tunic. Then he gave Bryden a worried look. 'You be careful with that thing,' he advised. 'It's awfully dangerous.'

'Don't worry, Evans,' Bryden promised him. 'I'll take *very* good care of it. I have a lot of plans for our little friend here.'

Lethbridge-Stewart was glad that the debriefings were finished, all of the goodbyes said. Hennessy and McMillan had cheerfully taken plenty of credit for their assistance, but he didn't begrudge them that. The more the regular forces were in the forefront, the better to keep the Fifth's invisibility to the public. There was no need for anyone outside of the military to know how close to extinction the human race had just come.

He was *almost* happy to be heading back to the reports that had undoubtedly been breeding on his desk while he'd been in the field. He opened the doorway to his outer office and stopped in surprise.

Sally looked up from the papers on the desk and gave him a broad smile. 'Alistair! I'm so glad you're back safely!' She jumped to her feet, and threw herself across the room to envelop him in a tight hug.

He kicked the door shut quickly behind him; didn't want any of the men seeing him like this! 'Sally,' he said, rather obviously, and with a certain amount of reserve. 'Ah… What are you doing here?'

She giggled slightly, and gestured at the desk. 'My job,' she said. 'My transfer came through.'

'It did?' It certainly hadn't been any of *his* doing… 'That was, um, quick.'

'Yes, well you're not the only one with contacts. I realised how unfair I was being to you, asking you to expedite it. I mean, while you were working so hard on saving the world and everything. So I talked to Brigadier Anderson—'

'Anderson?'

'Yes, you know, Brigadier Mary Anderson.'

Lethbridge-Stewart nodded. Of course he knew of her, although he'd never met the commander of the Women's Royal Army. He also remembered that Sally had once told him that Anderson had been her sponsor when Sally first enlisted with the WRA. With a sense of betrayal, Lethbridge-Stewart knew where this was heading.

'I explained it all to her, once I worked out she knew about the Fifth, and she got onto Hamilton. Turns out he owed her a favour or two, which I obviously didn't know,' Sally added, with her cheeky grin. The one that was usually kind of attractive, although not at that present moment. Less cheeky, more facetious. 'She nudged a bit, and here I am!'

'Yes,' Lethbridge-Stewart agreed. 'Here you are.' And he *should* be feeling overjoyed about it, he knew, and not the nagging pit of dread that currently rested in his stomach. Thankfully, Sally didn't seem to have noticed his lack of enthusiasm, probably putting it down to post-action reaction or something.

But what to do with her? He already had an adjutant, and Lieutenant Bishop was probably best left in that position, after all that was part of the reason he went through his training at Mons. Perhaps Lethbridge-Stewart could palm Sally off onto Dougie? The man could do with a secretary.

Brigadier Lethbridge-Stewart sighed. It seemed life in the Fifth Operational Corps had just got a lot more complicated.

Safeguarding the Legacy

By Andy Frankham-Allen

Twenty-Five Years of Doctor Who Novels

With the non-cancellation of the *Doctor Who* television series in 1989, it was only a matter of time before something was done to continue the Doctor's adventures. The comic strips in *Doctor Who Magazine* waited for no man and proceeded with companionless adventures, but what of Ace, who was last seen walking towards that big cup of tea in the sky?

Enter Virgin Publishing!

WH Allen, under the Target imprint, had been printing novelisations of the television stories since the early 1970s, and had often broached the idea of publishing original novels based on the series. Only two ever surfaced under the *Companions of Doctor Who* umbrella title; *Harry Sullivan's War* and *Turlough and the Earthlink Dilemma*. But this all changed in 1991, by which time Virgin had purchased WH Allen, when they got the rights from the BBC to publish original *Doctor Who* novels.

John Peel Reflects

'Twenty-five years ago, I happened to be the person who began the official original *Doctor Who* novels,' John Peel remembers. 'Editor Peter Darvill-Evans was determined to take these books as far from the famously skimpy Target novelisations as possible, aiming them instead at the older reader. His initial plan included a four-part arc centering on the Timewyrm, to be followed by a looser three-part story. I managed to pitch an idea he liked to kick off the Timewyrm run, and the series itself. I'd been a fan of *Doctor Who* for a long time, and a writer of novelisations for a few years at that point, and was certainly fan enough to want to be the first original novel writer.

'I also made myself something of a target for all of those convinced that the range wouldn't be the way they'd have done things.

'Peter and I discussed what the book would include, and the subject of sex inevitably came up. Peter (perhaps less than helpfully!) told me to use my judgment. "No explicit sex, unless the story calls for it," was all he dictated. He also wanted the book to begin as a possible new introduction for people who didn't watch the show but might pick up a novel (were there any such people?), so he asked for the book to start by assuming nobody knew anything about the Doctor.

'I took that literally, and had the Doctor accidentally strip Ace's memories, so that *she* knew nothing about the Doctor. As she recovered her memories, the readers would learn what she knew. I also had her stripped naked, to emphasize her fresh beginning, and the critics had a field day with that!

'Since the story would be set in prehistoric Mesopotamia (Peter wanted Gilgamesh in the story, and that was always one of my favourite myths, so I was happy to agree), I also wanted to demonstrate a lesson I had learned from *Doctor Who* itself; that other societies are often as alien as any science fiction we can dream up. I added a twelve-year-old prostitute as a character, and *that* attracted a lot of criticism! (To put that in perspective, incidentally, before 1889 the age of consent – if you can call it that – in New York City was ten.) I couldn't complain, since I'd introduced her specifically to shake people up and make them realise that the way we think now isn't the way everyone thinks, and certainly not the way people thought even as recently as 1889.

'Peter's plan was extremely successful. *The New Adventures* ran for sixty books after mine, which was a very respectable figure. And, twenty-five years on, new *Doctor Who* books and spin-offs are still being written. You're holding one right now, once again by me. All these years later.'

The Lost Girl – A Look at Dorothy 'Ace' McShane

Ace's television journey made it quite clear that there were some major issues between her and her mother. With so many hints it was hardly a surprise that her past was explored in so much detail during *The New Adventures* – some might say in *too* much detail. Her mother didn't care much about Ace's school life, and was absent so much that the school arranged for her to get a social worker. Often her mother's various boyfriends would look after her, which tended to mean Ace being around a lot of booze. She usually called her mother by her name, Audrey, while Audrey tended to call the young Ace 'Dorry'. At school she was called Dotty. Fourteen-year-old Ace idolised singer Johnny Chess (the son of ex-companions Ian & Barbara Chesterton), and after he rejected her attention she resolved to never like someone again without getting to know them first.

Following on from *Survival*, Ace was initially much the same as she was onscreen, fiercely loyal to her 'Professor' and always the first to throw herself into any adventure. Still her love of explosives continued, and in *Timewyrm: Exodus* she created nitro-9a, much more stable than the previous brand, but half the weight and half the explosive quality. In that story she also took up arms for the first time, shooting guns and blowing several Nazis away to protect the Doctor. She considered the Doctor her best friend and only family, but in *Timewyrm: Apocalypse* the first chink in their relationship appeared, after Ace learned that the Doctor knew that Raphael – a young man befriended by Ace on Kirith – would die, and did nothing to prevent it. She found herself very angry about this, certain the Doctor could have done something. It was the first of many such actions that would, ultimately, pull them apart. Nonetheless she still trusted the Doctor, after visiting his mind in *Timewyrm: Revelation* and learning how tortured he was by his past lives. At that point she was, apparently, in her early twenties, which possibly tied in with the obvious gap between seasons twenty-five and twenty-six. She was sure she was going to travel with the Doctor forever, but this changed in *Nightshade* when she met Robin Yeadon in 1968.

She fell deeply in love with Robin, a proper innocent, deeply emotional love, and when she decided it was time to stop travelling and remain with Robin, the Doctor refused to let her go. He *accidentally* materialises the TARDIS on an alien world instead of back on Earth.

Not long after, on the planet Heaven, in *Love and War*, Ace met a traveller called Jan Rydd. They fell in love, but unlike Robin it was more of a mad, passionate love and they got engaged. Jan was killed by the Hoothi – an act the Doctor had a huge part in. Ace is beyond unforgiving of the Doctor, even more so when she discovered he had always planned on sacrificing Jan. She accused the Doctor of being jealous of Jan and how she was going to leave the Doctor for him. She departed the Doctor's company, taking with her a device called a tesseract to remind herself of Jan. The Doctor keeps Ace's bomber jacket, knowing that she would need it again one day.

For Ace it was three years until she next met the Doctor in *Deceit*, by which time she had become part of Earth's Spacefleet, Special Weapons division. She was hardened and bitter, violence and sex being her currency. She discovered that the Doctor psychically drove her away from him in *Love and War* because he was infected by a protoplasmic virus which infected him on Tír na n-Óg (*Cat's Cradle: Witch Mark*), and he left the tesseract with her so she could contact him when the time was right to remove the virus. She remained with the Doctor to keep him honest, but Bernice Summerfield (an archaeologist who joined the Doctor on Heaven) was unsure about her. Ace, while travelling with the Doctor, was infected with a virus that boosted her immune system and prevented her from getting ill. She considered the twenty-sixth century her home. While visiting Haiti in 1915 (*White Darkness*) Ace was made to confront her violent tendencies. She shot a man called Richmann in self defence and continued shooting, emptying her gun, angry and upset over her wounded friend. She threw the gun away in fear of her own future. The violence got worse in *Shadowmind* when she wiped out the entire command crew of the *Broadsword*, who were possessed by the Umbra, and considered it the worst thing she has done.

Her nitro-9 was further advanced when she developed neo-nitro, small white spheres that were activated with saliva, and later the nitro-9a smart bombs.

In *Birthright* we saw the template for what will become a regular feature in *Doctor Who* from 2006 – the Doctor-lite story. In this book, Ace and Bernice had an adventure in Victorian London while the Doctor was off elsewhere. At the end of this adventure, when they see the Doctor again, he claimed to have spent the entire time in one of the TARDIS' rooms, but neither women trusted him. That distrust of the Doctor was potent enough to feed the Garvond in *The Dimension Riders*, a creature that lived off fear, hate and suspicion. Ace realised just how much the Doctor stood between her and Robin and then Jan, and remained only to one-up the Doctor. In *No Future*, she totally failed to charm Danny Pain, the front man of '70s punk band, *Plasticine,* which frustrated her – she was not used to being rejected like that. They encountered the Monk (whose name was revealed to be Mortimus), and he offered to take Ace back and save Jan, trying to steal her from the Doctor. Ace refused, and sided with the Doctor despite her distrust of him. She cheated time and prevented the Brigadier from dying in 1976. We also learned that she often felt like killing herself and she only drank to make herself feel vulnerable.

In *First Frontier* Ace finally got to have her second round with the Master, who had used Tzun nanites to remove his corrupted Trakenite DNA and restored his Time Lord regenerative cycle. Still infected by the Cheetah Planet (*Survival*), Ace was able to detect the Master, and she shot him in the back, unintentionally causing him to regenerate – an act that wipes out the Master's connection with the Cheetah Planet. At that point she was almost twenty-seven. In *Falls the Shadows* the Doctor and Ace discussed the way she had become hardened since she left him; he was worried about her but she told him that nothing touched her, and he responded that 'it should'. Despite her bravado, as soon as he was gone, Ace retreated to her room and cried for hours.

Ace finally left in *Set Piece*, and remained behind in 1870s France (as first revealed in the novelisation of *The Curse of Fenric*), and we discovered it was during her time there that the painting found in Windsor Castle in 1988 (*Silver Nemesis*) was commissioned. She decided to remain to keep an eye on the time rifts, and defended the Commune to save more lives. She took one of Kadiatu Lethbridge-Stewart's time hoppers. The Doctor, having taken a look at Ace's timeline, always knew this would happen. The Doctor, shortly after, met a thirty-seven-year-old Ace who was being courted by Count Sorin, the grandfather of Captain Sorin from *The Curse of Fenric*. In *Head Games* it was explicitly stated that the only companions the Seventh Doctor travelled with were Mel, Ace, Bernice, Chris Cwej and Roz Forrester, thereby setting *The New Adventures* apart from the Big Finish stories that later introduced other companions. Ace's time hopper could not take her any further than 2001, however in *Happy Endings* she visited Cheldon Bonniface, 2010, for Bernice's wedding to Jason Kane and slept with a clone of Jason (later leaving with him). She is reunited with her mother, and Robin, and finally made her peace with Audrey, promising to visit more often. By that point she was known as Dorothée Sorina-McShane, although she and Count Sorin were no longer together, and they only pretended to be married. She was thirty-one, six years younger than in *Set Piece* when she was being courted by the count – an apparent contradiction. She returned one final time in *Lungbarrow*, the final *New Adventure* for the Seventh Doctor, and discovers that the Doctor originally wanted to enrol her in the Time Lord Academy on Gallifrey. At that point she hadn't seen the Doctor for a year, and still totally believed in him. They parted company as close as they ever were, although both a lot older and wiser.

Continuing the Legacy

The New Adventures soon spawned a series of *Missing Adventures*, featuring older Doctors and companions. New companions were created for the incumbent Doctor, and *Doctor Who* novels continued, from Virgin Publishing to BBC Books, with other publishers creating spin-off novels based on lesser-known characters from *Doctor Who* novels. And in 2015 Candy Jar Books began publishing the *Lethbridge-Stewart* range, the first series of novels based on a character originating in the television series.

For twenty-five years original *Doctor Who* novels have continued the legacy began by *The New Adventures*, expanding upon what was seen on television. And now *The New Adventures* have their own legacy, with Big Finish Productions adapting certain titles into full-cast audio dramas. The final words go to Big Finish producer David Richardson. '*The New Adventures* were *Doctor Who* when there was no *Doctor Who* on TV. They were the very first original *Doctor Who* novel-length fiction on the printed page, and they pushed the format into brand new territories, telling the kind of stories that the small screen had never attempted. They also saw the *Doctor Who* debuts of many names who have since become the very heart of the massively successful revitalised show – Russell T Davies, Mark Gatiss, Paul Cornell, Gareth Roberts…

'The novels remain loved to this day because of the quality of the writing, and also because of the ideas and the imaginations of the authors. Great stories endure, and *The New Adventures* will live forever.'

Companions: Fifty Years of Doctor Who Assistants.
Now available on Kindle.
Updated version coming soon.

Available from Candy Jar Books

LETHBRIDGE-STEWART: MOON BLINK
by Sadie Miller

July 1969, and mankind is on the Moon. Both the United States and Soviet Russia have lunar bases, and both are in trouble.

Back on Earth, Anne Travers has learned she is about to be visited by an old friend from America, Doctor Patricia Richards. Lance Corporal Bill Bishop is aware of the visit, and is on hand to meet Richards.

She brings with her a surprise, one which the Americans and Russians wish to get their hands on. But the only man who can truly help Anne, Colonel Lethbridge-Stewart, is away in Scotland.

It's a game of cat and mouse, as Anne and Bishop seek to protect the life of an innocent baby – one that holds the secrets to life on the Moon.

'Once again, Anne Travers takes the lead in the proceedings while Lethbridge-Stewart is relegated to the background, but for this story that dynamic not only made sense, but is essential. Sadie Miller exhibits a natural knack for writing these characters, and has a strong voice with which to do it.' – Shaun Collins, Travelling the Vortex

ISBN: 978-0-9935192-0-8

Coming soon from Candy Jar Books

GANGSTERS: A LIFE FOR A LIFE
by Phillip Martin

Novelisation of the classic gritty 1970s British drama. John Kline is an ex-SAS officer recently released from prison who finds himself hired by the secretive DI6 police organisation to go undercover in the Birmingham underworld. Infiltrating a violent gangster organisation, Kline soon finds himself making some dangerous enemies, with his loyalties trapped between two opposing forces.

Gangsters is a novel of money, power and violence, the story of racketeers who grow fat on the profits of illegal immigration, drug trafficking – and death.

ISBN: 978-0-9954821-2-8